THE SIRIUS CROSSING

by the same author

THE DAY OF THE DEAD

The Sirius Crossing

JOHN CREED

ff
faber and faber

First published in 2002
by Faber and Faber Limited
3 Queen Square London WC1N 3AU
Open market edition first published in 2002
This paperback edition first published in 2003

Typeset by Faber and Faber
Printed in England by Mackays of Chatham plc, Chatham, Kent

A CIP record for this book
is available from the British Library

ISBN 0-571-21086-4

2 4 6 8 10 9 7 5 3 1

THE SIRIUS CROSSING

1

I once asked Liam Mellows why he did what he did. His reply was that sometimes you had a duty to the dead. He said you had a duty to find justice for them. I realized afterwards that he was wrong. You had a duty to find the truth. Two years after the day when Liam turned up in Kintyre, I finally found someone who could tell me how the whole thing had started, twenty-five years ago. His name was Harry Longsworth and he had been an air-force lieutenant at the time, but was now an air traffic controller at Luton. He didn't understand what had taken place, but he was an intelligent man and he knew there was something odd about it, and the memory had remained fresh through the years.

Bishopsway Air Support Base,
Northern England, February 1974.

Longsworth recalled how the whole thing made him nervous. He had been sitting in the dispatch room with the two Americans for almost two hours and in that time neither of them had said a word or, as far as he could see, had stirred an inch. The two of them were spread across several chairs in that informal athletic American way, both crew-cut and hard-faced, and both staring off into the middle distance with hard, bored looks. They were the kind of men who would have been surfers when they were younger, Longsworth imagined, and he had the unavoidable feeling that somewhere along the line they had taken all that flair and ability and split-second timing and had started to use it to kill people.

They had arrived just after dark in a C130 which had

landed on runway seven and taxied all the way to the perimeter fence at the northern end of the vast Bishopsway air base. It was a filthy night and in the roar of the engines and the spray the vast aircraft threw up, Longsworth almost missed the two figures running out from under one of the huge wings, coming at his open-topped Land Rover at a dead run and slinging their kitbags into the back before climbing on board. Longsworth had started to introduce himself but as he did so the plane's engines rose in pitch and it turned in a fast circle and immediately began to taxi back on to the main apron. Longsworth watched, puzzled, as it began its take-off run and then it was gone as if it had never been there. He turned to look at his two passengers and opened his mouth to speak but something stopped him. He started the engine and began to drive back towards the small empty stores building that had been requisitioned as a place for the two men to wait.

Longsworth knew little about the job. Colonel Clegg had told him to expect the flight, to meet two Americans off it and chaperone them for a few hours while they were waiting for another plane to pick them up. If Longsworth thought it odd that the transaction had taken place in the most deserted and under-used part of the base, he didn't ask any questions. Nor did he query the colonel's nervous, brusque manner, nor the fact that the chit that the colonel gave him for the jeep recorded that the jeep was to be used to transport crewmen to the other side of the airport, a patently transparent untruth. Longsworth had served under the colonel in Palestine and together they had finessed some unfortunate incidents involving civilian casualties. As soon as Longsworth saw the back of these two, he knew it would be in his interest to forget that he had ever seen them.

The trouble was that the two men made such an impression on him. Their battered flying suits without insignia, the paratroop bags at their feet, their air of steely competence. In the small room with the oil heater glowing fitfully in the middle of it, they seemed to grow in stature and to fill the whole place. Fortunately, Longsworth's ordeal wasn't to last much longer. At approximately 19.45 hours the two men rose, stretched and yawned. They picked up their gear and stood at the door, looking expectantly at Longsworth.

Longsworth drove them back on to the apron. When they were about a hundred yards from the perimeter fence, one of the Americans nudged Longsworth and grunted something by which he understood that he was to stop. He pulled up. The rain was driving down now with such force that Longsworth was soaked through and thoroughly miserable, though if either of the two other men felt any discomfort, they didn't show it. They waited like that for five minutes, then Longsworth saw an aircraft's landing lights appear above the runway as if they had just been switched on. Longsworth saw the shape of an aircraft appear out of the rain. It was a plane unlike any that he had seen before. A twin-engined jet with a short, stubby body, short, wide wings and an odd, downswept tail structure. In addition, the plane seemed to be painted in some odd, matt-black substance and it carried no decals or identifying marks. As the plane taxied to a halt, Longsworth noticed the muted sound of its engines.

In fact, the plane was an experimental jet developed by Lockheed at the request of USAAF, with a brief to develop a jet-propelled plane capable of dropping covert operatives into hostile territory without coming to the attention of the enemy. Speed and secrecy required jet engines but the aircraft had to be capable of slowing itself to turboprop speeds in order to drop paratroopers safely. That was where the short, wide wings and odd tail structure came in, allowing the plane to slow to stalling speed while sinking gently, nose high, through the air. The requisite speeds could be reached but there was a fundamental drawback involved – a drawback so fundamental that the project was eventually discontinued. It might have been discontinued after that night; that is, if the men who had commissioned the project had been aware that their brainchild was on a mission that night. In other respects, the aircraft was a forerunner of the Stealth aircraft, particularly in the use of radar-resistant matt surfaces.

Without a word, the two Americans slid over the side of the jeep and ran towards the plane. Longsworth watched them go. A hatch opened in the side of the fuselage and the two men threw themselves over the lip of it. As the plane turned on the apron, Longsworth felt a shiver running down his spine. There was something about this small black plane that stirred irrational fears in him. As it taxied away into the dark, he remembered the story of Charon, the ferryman who ferried the dead across the River Styx into the underworld, and thought that if Charon were to appear in the modern world, it would be in a craft such as this one, and on a night such as this.

The events of the rest of the night I pieced together from confidential records. I tracked them down in a little-used corner of the Library of Congress. The records belonged to the Lockheed Corporation, manufacturer of the aircraft, and weren't subject to national security. It's odd how, even in the most secretive organizations, someone is unable to resist the impulse to prepare a report or file a memo, and ironic how clever, secretive men are unable to stop themselves making records, even as they commit evil.

Eighty minutes later, the plane was over the drop zone. The pilot was confident he had avoided the Bishopscourt radar zone before turning hard starboard and coming in over Dundalk Bay. However, the weather bothered him. A weak high which had swept across Ireland from the Atlantic had formed a front right across the mountainous drop zone and the result was more turbulence than he was happy with. Had he been the experienced test pilot who normally flew the plane, he might have aborted the mission, because that man knew that anything less than flat calm exacerbated the flaw in the design of the plane. However, the pilot on this night had only flown the plane twice before and had only anecdotal evidence as to the potential problem.

The two operatives, who were by now standing by the red light and waiting for the hatch to be opened, were not thinking about the drop at all, but rather about the mission that awaited them. 'One minute,' the drop master said, holding up a finger. They nodded. The hatch slid open and they were looking out into the night, the wind tearing past the open door with terrifying speed. Suddenly the engine note dropped dramatically and the floor started to tilt in the direction of the flight deck. It was this sit-up-and-beg posture which made the drop possible. The fuselage bucked slightly in turbulence, then steadied itself. The red jump light turned green.

The design flaw was this: there was only a small gap between the fuselage and the starboard engine, and thus the jetstream, for the paratrooper to jump into. Even slight turbulence could force the jumping man towards the jetstream from the engine, and the jetstream would not let his body fall through it, but rather supported it, bouncing him along towards that complex tail structure which, because of the posture of the plane in the air, was lower than in a normal parachute jump. This is what happened. As the first man jumped, a gust of wind forced the aircraft six to eight feet to port. The man's body hit the jetstream and was flung back towards the tail with murderous force. The top vane of the starboard flap struck the man in the back of the neck like an axe and he was dead before he had a chance to realize what was happening.

Things happened very quickly then. The damaged vane forced the port wing to dip sharply as the second man jumped. He missed the jetstream but the sudden sharp dip imparted a cartwheel action to his body. He was alert enough to pull his ripcord but was unaware that he was still upside-down. The parachute wrapped itself around him and as his body plummeted towards the mountainside below, he fought frantically to free it. At two hundred metres the chute freed itself, but it was too late to prevent a sickening impact with the ground. As the man fought to stand up, he knew he was in trouble. He felt a terrible stabbing pain in his side. He realized immediately that he had broken ribs, perhaps even punctured a lung. He looked up and saw his colleague's parachute descending towards him and was able to see, just before the ground was reached, the unnatural angle of the head.

Within forty minutes he had found a hiding place for the body. Then he shouldered as much of the equipment as he could carry and started off down the mountain, towards the shadow of the border where the dark flame of war and slaughter by night had already been kindled by other hands.

2

My boss at MRU was fond of a bit of the old cloak and dagger and amused himself by placing his summons to me in the property section of *Horse and Hound*. I think it amused him to force a former student socialist to spend money on a blue-blood publication. It would have been just as easy to call me on a secure phone. However, *Horse and Hound* it was; old-fashioned to the point of being quaint, but reasonably effective nevertheless. The tag of old-fashioned to the point of being quaint would describe Somerville if you regarded Torquemada as old-fashioned and Vlad the Impaler as quaint.

The summons didn't come often, but when it did you were expected to respond immediately. And so I found myself driving down the M6, past the Lake District, on a rainy January morning with the weather forecaster warning of fog and the newscaster tolling death on the roads. The radio was in tune with my mood.

Oscar Wilde said something about not being too liberal when he was young because he didn't want to be overly conservative when he was old. Liam Mellows had introduced me to Wilde and the Dublin man's blend of excoriating insight and real compassion had always appealed. Substitute cynical for conservative and you've got me. Somerville knew I wouldn't take jobs which would be at odds with the tattered remnants of my liberal conscience, but he had a way of finding a job that would take you to the very limits of your supposed humanitarian instincts and then slightly beyond them, a little bit further every time.

At the end of the Cold War, people were looking at the Intelligence agencies, wondering what they were for and to a lesser extent, what they had been up to. Suddenly the mainstream agencies – MI5, MI6 – found politicians and journalists all over them. They would have been all over MRU if they had known of its existence. MRU is one of those organizations that is described as shadowy. Those of us who worked for it thought of it as a dark entity, devoted to doing the dirty work that other agencies wouldn't touch. It was responsible directly to the Prime Minister's Office, although sometimes you wondered if it was responsible to anyone at all. MRU was all about deniability. The PM denied that any such thing existed. And since the agency didn't exist, its operatives didn't exist, even if you were caught or killed. Especially if you were caught or killed.

The MRU didn't care about your ideology. They used ruthless right-wing psychopaths and people like me, who had started out full of *Boys' Own* romance that they were engaged in a daring covert war against evil men so that the citizenry could sleep easily in their beds. You could forgive the psychopaths more easily for what they did. They had personality disorders and mental illnesses to excuse them. The liberals among us had only a sense of romance and the inability to realize that our dreams were paid for with other people's blood.

I had trained as a journalist and it became what they call a cover, which is a kind of ironic term for something which is not in fact on the surface but is part of a deceit which enters your very soul. This cover involved my byline appearing for fifteen years on a series of travel articles in the national press. Colour pieces, sometimes quite analytical. Sometimes I was pleasantly surprised by my insight when I opened the paper on a Saturday. The articles were in fact written by Somerville and I doubted whether he had ever been to half of the countries in question. He could of course have had someone else write the pieces for him, but I think it amused him to do them. You never knew with Somerville. It might have been because it saved a few hundred pounds. He could be like that as well.

If that gives the impression that there was something homely and pleasantly eccentric about Somerville, there wasn't. He was an unfathomable, ruthless man. Over the years, I had worked out that his great strength was that he was totally indifferent to human suffering and death. It gave him great insight, of a sort, though I'm not sure if I wanted to pay the price. Somerville would probably say that in my case the price was half-paid.

The journalist cover gave me an existence in the real world and a reason to be in whatever part of the world Somerville decided I should be in. Maybe some day I would sit down and write about the real journeys I had undertaken. I wondered who would publish that account. A travel journalist in hell.

MRU was based at Gately Park in the Pennines. The headquarters was a compact stone-built country mansion with sprawling outbuildings. It overlooked a small valley which was owned by the Park and was farmed, at a small profit, by Somerville's right-hand man, Harry Curley. Typical Somerville. Perfect cover and a cash bonus. It was a lovely place in the summer and windswept and remote in the winter. Come to think of it, the place reflected much about Somerville. Charming on the outside, but capable of bonechilling bleakness. In the wintertime, it wasn't unusual to find Somerville and Curley leaning over a gate in the snow, eyeing up the ewes in lamb on the far hillside and working out fodder requirements. I'd seen them picking out men they judged fit to live and those that were fit to die with the same dispassionate husbandry.

It has always been an idea of mine that Somerville adopted much of the operational side of the Park from the South Armagh Provisionals. Like them, he had built huge galvanized sheds which were used for legitimate agricultural purposes. Like them, when the doors were closed, the scheming began. Mind you, the South Armagh boys were innocent enough when compared to the Park. It was rumoured that Curley, using a field lab, had perfected the CTT assassination. Carcinogen Transmission Technique. It was crude enough, involving a grain of degraded uranium hidden in a cigarette filter. Embassy Regal was the preferred smoke. The uranium lodged in your lungs. It was undetectable and effective within three months. I knew one SAS-trained loyalist jackal who had gone that way, although it was doubtful that any of his handlers suspected.

Curley was an original except when it came to those dumb abbreviations that were loved by spooks and military types. CTT indeed.

I took a last look at myself in the mirror as I entered the gates of Gately Park, as though to remind myself who I was before I subjected myself to whatever dark scheme was hatching in Somerville's mind. A lean face, a bit of grey at the temples. Blue-grey eyes, part of the Celtic heritage. Hard eyes. Small scar on the temple – small arms fire in Angola, where a spent slug had flattened itself against my skull. More scar tissue barely visible around the ear. A flashbomb I thought I had defused and had placed in a bag beside my ear in the back of an APC. Pretty damn stupid but I did have the best part of a bottle of Chechen vodka in me and it was only ten o'clock in the morning. When those boys offered you a drink, you didn't refuse.

All in all, it was a serviceable face; a bit weathered, a bit battered. Reasonably anonymous. But starting to acquire that cynical look you get with men who have seen too much death. The look that says it doesn't matter any more, we're all going to die. The look of the man who throws a bomb into a crowded restaurant or orders an air strike on a refugee camp. I told myself that I had kept my conscience intact, that the man I saw in the mirror wasn't the man inside. But as Oscar said, only the most superficial people don't judge by appearances.

*

An hour later, the dark deeds emanating from the Park seemed a long way away. I was standing on the small terrace, looking down on the valley. The sun was shining and across the valley the mountain grasses blew in the cold breeze. Far below me, I saw the chimney of a derelict mill. The mill made bricks and the bricks paved a path which followed the ridge of the mountains for eighty miles and which had been a busy thoroughfare walked by men in search of work from medieval times until the Industrial Revolution, but which was now untravelled except by walkers.

'And ghosts,' Somerville said, coming up beside me.

'I'd rather you didn't finish my sentences when I haven't actually spoken them,' I said.

'Then don't be such a sentimentalist,' he said mildly. He was a slight man in his early sixties, wearing a fisherman's tweed hat with flies in it and a wax jacket. He looked like something you'd see in a slightly antiquated version of *Rod and Line*. Kindly eyes under bushy eyebrows. Probably a pipe and a photograph of his grandchildren lurking somewhere in his pockets. Only a fly-fishing *aficionado* would have noticed the macabre aspect. It was Liam who had pointed it out to me. Liam had, at some stage, fished the great western lakes of Corrib and Mask. 'You see what that fucker's wearing in his hat?' Liam said. 'The fishing flies? You know what they're called? They're all variations on the one fly.' It was true. The fly was known as the Bloody Butcher.

Somerville patted my stomach with an avuncular chuckle. An evil enough sound when you knew the man.

'We're not keeping you fit enough.'

'I'm all right,' I said. 'What I lack in fitness I make up for in experience.'

'Still,' he said, 'keeping fit is important.'

We went into Somerville's office. It was book-lined. An old Remington typewriter sat on an untidy desk. There was a wax jacket and a tweed cap on the old hatstand. A gentleman farmer with a taste for bookish things was the impression that the outsider would take away.

'I assume there's a reason why I'm here.'

He ignored me.

'I particularly enjoyed your Cuban sportfishing piece,' he said, lighting an obnoxious old pipe and looking particularly pleased with himself at this new addition to the country cliché.

'Marlin,' he said, 'the king of fish. Beautiful photographs too, I thought.'

'I've never fished for big-game fish in my life,' I said, 'and you know it.'

'Indeed I do, indeed I do,' he chuckled. 'In fact, I had the opportunity myself a few decades ago. Cuba really is a most beautiful place.'

I didn't doubt that he had been there. Havana, Berlin, Hanoi. Anywhere there had been big politics, big intrigue, the old bastard was likely to have been there.

'More of a trout and salmon man, like myself.'

'Not really alike, it has to be said.'

He gave me a small, thin smile.

'Ireland,' he said, 'that was where you used to go.' He grimaced. 'I don't really go for the misty Celtic thing myself, but there's no accounting for taste. When was the last time you were there?'

'Ireland? A few years.' I was wary. I didn't know if he knew about my friendship with Liam Mellows. Or the deeper friendship with his sister. It would be naïve to assume that information hadn't reached him and been stored up for future use. And I was right.

'You have a particular regard for Ard Mhaca,' he said, 'particularly the southern half.'

I was only half-surprised at his use of the Irish term for County Armagh. It was the kind of thing he liked to bring into a conversation, knock you off guard, make you think he knew more than he did.

'South Armagh,' I said. 'You mean South Armagh.' He

gave me a smile that was half a grimace. You could see the skull under his skin. It seemed too close to the surface.

'Yes. Bandit country. Never liked that term myself. Smacks of melodrama a bit. One does somehow resent the capacity of military men to remove the mystery from a place. Anyhow, I need somebody to go there.'

'Why?'

'Ah, the legendary bluntness,' he said, pulling on his pipe and leaning over the desk, his eyes twinkling.

'Ah, the legendary twinkly old squire act,' I said, getting annoyed.

'Yes, well,' he said, sitting up. 'There's a body in there. Ravensdale Forest which, I know, is strictly speaking across the border in the Republic, but local knowledge is what I'm after. I want you to find it and bring it back along with any possessions you might find on it of course.'

'Nairac?' The young SAS officer had been abducted in the early seventies and killed. His body had never been found, but it was presumed he went through the mincer in a local meat plant. He was a bit of a legend in the services, but I always thought he was foolish and a danger to himself and others. Obviously Somerville felt the same.

'No, not Nairac. I wouldn't waste an operative on that gung-ho fool.'

'Thanks,' I said drily.

'Nairac,' he snorted. 'This is far more important than Nairac. I want you to find him and bring me everything that you find on him. Unread.'

'Documents, in other words.'

'Documents, yes.' He clearly hated having to tell me anything at all. He didn't have to worry. I had no intention of going.

'You know how I feel about Irish operations, and as far as this one is concerned . . .'

'The operative concerned was parachuted into Ravensdale Forest in 1972.'

'1972? For God's sake, Somerville,' I said. 'How do you expect me to find a body that's been lying in a forest for decades?'

'Keep your shirt on,' he said mildly, 'I wouldn't ask you to do it if it was impossible.'

I treated that with the contempt it deserved.

'There were two operatives,' Somerville went on. 'The second operative was injured in the landing as well, but he managed to drag the body to a cistern. According to the account that he gave in hospital, he then tumbled the stone of the cistern over the body. "Safe for a hundred years" was the phrase he used, I believe.'

'I don't suppose there would be any chance of talking to this operative?'

Somerville made an elegant gesture with his right hand which suggested a circle closing. I had seen this before. It was his way of saying that the man was dead.

'It took three days to find him and get him out. He was weakened by his injuries and by exposure. Unfortunate.'

I didn't know it then but Somerville was lying. The man was still alive. And he had fullfilled at least part of his mission.

Unfortunate. It was the strongest epitaph you were ever going to get from Somerville. He wasn't a man given to graveside eulogies.

'Any map co-ordinates?'

'No.'

'General location? Something like that would be nice.' I didn't ask why the two operatives had gone parachuting into a forest in the dead of night when there was a perfectly good network of minor roads in the area. You'll find that secret services are inclined to operate to a highly rarefied logic which only occasionally makes sense when exposed to what the rest of us call common sense.

'No, but I have come up with rather a clever theory.' Somerville looked pleased with himself, which always worried me.

'Our friend said that he buried the body in a cistern. It seems unlikely that it really was a cistern. However, the area is littered with stone-age souterrains. Burial chambers. Rather apt, don't you think? I'm working on the assumption that it was one of these souterrains that the body was deposited in. Now. Look at this.'

Somerville took a round cardboard tube from under his desk. He took an old piece of paper from it and spread it with something approaching reverence on his desk. It was a beautiful object, an early nineteenth-century archaeological map. It was beautifully drawn, castles and ancient sites carefully inked in by hand, the forest represented by exquisitely drawn, minute trees.

'Thought you'd be impressed,' Somerville said. 'But the chief advantage for us is that it shows souterrains that aren't listed on more recent maps. We reckon that our man landed up here.' He pointed to a mountainous area at the top of the forest. 'And as you can see, there are four souterrains in that area. Shouldn't take you more than a night to visit all of them.'

'Who says I'm going?'

'Don't be tiresome, Jack. You are going and you know it.'

'How does that work?'

'I'm getting a bit old to be making threats, to be honest with you, Jack. But I can if I want to. You've been in this business long enough to know what you're doing. All your choices were made a long time ago and you chose to stay with this kind of work. You can't leave this world now. It won't let you go. I'm sorry about that. I really am.'

He really did look old and tired, and for a moment I felt sorry for him and almost stretched out a hand to comfort him. What I should really have done was reach into my shoulder holster, take out the Glock and empty it into his dessicated, evil old body. I know that now. And some part of me knew it then.

*

Outside, he seemed to cheer up.

'You'll get everything you need through the usual channels. Full logistical support . . .' He held up a hand. 'All right, all right, Sir Galahad likes to operate on his own. But one has to say these things. By the way, we're doing *The King and I* in the village hall tonight. You should stay. It's really rather good.'

The thing that concerned me about the operation was why this man was so important after so many years. And if he was important, why did they not send in an army team to get him back? It wouldn't be the first time a covert team crossed the border on nefarious business. At one stage, they were crossing it as often as the twice-daily Dublin–Belfast train. Even in the mirror world of covert operations, there was something very strange about this one.

3

It was a long drive back to the west coast of Scotland, but I did it that night. I felt somehow grubby after the whole meeting and I needed the clear air of Kintyre to cleanse me. It was close to dawn as I rounded the curve at the top of the road above my croft and even in the murky pre-dawn light the confluence of sea and sky and mountain was enough to reduce you to awestruck silence. The croft was a simple building – three rooms, an outhouse and a large stone barn which I had renovated. But the big advantage of the place, aside from the remote location, was the small pier that came with the property. A path led down from the house, a tunnel really, between tall, overgrown fuchsia and whitethorn bushes. The path led through a gully and you emerged on to what was effectively a secret harbour. There was a cut granite storehouse, a slate-roofed boathouse and a small granite pier. No matter how hard it blew – and the north-easters coming down from the Norwegian coast and Siberia knew how to blow – it was always calm in this little anchorage. In 1981, I'd paid a modest sum for house, harbour and eighteen hundred acres of heather. The year before, I had bought the *Castledawn* and at the time it seemed the perfect place to berth a fifty-foot, clinker-built trawler-turned-houseboat. She might not have been a thing of beauty as a houseboat, but as an elegant seagoing working boat I don't think you would find anything more lovely. A high seabreaking bow and a low, upswept ducktailed stern. I had spent a summer and an autumn turning her into a boat you could live in, working long hours with high-pressure steam hose and sander to get rid of the smell of herring and diesel oil. Honest enough smells, but visitors seemed to find them a bit overpowering.

As I walked down the tunnel from the house, I wasn't expecting company. I was looking forward to a hot shower and a warm bed, but when I rounded the corner at the bottom of the path, I knew there was someone on the boat. I wasn't too worried. If a professional assassin had been after me, he would have taken me out on the path and I wouldn't have known a thing about it. And it was unlikely an assassin would have been responsible for the thin plume of smoke rising from the galley chimney. But somehow I found I had a gun in my hand. Just in case.

I needn't have worried. I smelled the black bacon as soon as I hit the gangplank. It came, dry-salted, from Fermanagh and nothing could compete with it for mouthwatering aroma. Only one man would have thought of bringing it with him from Ireland. Particularly when he was being pursued by ruthless gunmen.

'Hope you found the eggs, Mellows,' I shouted out.

'I found them under the hens,' Liam shouted back cheerfully through the galley window. 'Hens indeed,' he went on. 'Some secret service man you are. Keeping hens.'

'Fully organic,' I said, noting that he had put on enough food for the two of us. 'How did you know I would be back today?'

He gave me a shrewd, countryman's look.

'Somebody had to be here to let the hens out of the coop.'

In fact, when I wasn't there, Jackie Irvine, my elderly neighbour, was happy to look after the chickens and grumble to them about why people had to go off gadding about the world in the first place. But I let it go. The food smelled too good and Liam shovelled it on to plates with a triumphant grin. I swallowed my curiosity and tiredness and tucked in. When we had finished, Liam leaned back in his chair and looked around him. He had never been on board the *Castledawn* before, but I could tell he liked what he saw. However, a grunted 'Good workmanship' was all the compliment I was going to get from him. I waited. He got up and wandered around the cabin, looking at the paintings. There was a small Brancusi which I'd paid for in Zurich with a handful of uncut diamonds I'd scooped up from the desert floor that time in Africa. There was a seventeeth-century oil on board from the hand of an unknown Venetian artist, depicting a woman with a subtle, murderous smile. The owner of that had left it with me for safekeeping, then thrown himself from a fourth-storey window in his Belgravia house. At least, the inquest had concluded that he had thrown himself out of the window, although I had my suspicions. I loved both of the paintings but felt compromised by their origins. The other painting was different. A five by four-foot McSweeney: a bog scene set in the west of Ireland. It was almost abstract, because that was the way he saw it, and you could lose yourself in the colours and the endless western sky. I think the best thing about it was that the painter had given it to me himself. I remember protesting and the words coming out wrong. I meant to say that it was worth too much. In fact, what I said was that I wasn't worth it. 'You are,' he said, turning away with a twinkle in his eye. 'Just.'

But Liam couldn't stay lost in the McSweeney for ever. He turned to me and threw a photograph, a black-and-white print, on to the table. I picked it up. It was a surveillance photograph of two men standing outside what looked like a military hanger. Neither of them seemed aware that there was a camera on them. One of them was a heavy-set man in a raincoat. He had a heavy, jowly face and small, shrewd eyes. It was unmistakably a policeman's face and not the sort you wanted to see looking at you across a plain table in an interrogation cell. There was a brooding sense of violence about him. The other person in the photograph was Liam.

'Who is that?' I asked.

'Whitcroft,' he said. 'Special Branch.'

I nodded. I had heard the name. Ronnie Whitcroft was

something of a legend in Special Branch circles and had once been considered for MRU work. He hadn't passed the physical but had gone on to head the fight against the IRA in the border area. They feared and respected him. Two members of an IRA unit had been killed when their own bomb went off a few years ago, Liam told me. One body had been found immediately. The other body had been found several days later, under rubble. Except that wasn't what had really happened. The second man had been found unconscious but alive, brought back to Newry, revived, interrogated, and then beaten to death in order to replicate the injuries of a man killed by rubble. His body was dumped under a collapsed wall at the bomb site. That had been Whitcroft's operation and he had done the interrogating. Not the man any IRA member of an Active Service Unit exchanged pleasantries with in the street.

'It's a fake,' Liam said bitterly, 'I can't prove it, but it's a fake.' There was an edge in his voice that I had never heard before. Fidelity is the virtue prized above all in Liam's world, and the implication that he was betraying his comrades to the enemy was the worst possible slur you could put on him. Especially when it seemed that his friends and comrades believed that he had betrayed them.

Liam explained what had happened. The photo had been in among documents that the IRA had recovered following a helicopter crash near Bessbrook helibase in South Armagh. The outdated Lynx helicopters crashed much more often than was admitted by the Ministry of Defence and this one had left debris scattered across fields. Two pilots had been injured and the word on the grapevine was that one had died. A farmer had found a briefcase in a field and passed it on to an IRA Active Service Unit. The photograph had been among other documents. According to Liam, much of the other information was good, and it had been assumed that the photograph of Liam and Whitcroft was the real thing. There is nothing the IRA hates more than an informer, and when someone of Liam's prominence turns, their cold fury is intensified. I looked at the photograph again. It had a look of authenticity about it. Liam was in real trouble.

'Who's after you?'

'Apart from everybody?' He smiled wearily. 'They put Canning and Marks on me.'

Canning and Marks. Names to fear. They were known as the border nutting squad. Cold executioners. They were both of farming stock and would put a bullet in you or worse with the same lack of emotion as a farmer's wife would show when wringing a chicken's neck.

'Nearly got me too,' he said, 'before I knew about this photo. Came after me with SLRs. You remember the Alfa?' Liam, unlike many of his comrades, was fond of the good things and a fast car was always one of them. He had an Alfa Romeo Spyder that was his pride and joy.

'No!'

'Afraid so. Involuntary air conditioning. They riddled it. Somebody was looking after me, Jack.' For a moment I thought he looked defeated, then he started to laugh.

'What's so funny?'

'It's just Canning and Marks. I've known the two of them all of my life. Many's the operation we went on. I just can't believe the way they're going after me. It's almost a compliment. The dedication of the two of them. I should be flattered.' He turned serious again.

'Somebody's out to get me, Jack. I've got to prove that photo is a fake and then I've got to find out who planted it, and why.'

'Should be obvious who planted it,' I said. 'Army Intelligence, C3, MI5 – take your pick. The IRA turning on its favoured son. Enough to make their mouths water.'

'I wonder,' he said, 'I wonder.' I wondered if he knew or suspected something else, but the pale, wintry sun was well above the horizon now and the sleepless night was catching up on me. I yawned. Liam grinned. His capacity to go without sleep was legendary.

'Better hit the bed,' he said. 'I can't believe the way you Scottish boys need sleep. You're like a teenage girl sleeping half the day with fairies dancing in your head.'

His reference to teenage girls seemed to strike a chord in Liam. His mouth set and he turned silent. As I went to bed in the forward bedroom I had built for myself, I looked out the porthole and saw Liam standing on the deck, oblivious to the sleet that was now driving in from the sea. When Liam was sixteen, his fifteen-year-old girlfriend had been shot dead by a British paratrooper when she was on her way home from school. Witnesses described how the man had taken careful aim at the laughing girl in the convent school uniform and shot her through the heart, then turned, grinning, to his comrades. Later, it had been claimed that she had been killed in an 'exchange of fire' with the IRA. It was a lie. She had been cold-bloodedly shot down and then her murder had been covered up. Sometimes a man puts on a uniform and it ennobles him. More often he puts it on and it turns him into a slobbering repository of evil and hatred. I wondered which category Liam Mellows considered he belonged to. I wondered which category he considered I belonged to. I sighed and got out of bed. There was one job I could do for him before I turned in. I slid back a teak panel in the aft bulkhead to reveal my computer and satphone. I turned on the computer and dialled a Milan number. While I waited for it to boot up, I remembered how I had renewed my acquaintance with Liam.

It was 1987 and I was in the bar of the Cross Keys pub in County Antrim, when three men entered. It wasn't just their grim demeanour that made me think that they weren't in for a night's drinking. It was the Kalashnikovs that two of them were carrying and the Glock revolver that the leader was carrying in his belt, and the black balaclavas they were all wearing. The leader moved among the people at the bar, asking strangers for identification and I realized that this was a dark parody of the police and army checkpoints that were so prevalent at the time. When the leader got to me, he looked at me for a long time. He looked at my driving licence.

'What are you doing in these parts, Mr McElhinney?'

'Tractors,' I said, trying to sound nervous, or at least the kind of nervous a Mr McElhinney selling tractor parts would feel being confronted by an armed man and not the sort of nervous a man who was well able to recognize his interrogator's custom-handled Glock revolver since he had one of his own tucked into his shoulder holster.

The Glocks were customized in a back-alley shop in Windhoek, South-West Africa, by a small, mild-mannered man in a cardigan who could get you anything from a Challenger tank to a kilo of weapons-grade plutonium if you had the money. And in Africa, somebody always had the money.

'Welcome to the occupied six counties, Mr McElhinney,' the man said, and smiled. He moved on and the other two went with him. After a few minutes, they slipped out into the night. I breathed a sigh of relief and was about to order a stiff drink when the barman appeared at my elbow with a glass of Redbreast, neat.

'Where'd that come from?' I said.

The barman nodded in the direction of the door where the three men had just left.

'The boys,' he said gruffly.

'The leader?' I asked. The barman nodded. He wasn't going to get into a discussion about the matter. He went to the end of the bar, and only the occasional glance in the bar mirror when he thought I wasn't looking betrayed his curiosity. I swilled the peaty liquid in my mouth. I'd learned to drink it while trapped in a curfew-hit obscure Sudanese town. I couldn't get out but I met a flinty Irish missionary who was in the same situation and had learned a long time ago to temper the hardship by slipping a crate of whiskey in with the shipments of pamphlets they sent him from Dublin. Only a few people knew of my taste for the amber fluid. Only a few.

Outside, a lonesome wind carried rain down from the ancient boglands stretching out in front of the warm bar and once again I wondered at men prepared to fight and die for such an impoverished and Godforsaken scrap of earth.

I shivered and pulled the collar of my coat around my neck. It was as dark as the inside of a cellar and I fumbled putting the key into the lock as I got into the car. As I reached for the seatbelt, I heard the unmistakable soft metallic click as the safety catch of a custom Glock automatic was slid to the off position and felt the cold steel of its barrel caressing the back of my neck.

'A tractor salesman, Jack? Not the most original identity I've heard you come up with.' The voice was soft with a deceptive lilt of laughter in it. Deceptive because the last thing that many men had heard was that same lilt.

'Thanks for the Redbreast, Liam. It was a nice touch.'

'What sort of Irishman would forget a friend's favourite drink?'

'It's a pity you couldn't have sat down and had one with me.'

'There's still a war going on, Jack,' he said, 'and sometimes friends find themselves on different sides.'

I wasn't sure if it was my imagination or if the pressure of the gun barrel against the back of my neck had increased slightly.

'I'm not here on war business, Liam.' The gun stayed pressed against the back of my neck for a moment and then it was gone. We might have found ourselves on different sides in a very dirty war, but the kind of trust that existed between us transcended even that. I knew that Liam Mellows set a lot of store in comradeship. He might have been completely ruthless, but he was the most loyal friend I had ever had.

I realized that Liam hadn't even asked me what I was in

fact doing there. Once he knew I wasn't there as an enemy, he had no interest. I decided to confide in him. I told him I was looking for a surveillance pod dropped from an overflying American Awac spy aircraft.

'More imperialist junk dumped by the US empire,' Liam said. I was inclined to agree with him. I had seen the effects of American carpet bombing in Cambodia at first hand.

'As far as I'm concerned, Liam, it could just lie here and rot. The problem is that it's full of radioactive material.'

'Dangerous?'

'Not if the container is intact. Still, it's not the sort of thing you want lying around.'

Liam got out of the back seat and climbed into the passenger seat.

'Is that who you're working for now? The Yanks?'

'They borrowed my services from my boss, apparently.' Liam didn't say anything. I knew he disapproved of my lack of an ideology. But he also knew there were things which I wouldn't do.

'OK, Jack, let's go and find your surveillance device.' I started the engine and he pointed to the road leading across the bog.

Liam didn't have much to say on the drive and I respected his silence. After a few miles, he motioned me to stop outside a small farmhouse.

'Come on,' he said, 'there's something I want to show you.'

Ten minutes later, accompanied by an elderly, morose farmer, we had found the surveillance pod. It was intact and fulfilling a task it had never been designed for, that of filling a gap in a threadbare hedge and preventing a herd of scrubby mountain cattle from heading for the hills.

'You may give Peter Joe here a few bob for taking it out of his hedge,' Liam said. The old man took the money and grunted something to Liam. The area around the Crosskeys was one of the few areas in the North where you could still hear Irish spoken. Liam spoke back, a few soft words.

'He says he's got some poteen back at the house, some of Big Flynn's, if you're game.'

I thought about it. Poteen was harsh stuff and a bad bottle could kill a man, but Big Flynn was a legend in the making of the illegal spirit, and he had a recipe handed down from father to son where a little honey was blended with the finished product. At least it killed the taste.

'Come on then,' I said, nodding at the retreating back of the farmer, 'before Peter Joe has it all gone.'

But there was more to Peter Joe than met the eye. Once we were sitting in his kitchen with a turf fire in the grate and a bottle open within easy reach on the hearth, the old man thawed. I learned many things that night. How to catch a salmon with a flashlamp and the two-pronged fork they called a graip. How to make a rope out of twisted straw that would hold a man's weight many times over. How to trim a bullrush to make a rushlight that would burn all night in the teeth of a gale. I learned the places to ambush a man in these low-lying windy hills, and the places where you could bury him so that the ever-moving bog would not deliver up his body. For Peter Joe was older than he looked and as a teenage boy he had fought the British in these very hills. Liam flashed a weary smile at me.

'And he hasn't stopped fighting,' he said.

All through the night, Liam had said very little. Out of the corner of my eye I saw that he was staring into the fire. I could see the lines on his face and it reminded me that Liam had been fighting for a long time, had killed, and had seen his comrades killed. I had a feeling that he was suddenly wondering what it had all been for. As we left the small house in the early light, he said something so softly that I almost didn't catch it and indeed I wondered if the words were addressed to me or to himself.

'It's over,' he said.

'What's over, Liam?'

'The war in Ireland is over, Jack, and all that goes with it, good and bad.'

'You think so, Liam?'

'You can smell it on the wind.' He laughed bitterly. 'And guess who won? Not the soldiers on either side, but the shopkeepers. The bread-and-butter boys who spent the past thirty years cowering in their beds. That's who won.'

'And we're getting old.'

'Aye, that we are. We're getting old and we'll be condemned and forgotten.'

'Still, when this one is over, Liam, maybe there'll be time for one more campaign. Both of us on the same side this time.'

'Aye, maybe,' he laughed. 'Just one more campaign. One more good campaign.'

Neither of us really believed it at the time, but there would be one more campaign. A good one it may not have been, for both of us were to pay a dear price, but perhaps it was good, if the erasing of one small part of the evil of your own time is a good thing.

As I walked down the lane away from the house, I turned and saw Liam jump a five-barred gate and stride, whistling, across a rushy field with no trace of the weariness he had betrayed earlier. He had old man Kalashnikov's bitter and durable little darling slung over his shoulder and if he had any concerns that half of the British Army and the whole of the RUC were determined to see him dead or rotting in prison for the rest of his life, then you would never have guessed it.

Two months later, I would find myself wounded and alone in the loyalist badlands of Portadown. It was Liam who came to get me, and his sister Deirdre who tended to me until I was well again. Sometimes, in my bad moments, I wondered if my life was worth saving twice over.

After I had made my call I slept for several hours and woke at dusk to the smell of fresh coffee. I got up, showered and went into the galley. The table was laid for dinner. Philippe Starck cutlery. Nineteenth-century German leaded crystal glasses. I poured a cup of coffee.

'Are you trying to feed me or seduce me?' I said, joking, but Liam gave me a level look.

'A bit of both, I suppose,' he said. 'I'm going to need a bit of help on this one, Jack. And it would seem that I don't have anybody else to turn to.'

'As to that,' I said, 'I've already started on the help, so get the dinner on.'

Liam was a good cook. 'Deirdre taught me,' he told me once. He was one of those men who, in a traditional society, felt no embarrassment about doing things that were regarded as woman's work. Perhaps his supreme confidence came from the fact that no one would dare laugh at him. Not twice at any rate. He had done a Breton chicken dish, cooked very, very slowly in the oven while smothered in three different kinds of mustard. It was delicious, but I ate it with mixed feelings. I'd grown fond of my little brood of chickens and almost thought of them as individuals, although I didn't have the heart to ask Liam which one was on the plate in front of me. Liam chided me for my unimaginative stock of wines. I replied that it was the best cellar you'd find on a seagoing trawler this side of Lerwick.

In a story that was like something out of a bad romantic novel, Liam had been seduced by the beautiful daughter of one of the local Anglo-Irish houses. As well as the more obvious benefits of the relationship, she had introduced him to the fine Navarra wines that her Spanish *emigré* cousins had been cultivating since the previous centuries. Mind you, the benefits of the relationship had flowed both ways. One night, a local Active Service Unit had grabbed the girl's brother, who was a part-time policeman and full-time bastard. He was destined for a bullet in the head until Liam intervened. With the brother at his feet, trussed up in two plastic binbags, Liam had shaken hands with the girl's father. The young man's life would be spared as long as he never set foot in the area again. Both sides kept their bargain.

I stretched out my legs under the table and leaned back contentedly against the bulkhead behind me. Liam fetched glasses and a bottle of Redbreast. But we weren't going to get the pleasure of the whiskey. As I stretched, a light caught my eye. Car headlights were travelling up the headland towards the house. I knew there might be an innocent explanation. I also knew there was no reason for a car to be on the narrow road at this time of night. I had one elderly neighbour who positively discouraged visitors and I hadn't exactly advertised my own presence.

'What is it?' Liam asked sharply. I nodded towards the lights. I could see him assessing the situation. He turned towards me and raised his eyebrows slightly. It's odd how, once you've been companions in mortal combat, an understanding starts to flow between you. I knew that Liam had registered the car as hostile and was asking me whether we should take on its inhabitants. I shook my head. Age taught you the wisdom of tactical retreat as opposed to the unnecessary engagement of what might be a superior force.

I reckoned we had ten minutes before the car reached the house and another five before they found their way to the boat. I hoped the engines would start first time. I was reasonably confident. I had spent a fortune on the twin Perkins diesels to make sure they were ready for just such a situation. I hoped my confidence wasn't misplaced. Without the engines, we were sitting ducks. I made my way to the engine room as Liam climbed on to the pier and made ready to cast off. In the engine compartment, I held in the preheat switch until I got a green, took a deep breath and hit the start button. I needn't have worried. The starter rumbled, coughed and the big diesels kicked into life with a confident throaty rumble. If I'd had more time, I might have stood there and soaked up that well-engineered sound. But I didn't have time. When I got to the wheelhouse, Liam had already cast off one cable and was holding the boat to the pierhead by the other, his back braced against the pull of the tide. I slid back one of the side panels and shouted to him to get on board. There was a narrow channel between razor-sharp rocks that had to be navigated before we hit the open water and we were still vulnerable. I throttled the engines back and swung the *Castledawn* away from the pier. I shut my eyes and tried to picture the channel, then opened them again. 'Dinnae go at the bastard like it's an obstacle course,' old Jackie had said, 'you can feel it here, in your arms. If you let the current carry the boat, you'll nae hit a thing. You just got tae feel the boat.'

As I eased my way down the channel in the dark, Liam knelt on deck with my big Praktica night-vision binoculars clamped to his eyes. A sudden squall of rain blew across the channel and I could see him trying to adjust the binoculars, but even the Prakticas couldn't penetrate the sharp sleet. In a minute, he was in the wheelhouse.

'Four of them, I reckon,' he said, 'in a four-wheel drive. They're at the house.'

I grunted, keeping my concentration. They had made better time than I had expected. The squall passed over and I could see the line of foam where the razor-sharp rocks ended and the open sea began. I resisted the temptation to open up the engines and make a dash for it. The space was too tight and speed limited manœuvrability. I even resisted the temptation when I saw sparks fly from the metal of the winch on the foredeck, followed by the ricochet sound of a hornet's whine, and when the next bullet passed through the wheelhouse door and embedded itself in the engine control stand. Obviously they had found a gap in the weather to shoot through. It also meant that they hadn't come as far as the harbour but had started shooting from the croft, using the height to their advantage. An SLR on single shot, I thought, and good shooting at that. I heard the flat sound of an automatic pistol from the aft deck. Liam hadn't much chance of hitting anything, but it might throw them off a little. I heard more bullets strike the infrastructure. More than anything, I was worried about the expensive array of electronic equipment bolted to the roof of the wheelhouse. A stray round could remove a lot of the communication capacity of the boat, not to mention cost a fortune.

The firing seemed to stop. I think we were outside their range. As I rounded the last dog-leg of the channel, Liam ducked into the wheelhouse.

'Can you not make this tub go any faster?' he said. In answer, I slid the brass arm of the speed control to top and there was a noticeable jolt as the stern of the trawler dug in. She was never going to win a powerboat race, but for diesels the engines were fast, torquey and responsive.

'You see anything?' I asked.

'Not really,' he said. 'But they were professionals. Even from the shooting you could tell that.' He held up the Prakticas. A slug had glanced off the right-hand eyepiece, bending it without fracturing the lens.

'Ricochet,' he said grimly.

'Somebody is really unhappy with you,' I said.

'You're not kidding,' he said. It was a miscalculation we were both to regret. The assumption that the men were after Liam. If I had thought, I would have realized that they were familiar with the layout of the croft, and that they opened fire on the boat, indicating that they knew who owned it.

'I have to get back to Ireland,' Liam said fiercely.

'Funnily enough,' I said, 'that's where I'm going.'

For the first hour I busied myself in the wheelhouse. I liked to keep the boat in a seaworthy state but there are preparations you need to make for the most elementary of journeys and I hadn't made any. I checked the weather forecast and instruments, particularly the Satnav, then, Luddite that I am, I got out a set of charts and plotted a course for the coast of Ireland. Just in case the navigation satellite crashed. Or something. The truth of it was, I liked the feel and look of charts. The feeling that men have carried out this process through the centuries. If I'd had the time, I probably would have climbed out on to the deck and plotted a course from the stars as a third failsafe.

I set the automatic pilot, checked the Decca screen for other ships in the area, then called below to where Liam was engaged in the kind of activity you'd expect from a doughty Irish rebel: washing the dishes. He was whistling the 'Bold Fenian Men' while he was doing it, but I'm not sure that the dead generations of patriots would have approved. I told him to come up and take a watch while I went below to check something. He replied with a dissertation on the best way to dry fine crystal and the vital importance of not placing delicate glasses rim-down when you were draining them. I called him a few names and he came up to the wheelhouse with the look of a put-upon housewife.

Before I went below, I toured the boat. There were a few bullet holes but nothing vital appeared to have been hit. I checked the engines. Oil pressure was spot on and the tanks were full. I went into the forward stateroom. At least in nautical parlance, that's what you called it, but to be honest I thought of it as a bedroom. I booted up the computer again and got the satphone aligned as best I could in the pitch of the waves. The man I rang was called Paolo Casagrande. He had been on the fringes of the Red Brigades in the early seventies and seemed to have operated on the murkiest of murky right-wing counter-Communist operations in the following years. I knew that it might not have been Paolo who had hanged Roberto Calvi, the Vatican banker, from Blackfriars Bridge in a fake suicide, but he knew the men who had done it and he knew the reason why. As a student, he had been at the cutting edge of fashion and art photography and he had kept up his interest in the subject, now operating as Europe's leading fine-art photography dealer. He was one of the shrewdest men I knew and had emerged with his health and fortune intact from one of the darkest periods of European post-war intelligence. Earlier that evening, while Liam had been preparing dinner, I had scanned the photograph of Liam and Whitcroft and e-mailed it to him.

'*Caro* Jack,' Paolo said warmly as he answered the phone, 'how are you? Are you still in the whore's life?' 'The whore's life' was Paolo's term for covert work. It fitted.

'Afraid so.'

'Why don't you come and work with me? You know I need an art buyer.'

The offer was genuine and had been made before. I didn't say anything. Paolo sighed.

'OK, my friend. You'd rather earn your money on your back. They say that you can become addicted even to that. Now, you send me faked-up picture of two men, Irishmen perhaps?'

'Perhaps.'

'Jack, Jack, this sentimental attachment to Ireland will get you killed.'

'Why fake, Paolo? Is it obvious? From a technical point of view, I mean?'

He made an impatient sound.

'No. From a technical point of view it is impossible to tell. The techniques are too good, my friend. No, you must thank the old masters.'

'Explain that one.'

'Chiaroscuro.' Chiaroscuro. The interplay of light and shade. The late Middle Ages had seen painters start to master it. At the time, their technique was seen as a marvel.

'If you enhance the photograph and study the shadows, you will see that the light source for one man – the policeman, no? – you will see that it is coming from, let us call it the eastern quadrant. It is shining from his right. If you take the other one – the good-looking, sad man – the light is falling on him from a different direction, the north-west. Unless there were two suns in the sky that day, then the images of these men were taken in two different places and combined. How do you say it? One was superimposed. I would guess, my friend, that this man should not be seen talking to policemen, yes?' He chuckled. 'No matter. I help you, *caro*, yes?'

We chatted for a while and then Paolo had to go. There was no charge for his services. In this world, you used your expertise to build up credit that you could call upon in time of need. Sometimes it worked, sometimes it didn't.

Paolo e-mailed through the enhanced images. I brought them up to the wheelhouse and showed them to Liam. It was obvious, once it was pointed out to you, but Liam was silent. I knew what he was thinking. Chiaroscuro wasn't going to cut much ice with the boys that were after him. He needed more. I patted him on the shoulder.

'It's a start,' I said. 'Not much of a start, but a start none the less. We've been in worse places.'

'We have,' he said, with a half-laugh, 'we have that. Remember Swartzhoek?'

It was a rhetorical question. You didn't forget things like that. I had met Liam there and we had forged a bond which transcended politics. As the little boat sailed steadily into the gentle North Sea swell, my mind drifted back to Swartzhoek.

4

It was spring in South-West Africa, 1978. The country they now call Namibia. Not that you would know it was spring, for the searing winds, choking red dust and blazing sun were the same all year round and it hadn't rained for twelve years. South-West Africa was a hell for all but the little bushmen who caught what little lived in the burning desert and found ways to cook and eat things you wouldn't even dream of eating. These small people struck me as possessed of a clear-eyed wisdom that the Westerners who ventured there only dreamed of. I had to earn their confidence by eating the things that they ate and by keeping up with them on their treks from dry riverbed to dry riverbed. They taught me the stark beauty of the place, and to see it with their eyes. They were always ready to help outsiders and in return the outsiders hunted them down like rats and slaughtered them for sport. Liam was the only other white man I had seen who established a real rapport with them. He knew how to make them laugh – God knows how – and he teased their tiny gap-toothed women with a line of vaguely suggestive mime that left them bent double with laughter.

I was a young operative, a bit wet behind the ears, and labouring under the delusion that I was working in the cause of justice, liberty and democracy. I had a lot to learn.

It wasn't a happy country at the time. SWAPO were trying to establish the independence of their country in the face of South African resistance, and the land swarmed with regular and irregular armed forces. Desert wasn't worth much, but there were places in the desert where you could pick up diamonds by the handful, and the mineral wealth of the place was reckoned incalculable. I had been sent in to contact a resistance leader and persuade him to throw in his lot with SWAPO. I'm not sure if the real purpose of this machination was to help SWAPO free their country or if there was a deeper geopolitical ramification that I was unaware of, but I had carried out my task and had left a by now very nervous guerilla leader in no doubt what the CIA, FBI, MI5 and God knows who else would do to him if he didn't comply with my gentle suggestion.

I was waiting in Swartzhoek for the big Hercules that would bring in supplies for the town, and take out those with enough dollars to pay for it. Swartzhoek was a small town with a frontier atmosphere, a place which would barely have existed if it hadn't been for the airstrip. As it was, it only had a few hours left to exist on that hot January day as I sipped a Spanish Cinco Estrella and scanned the skies for the big transport plane. There was only one other person in the bar, a white man with the broiled look that fair-skinned people get in a place like this. I noticed that he had a copy of St-Exupery's *Night Flight* open on the table in front of him, and thought that Swartzhoek was the wrong place to get lost in Franco-African desert romance, but I kept my thoughts to myself. It was that kind of place. You kept your own business to yourself in a place where staying alive was the biggest business of all.

I finished the Estrella and strolled down to the airstrip. The plane was due. I noticed a pile of boxes of the distinctive shape they use to carry armaments which seemed ready to to be loaded on to a plane. Again, not an unusual sight in these parts. The European from the bar passed me. I saw his eyes sweep across the boxes and I knew they were his. He carried himself well, and I realized with a shock that for all his man-of-the-world look he couldn't be much older than twenty. I stopped looking at him because I heard the sound of the Hercules in the distance. A group of about a hundred young African soldiers, some of them with wives and children, started to pack up their gear and get ready for boarding. The Hercules didn't hang around. Everybody watched as the plane banked round and lined up for the runway. It was about half a mile out when all hell broke loose.

A long line of red-coloured sand dunes ran to the north of the runway. In fact, they were more hills of sand than dunes, maybe three or four hundred metres high. As I watched the plane come in, I thought I heard a competing engine note. I looked towards the dunes and my heart stopped beating. Behind the red dunes, rising slowly and menacingly above them, I saw four Bell Huey Cobra attack helicopters. They looked like something from another, wicked era. Monstrous science-fiction insects, their crew wearing reflective visors, the red sand whirling beneath them as they advanced across the desert floor, the multiple machine-gun pod slung beneath them moving from side to side as though seeking its prey. I just had time to see the tracked support vehicles speeding down the sides of the dunes before they opened up with side-mounted rockets. Everything seemed to happen in slow motion. Women and children screaming, cursing men trying to unsling rifles, then the smell of burning fuel, the smell of burning flesh.

I stood mesmerized as the big Hercules, committed to landing, and moving with desperate slowness, tried to escape. It went past me so close, I could see the pilot fighting the controls as it banked away from the airfield, its four engines screaming, almost standing on a wingtip so that its vulnerable underbelly was exposed. Almost casually, one of the choppers turned towards it, the gun pod seeking out the big plane, almost as if it was sniffing the air for it. I watched the tracer bullets stitch their way across the wing of the plane. One engine burst into flame, then another. It was enough. The wing tip hit the ground and the plane cartwheeled, bursting into flames with a hollow crumpling noise. I felt a pressure on my arm and I turned. The young European was standing there. Despite the mayhem all around him, I felt his eyes searching mine. It felt as if he was examining my soul, seeing if I was worth saving. I passed the test. He nodded at me to follow him. With the oily smoke of the burning aircraft for cover, we began to run. I understood that he was heading for the dry riverbed that ran north from the town. It wasn't much cover but it was something.

We ran through a small courtyard. There was a rocket hole in a wall and a blackened rocket fin on the ground, but no other sign of war. Except for the young mother and her two children lying on the ground in the middle of the courtyard. Neither child, a boy and a girl, could have been over five. In fact, the mother couldn't have been more than seventeen or eighteen. There didn't seem to be a mark on them, but they were dead and the little girl still had a doll in her hand. I looked at Liam. His face was red as if it embarrassed him to be alive in the presence of the innocent dead.

'Bastards,' he said. 'Fucking bastards.' He leaned over and shut each pair of eyes gently. Then he blessed himself and stood in silence. I had to draw him away as the sounds of war drew near.

As we closed on the wadi, he stopped at a small shack. He emerged from the shack with a M16 machine-gun and stand, a box of bullet belts for the M16, a small but strong-looking bushman who seemed to come along to carry the ammunition, and a Kalashnikov which he tossed to me. We ran for the wadi.

We might have made it. There was a fair bit of scrubby undergrowth in the wadi and we covered about quarter of a mile at a trot. But there is an instrument of war that the First World brings to its conflicts with weaker nations, weapons which it leaves behind on the land like a deadly crop which feeds nobody and kills without distinction. They are assembled by housewives for pin money in discreet factories in Rotherham and Birmingham and Daid County and in secret towns in the Russian interior, and everywhere else the arms industry plies its evil trade. Landmines cost nothing to make and are sold cheaply in their millions. The one that Liam put his foot on was an old Russian model, and that was important in that it was a crude device which didn't explode straight away. Putting your foot on it armed it and you had to take your foot off it before it exploded. Liam had obviously come across it before, because he froze, standing awkwardly in the wadi with the M16 still in his arms. As if things weren't bad enough, the bushman shouted something and raised his arm. We could see where he was pointing. An angry engine noise and a cloud of dust showed where one of the Hueys was starting to work its way down the wadi.

I looked at Liam. He met my gaze with the same calm look I had seen earlier. There was a quizzical look in his green eyes. He had judged me a worthwhile companion earlier on. Would I live up to his assessment of me? The old bushman seemed to be looking at me as well, with the same air of being a disinterested observer. I looked down the wadi towards the chopper, then I threw the Kalash to the bushman and knelt to examine the mine. The bushman knelt at the other side just to make sure that the mine would get all of us if it went off. I could see what I had to do. As I said, the mine was a crude device, designed more for vehicles than men. There was a sprung lever on top of it. When you lifted your foot off, the spring forced the lever back up again and the charge went off with enough force to disable a tank track. Crude but effective.

I could see what I had to do. Liam was wearing boots with a Western heel leaving a big enough gap between the heel and the sole to put something narrow through the gap and weigh it down at either end. It would hold the spring down for long enough to enable Liam to step off it. The only thing was, we were in one of the most barren spots on the face of the earth and the twiggy, underfed bushes growing in the wadi weren't going to provide the necessary rod. I felt the bushman tugging at the small rucksack I had on my back. It took a few seconds to realize what he meant, then it hit me. The rucksack was the old-fashioned kind, with flexible steel rods sewn into the material to hold its shape. I hauled the rucksack off and began to cut the seams. As I did so, I saw the bushman start lifting rocks and weighing them in his hand, looking for something that would weigh down either end of the rod.

I began to curse the efficient German machinist who had put the rucksack together. I looked up and saw that the chopper had covered a lot of ground since the last time I had looked. The bushman put two good-sized rocks down beside me. The rod wouldn't come. There wasn't enough time. I heard Liam say something to the bushman. To my amazement the bushman flipped open the ammo box and began to feed a belt into the M16, as Liam raised it into a firing position. I couldn't believe what he was doing. The M16 was designed to be fired from a tripod. Even if you could fire it while holding it in your hands, the kick would make it impossible to aim. And another thing. It would throw you off your feet, meaning that the mine would go off and kill all of us. And even if, by some miracle, none of these things happened, the helicopter still had more firepower. Liam looked down at me. He was grinning broadly, and I knew at that minute exactly what I should have done. I should have stood up and taken to my heels and got as far away from this madman as I possibly could. Then two things happened at once. The steel rod came free of the material and the chopper rounded a bend in the wadi, the rotor noise suddenly deafening, a wall of dust blowing towards us. We hadn't been seen yet, but it wouldn't be long. I bent to the ground and started trying to insert the rod between Liam's instep and the detonation lever of the mine. The rod was slightly too big. I leaned back and wiped the sweat out of my eyes. There was a change in the rotor note of the chopper's engine. It had seen us. I looked up at Liam. The grin was wider. The rotor wash was sweeping his hair back. He opened his mouth and, although I couldn't hear him, I knew he was laughing. He leaned forward in a crouch and I saw his finger tighten on the trigger. I couldn't have run even if I'd wanted to. Even the chopper seemed to hesitate, as if uncertain.

It's a scene I'll never forget. The man facing the machine. As I bent to try and insert the rod again, the barrel of the M16 began to spit fire. I could feel what he was doing, taking all the kick of the gun on one leg and resting the other lightly on the mine mechanism. This time, I heard him laughing. I slipped the rod under his foot and felt rather than saw the bushman clamping it down with one of the big rocks. I reached for the other rock and put it in place. The noise and dust was incredible. I could feel bullets from the chopper thudding into the ground behind me. I knew I should roll clear, but instead I stood up slowly. Some instinct told me that I would be cut down if I ran. I saw that the chopper must have been hit. It was yawing from side to side, making it difficult for the gunner to aim. Liam was firing in short bursts, the bushman feeding the big gun. The pilot must have thought the whole thing as crazy as I did and he decided to cut and run. It was a mistake. Liam loosed off a long, sustained burst. Lumps of perspex began to fly from the cockpit. There was a bang and a scream of tortured metal as the tail rotor shaft snapped and the tail rotor scythed off into the burning sky. Without a fulcrum, the chopper began to spin, soaring into the sky in what seemed like slow motion, the merciless barrel of the M16 following it. A spurt of fuel, followed by a spurt of flame, and then it was all over. For one terrible moment the rotor blades turned above what seemed like a ball of fire and then the Huey plunged to earth, hitting the sand with a dull, lethal noise, the fuel flaring up into the sky.

Liam lowered the barrel of the M16 and stepped forward. He stopped dead still, then turned, looking down at the ground with a wondering look in his face. The steel and rocks had restrained the deadly mine.

'Fuck me,' he said. 'I'd forgotten about that.'

*

It took us a month to reach a port from where we could get back to Jo'burg and thence to Europe. Liam never told me what he had done there, but a few months later the back-streets of Belfast began to reverberate to the sound of RPG7 shoulder-fired grenade launchers. South-West Africa was awash with them, brought in by the Cubans. Neither did he ask me what I had done there. We had forged an unbreakable bond, based on the fact that we would never quiz the other, sharing trust that there were boundaries we wouldn't cross in a world where violent death was a constant companion.

But as we left the coast of Scotland behind us on that dark night, I had a feeling our friendship was moving on to a new level, one where we'd have to let each other into our separate worlds. I made strong black coffee and poured a good shot of Redbreast into each. Normally boats and alcohol don't mix, but I felt we deserved it, and we were a bit too restless for such a small space. The realization that there are people out there prepared to kill you does that. We were crossing the North Channel when I sent Liam below to get some sleep. As I checked the instruments again, the smell of phosphorous stung my nostrils. After both world wars, thousands of tons of munitions had been dumped into the Beaufort dyke and in places the sea was a stinking chemical soup where the shells were leaking. I opened the door to clear the smell from the wheelhouse and heard the whistle of wings overhead. Brent geese probably, heading for some Baltic feeding ground remote from the spoilheads that surrounded the Irish Sea.

The hour before dawn always put me in this morose kind of mood. To dispel it, I began to review my operation. It seemed fairly simple. Find an hotel in the area, and do a recce of the Ravensdale area, using my journalist credentials. The angle? Perhaps the hidden beauty of the border area. That would do. Try and pinpoint the souterrain, get in quick, at night, recover the material, get out, go home. Sounded easy. The problem was that things never went simply on these kind of operations. There was always a snag, sometimes a deadly one. You also had to be aware of hidden agendas and I had absolutely no doubt that there was a hidden agenda here. I knew I would have to stay flexible, react to situations as they arose. Structured plans were likely to get you killed on operations like this.

The other thing was Liam. To be seen with him was a liability, but he would know that himself and wouldn't put me in a spot. But I suspected that he wouldn't be able to operate on his own without support.

By first light, we had passed the coast of the Isle of Man and I set a course for the County Down coast. A fishing boat was unlikely to attract too much attention in the Irish Sea fishing grounds frequented by the Kilkeel and Ardglass fleets, and that suited me fine. Liam came into the wheelhouse with hot coffee just as the cold winter sun was clearing the horizon.

'We'll be within landfall about lunch-time,' I said. 'We'll work our way up the County Down coast and land around Carlingford lough.'

'Suits me,' Liam said. 'I've got an appointment with a Special Branch man.'

'You think Whitcroft has some connection to the photograph getting into circulation?'

'Just an instinct. Well, more than an instinct. I took another look at that photograph last night. There's something in the man's eyes. I don't know what it is. He's just looking too pleased with himself.'

I started to speak but Liam held up his hand.

'I know, I know, there's a thousand ways that the photograph could have been taken without Whitcroft's knowledge, but I have a powerful instinct.'

I knew that this wasn't just talk. Liam did have an uncanny knack of looking at a situation and intuitively working out what was happening. Travelling across the Namibian desert, even the bushmen sometimes deferred to him as if they recognized and valued this quality in him. And to the bushman, intuition was not an abstraction: it was something they relied upon for life itself in the harsh desert landscape.

'So, what do you do?'

'Make contact with Whitcroft.'

'Dangerous game, Liam. Whitcroft is shrewd. If the boys get to know that you contacted Whitcroft then you'll never convince them you haven't turned.'

'I know. I've thought about it. It might even be Whitcroft's game. But the way I see it, I don't have a choice.'

He was right. He had to know what Whitcroft was up to. He had to figure out the game. And the way to figure out the game was to play it. In some way, I could see that Liam was almost looking forward to it. Mental chess with a formidable adversary, the game weighted towards your opponent and the forfeit in the event of failure being your own life. Liam possessed a powerful intellect, but he was too much drawn towards the dark ironies of the intelligence game, lingering over them and enjoying their appalling attraction. It was dangerous to get too close to the terrible romance of it all and I told him so. You lose sight of the bullet or the prison cell that lies at the end of the game. He looked at me with grim amusement in his eyes.

'You're missing one thing, Jack, one vital element.'

'What's that?'

'The fact that Whitcroft feels the same way about it. He likes to play the game and damn the consequences.'

'You don't know that.'

Liam tapped the photograph with his fingernail.

'I do know it, Jack. The man that sent out this photograph is playing games. He's putting it up to me. It's not just a ruse to turn my old friends against me. It's an invitation to play.'

I knew what he was talking about. It was all part of the covert game. Bluff and counterbluff. I had been in a Washington restaurant with a friend for lunch one day. The kind of restaurant with dim lighting and expensive mahogany and brass fittings and discreet staff. The kind of restaurant where, if you didn't know every person in the room and what they did, then you knew nothing that was worth knowing in that most imperial and intrigue-laden of capitals. My friend had nudged me and drawn my attention to two men in an adjoining booth. One was Kim Philby, the man who, apparently, had betrayed almost every move the West had made over thirty years of the Cold War. The other man was James Angleton, head of the European bureau of the CIA. Here was the game writ large and I would have given my right arm to know what the two men talked about on their regular lunch meetings. Whatever was said, insiders maintained that Philby turned and twisted his former pupil with such mastery that Angleton ended up destroying the organization he worked for in a fit of grand paranoia, a twenty-year search for the Soviet mole within the CIA. Others said that the mole was a mirage, a chimera created by Philby, knowing the long-term effect it would have on Angleton and the CIA. Others again said that in fact Angleton himself was the mole. The game is endlessly complex and can be played at as many levels as you think you can handle.

However, the game can't be played if you don't get the basics right and our problem right now was a place to land. The converted trawler houseboat was reasonably conspicious, but normally I could land at any port or marina and make a show of cheerful eccentricity. This time, however, I had a wanted man on board, one who could hardly afford to draw attention. I put the problem to Liam, expecting that he would come up with something heroic like swimming two miles to shore in the dark, a Kalashnikov clamped between his teeth. I mentioned this to Liam and he looked at me as if I had two heads and asked if my phone was secure. It was, and he went off to use it.

It was dusk at that point and we were following the County Down coast, past the industrial overspill of Belfast and the salty, wild beauty of Strangford, and I set a course for Carlingford. Strangford. Carlingford. Old Viking names that delineated the history of brutal invasion and counter-invasion along this coast over the centuries. But as we sailed into the dusk, the shoulders of the Mournes started to appear, blue-coloured in the fading light. The water beat gently against the hull, a trail of phosphorescence formed in our wake, stars started to appear in the clear sky, and I wondered whether it was some unspoken yearning for this gentle landscape that drew the bloodthirsty men down from the north to kill and pillage.

I noticed that the aerial for the satphone had retracted and Liam came up looking pleased with himself. If I'd known the reason for his inscrutable smile, I might have questioned him a bit further, but he gave me a precise set of co-ordinates and grid references which meant that I was busy with the Satnav and the charts for the next twenty minutes while Liam carried his holdall up from the cabin and weighted it down with a few angle irons.

'If the coastguard or Brits stop us, then it goes over the side,' he said, grinning again. 'There's one or two things in here might raise an eyebrow.'

I said nothing. God knows what he had in the bag. As we cut across the mouth of Carlingford lough in the dark, I kept my eyes open for the semi-rigid Sea Otter inflatables the marines used around here, but there was no sign of them, nor of the converted minesweeper which was their base and which patrolled the lough in some odd, old-fashioned gun-boat view of relations between the north and the south. There were better ways of guarding these waters and they knew it, but it pleased them to have an old-fashioned honest-to-God gunboat sitting in the middle of it, just to let people know what was what.

It had turned cold and a squally south-easter was beginning to lift the crests of the choppy waves. I turned my attention to the navigation of these treacherous waters, with their shifting sandbanks and untrustworthy rip tides, and it was after midnight before a small, semi-derelict wooden jetty appeared out of the spray and darkness and Liam shouted as he saw a hooded torch flash three times from the shore. It felt like something out of a World War Two drama and I felt as if I should have a commando cap on and black-out camouflage on my face, but the man who had planned the operation made sure it went smoothly. A small man in his early forties drew his hand across his throat to tell me to cut off the engines and then two other men took cables from Liam and used the forward momentum of the boat to guide it into a dark, roofed-over dock with enormous doors which closed on us as soon as the stern had cleared the entrance. I tried to make out details, but there were only the navigation lights to cast a dim light into the darkness and I suddenly started to feel trapped and at the mercy of unseen forces. I had the Glock in the small map compartment under the wheel and I reached in and rested my hand on the butt. As my eyes got used to the light, I saw that Liam had leaped on to the dock and was talking to the small man I had seen outside. Something about the stance suggested that they were not particularly friends but rather business rivals who liked and respected each other but knew that friendship had limits in whatever territory they operated in.

I heard a switch being thrown and a harsh light was cast over the area. I hesitated, then withdrew my hand from the pistol and stepped out on to the deck. I climbed on the rail and leaped on to the dock.

The small man swept a glance over me with a swiftness which suggested he didn't need much time to sum up a man. He had dark, shrewd eyes and pockmarked skin. He was wearing a sweater and jeans, nothing to mark him out, but there was a tension about him, a sense of stored energy.

'Jack, this is Paddy Regan.' I knew the name as one of a group of what were loosely referred to as smugglers in the border area. People had been smuggling there since the border had gone up but some people maintained that there was a history of defiance of the law that went back so many centuries that it was almost genetic by now. Large-scale oil smuggling, abuse of European premiums, tax avoidance, subornation and bribery of Her Majesty's officials, unashamed fraternizing with known paramilitaries . . . it was a murky world, but, as I learned, when you met a man as erudite and clever as Regan, you could see that it held the same fascination that drew people into covert work. Except that Regan had extended into property and investment, and had an unashamed liking for money in place of the half-baked ideologies and white-knight complexes that drove the rest of us.

Regan asked me what I thought of the dock. The whole place was cut stone, but the roof was of corrugated iron.

'It was a famine work,' he said. 'It was meant to be the mouth of a canal but this was the only part they built. I threw an old roof over it and a few doors. Handy now for a bit of quiet business, and you'll forget that you ever saw it.' The last remark was made in a mild tone, a casualness that didn't fool you. The really dangerous ones never needed to raise their voices.

'I hear you're a friend of Deirdre Mellows,' Regan said, with a tone that suggested being a friend of Deirdre's was good enough for him.

He turned to Liam.

'I got both of you a car,' he said.

We went outside. Liam's car was a BMW M3. Hardly the sort of car you wanted if you were trying to avoid drawing attention to yourself, but fast enough to get you out of trouble.

'This is for the Scotsman,' Regan said with a grin on his face. I turned to see what was probably the dirtiest, most battered Land Rover I had ever seen in my life. Liam laughed at the expression on my face.

'There's a bit of slurry on her,' Regan said, 'but I'd be used to the smell myself.'

You had to just smile and let them have their fun. In fact there was nothing decrepit about the Land Rover, and I would have reason to be grateful for its capabilities. I brought both of them into the wheelhouse and poured them a drink while I went down into the bilge and secured some of the tools of the trade from their hiding place. When I came back up, the two men had poured themselves another drink and neither showed any appreciable signs of leaving the warm sanctuary of the wheelhouse. I joined them. We talked quietly for a few minutes, then Liam turned to me.

'Regan says that Deirdre is home.' I felt a dryness in my mouth. You'd think that as you get older you would lose all those heart-fluttering sensations you felt as a teenager. But you don't. I knew that Deirdre had been working as an administrator in an aid organization and I knew her work took her all over the world, and it seemed somehow easier that I never knew where she was. Now she was close, probably within a ten-mile radius.

'I met her in Dundalk the other night,' Regan said. 'I think she got herself suspended from work. She's waiting for them to decide what to do with her.'

Deirdre had always been interested in that kind of work, but from the start there had been nothing starry-eyed about her. She pointed to the fact that most of the acts of so-called charity during the Irish famine were motivated by self-interest dressed up in one form or another, and she knew that many humanitarian interventions did far more harm than good, but she said that focused, intelligent work could save lives. This time, it seems, she'd become just a little too focused. Regan explained that a local hard man in Somalia had a warehouse packed with grain which he was using to control and exploit the market. People were starving but he wouldn't release it at an affordable price. So Deirdre released it, crashing one of the armed jeeps they call technicals into the compound and through the wooden wall of the warehouse, holding off the warehouse guards with judicious use of the 12mm cannon mounted on the back of the jeep. She got out of Mogadishu on an Arab dhow and persuaded a passing American frigate to take her to a friendly port. Apparently she was still continuing a chess game by correspondence with the skipper of the dhow.

For all of the feelings that the mention of her name had stirred up, I couldn't help laughing. Liam looked suitably disapproving at first, but the mention of the chess game weakened his angry protectiveness and in a minute he was laughing the same rueful laugh.

'Has she changed much, Regan?' I asked. There was too much feeling in the question and Regan glanced at Liam before replying.

'Not at all, *a chara*,' he said, rising from his chair and slapping me on the back, 'not at all.'

5

I finished the last few yards, before the ridge, on my belly. The last thing I wanted to do was create a profile on the ridge. Just before I got to the top, I stopped to screw the anti-reflective filters on to the Zeiss binoculars I'd bought that morning. I edged over the damp turf until I could see the whole of south-east Armagh spread out below me. In the distance above the army base on Dromad mountain, two Lynx helicopters were circling in a protective fashion, five hundred feet above a heavily laden Sikorsky delivering supplies. The base wasn't there solely as part of the military infrastructure of South Armagh. It was a test base for surveillance equipment and sophisticated listening devices, to see how they would perform under real battlefield conditions, a refinement which added a few million to the price of the item in question, I suppose. Swinging round to my left, I could see the wooded slopes of Ravensdale. I reckoned I would be safe enough up there from whatever technological marvels were peering at the woods from the top of Dromad. Electronics are all very well, but people start to depend on them and forget the high failure rates of electronic warfare devices. Useful tools do exist, but that is all they are, and they are no substitute for human skill and experience. The slopes of Ravensdale are covered with trees, and if a boffin anywhere has come up with a device which can see through a tree, I haven't heard of it, and the mists which generally shrouded the upper slopes at night were equally resistant to inquisitive eyes.

I spent the afternoon doing a careful reconnoitre of the whole area. The sites of each souterrain were hard to find among the jumble of rocks that littered the mountainside. I thought about Paolo and what he had said about the photograph, and started to think about the problem laterally. If I were burying a body four thousand years ago and was looking for a site which provided mystical significance, I wouldn't plant it in the middle of a bog. Nor in a shadowy hollow if I was part of a society which regarded the sun as the giver of life. I went back to looking at the landscape, searching this time for sites which would have the longest exposure to the sun. I found the first souterrain within five minutes and as soon as I developed an eye for the task, it wasn't difficult to locate the other four likely targets. I decided to get off the mountain. I would have to come back the next day and mark them so that I could find them in the middle of the night. It didn't pay to stay in your target area a minute longer than necessary.

What happened that night seemed inevitable. Even before Paddy told us that Deirdre was back, I had decided to stay at McKevitt's in Carlingford. It was a small hotel in a quaint town that attracted travel journalists, archaeological buffs and hill walkers in equal measure and so provided good cover, but I had a less professional motive for choosing it. What is that Chinese curse? That you get what you wish for?

I realized when I started the Land Rover that it was something special. There was so much under your foot that it was hard to keep the thing on the road until you got used to it. I drove into Drogheda and down through Dundalk before turning off for the Cooley peninsula and gave two young lads in a GTI the shock of their lives as I burned rubber at traffic lights and left them standing, laughing like a hyena at their stunned faces in the rear-view mirror. It wasn't the way to keep your cover intact, but the best operatives I had ever seen were the ones who were able to let off steam on an impulse that went against everything they had ever been taught. I suppose it kept them from taking themselves too seriously. And besides, I drove into Carlingford like the middle-aged man in a wax jacket that I was.

I did all the things I'd done before. I booked into McKevitt's, where the owner recognized me as the hill walker and amateur art historian he had met before. I had lunch at the bar, wandered around the harbour and looked at the ocean-going yachts that swept down here in a fast arc from Scandinavia, driven by the same cold winds that brought their Viking ancestors. It was a small village with narrow medieval streets, dominated by the bulk of the Carlingford mountains behind it, and it didn't take long to walk around. I went to the library and read up on souterrains until the library closed and I emerged not much wiser than before.

PJ's is one of those pubs that seems to transcend the idea of a pub and take it into some other realm of comfort and ease. A small, low doorway into a tiny bar with groceries stacked behind the counter, opening out into a long, narrow low-ceilinged room with comfortable chairs and low tables with a fire burning at the end. There are nautical bits and pieces dotted around the place, and there's a gleam of brass and mahogany that captures the flickering light of the fire. I waited until it was almost dark before I went in. I ordered a Redbreast and a bottle of Guinness as a chaser and sat by the window, watching as the light faded and the wind drove spatters of rain against the window. It was quiet at first, but as the evening went on, people began to drift in.

Like I say, there was more than one reason for choosing Carlingford, more than one reason for being in PJ's, and as the night went on I began to lose myself in nostalgia, staring into my glass and not watching the door as I should. I only glanced up as the door opened and two men came in, and again as a group of women came in, laughing among themselves. But I sat up and took notice as I saw the face of one of the men reflected in the mirror of the outer bar which was otherwise separated from me by a partition. It was Whitcroft, the Newry detective. It couldn't be a coincidence. Among the raised voices of the group of women behind me, I heard a voice and the tone of it froze me on my stool. Without thinking, I turned towards them and caught Deirdre Mellows in profile, and for a few seconds was able to look at her without her knowing. She was laughing and telling a story, her eyes flashing and her black hair hanging forward over her face, a little older, but that had just given her face strength, filling out the high cheekbones a little, slightly softening the bow shape of her lips. The first thing you saw was her beauty. The second thing you saw was her strength. She finished her story and as her friends were laughing, sat back and felt my eyes on her. The colour drained from her face, except for two small spots high on her cheekbones. The expression in her eyes suggested someone who had always known that some day fate would show its cunning hand in her life, and now it had. Her lips opened and I shook my head in a barely perceptible motion. Don't. Don't look at me. Don't speak to me. I was aware of Whitcroft and the other man sitting in the next bar, in such a position that the mirror behind the bar enabled them to see everything that took place in the back room. I knew they weren't watching me, so it had to be Deirdre. I turned back to the bar and tried to take a drink from my bottle without dropping it. I sat there with my back to her for ten minutes while I finished the drink and it was the hardest ten minutes of my life. Without looking at her, I slid off the stool and left the bar by the back door.

I waited in the back yard. Through the window of the bar I could see her talking to her friends, although once she turned to the window and stared out into the darkness, unaware that I was there, and her face suggested that she was looking into a void.

I saw her pick up her handbag and go through a mime with her friends, touching her stomach to indicate that she wasn't feeling well. The door opened and the sound and the light of the pub spilled out into the yard. She stood on the threshold of the pub as if she stood at the very portal between the light and the darkness and then she closed the door behind her and stepped into the dark. I moved forward and put my arms around her and drew her into the shadow of the turfshed beside the bar door. I put my finger to her lips to indicate silence. We stood there without moving. I could feel my hand on her ribs, the lightness of the bones, a faint pulse. She did not move into me, nor did she move away from me. I lowered my face towards the top of her head and inhaled the smell of her hair and I swore in that rainwashed yard I could smell sunlight and apple blossom and a more innocent time. The door of the bar opened again and this time she stiffened and moved towards me. Deirdre had lived with the consequences of subversion all her life and knew when she was close to danger and what to do about it.

I watched as Whitcroft emerged and stood in the yard. There was no way he could see us unless he entered the turf-shed. I could smell his cigarette. In the light of the tip as he drew on it his features appeared feral and shifty. He spotted the gateway and made his way towards it and out. I felt Deirdre relax and start to turn towards me. I dug my fingers fiercely into her to stop the movement, shaking her slightly. Don't move. Don't fucking move. Something in her told me that she was offended, but there was nothing I could do about that. We waited. Two minutes, three minutes. She shifted restlessly then froze as the bar door opened a fraction and a shadowy figure slipped out. It was Whitcroft's companion and there was no mistaking the heavy police-issue Walther in his hand. They were professionals. They had given us just enough time to break cover. The second man would have had us. He stood absolutely still for another minute, then moved stealthily across the yard and out of the gate.

It felt as if we had been standing there for ever. It was ten minutes before I released her. Telling her to stay there, I crept down to the seafront. I saw Whitcroft and the other man standing beside a green Rover. They were too far away for me to hear what they were saying, but it seemed they had given up on the search, as I saw them get into the car and drive off. I turned to go back, then found Deirdre at my side. I thought there was something I should say but the silent danger of the yard seemed to have somehow short-circuited the years between us, the catching-up, the surveying each other for the damage those years had done. We walked slowly together towards the castle that dominated the harbour and as we walked she slipped her hand into mine. As we stepped into the shadows of the castle, she turned to me, her grey-green eyes searching mine as if to find out how much I had changed. I met her gaze without flinching. She reached out one finger and traced the scar on my temple. Her finger traced the outline of my cheekbone, then touched my lips, and I saw her smiling at me with a look that was frank and open and teasing at the same time. And I pressed into her, knowing I needed no second invitation, for when she gave herself she gave herself completely. I buried my hands in her hair and she responded violently and the years of regret and wasted opportunity between the two of us melted away as my hands sought her breasts and her thighs and she writhed against me.

There would be time afterwards for talk. To hear about the years of work in remote, unheard-of places. To hear about the months of building up projects to conquer disease and hunger only for uncaring governments and militias and local warlords to destroy everything. I think it was this we had in common, that we both thought we could change the world and found out that we couldn't, and this fact had made me cynical and had made Deirdre sad, and we were rough with each other in the damp grass in the lee of the castle, Deirdre biting my lips and drawing her nails down my back until it bled, and then it seemed we found each other in the darkness and found a rhythm, moving slowly now and speeding up and Deirdre made a noise in her throat that was half-laugh and half-sob and then she drew me to her and made a noise that was neither.

Afterwards, we lay on the grass, looking up at the stars above the ancient walls. I felt her shaking and I went to wrap my coat around her, but she turned to me and started to laugh uncontrollably.

'Look at me for God's sake,' she said, 'lying on the wet grass with my skirt around my ears and the face pulled off me with beard rash. You'd think I was fifteen.'

'I wish I was fifteen,' I said ruefully, realizing that something seemed to have gone in my back and I had skinned my elbow on a stone, and that my left leg seemed to have gone permanently to sleep and was refusing to respond to any signals coming from my brain. And then I was laughing too.

I was pretty sure that Whitcroft didn't know who I was, or that I had any connection to Deirdre or Liam, so we made our way back to the hotel, coming in through the back exit. In my room, I poured us both a drink and lit a fire in the smoky old hearth and we sat side by side in front of it, and we told each other what we had been doing in the years since we had seen each other, or at least as much as we thought it was right for each other to know. There were a few episodes that I had never really talked to anyone about, and she seemed to sense this and didn't pry. There were a few episodes in her life as well, the unmentionable details of war in famine-stricken countries, and I let her talk about them or not, as she would. To tell the truth, we were like teenagers, the way that teenagers talk about themselves and their hopes and dreams without self-consciousness. We both knew it was an interlude and we would have to pick up the threads afterwards and neither of us really thought there could be any future in it. I started to say this but she put her fingers to my lips and stopped me.

'Don't say it,' she said, 'you don't need to.' She was silent for a moment and then she spoke again.

'Those men?'

'They weren't following me, Deirdre.'

'Me?'

'I'm afraid so.'

'Liam?'

'Yes. He's back in Ireland and in a bit of bother. I assume they're hoping that you'll lead them to him.'

She didn't say anything for a while, then she sighed.

'I wish it was all over,' she said. That was all she had to say on the matter and I didn't intervene. She had been around war for most of her thirty-one years and she was capable of taking her own counsel on what should be done. She could look after herself in her own way. I could help her, but I had to wait to be asked. After a while, she said she was tired. I sat on the bed and watched her undress, which she did in front of me, unselfconsciously. When she was finished, she gave me a coy look, then put her hands over her head and twirled.

'Do I please you, good sir?' she said.

'You please me mightily,' I said with sincerity, for she was even more beautiful than I remembered. Her slender girl's body had filled out, without losing any of its tone, and the shadows cast by the fire danced on her naked skin.

'Flatterer,' she said, looking at herself in the mirror with her lower lip held between her teeth in a frown of girlish concentration. Then she turned and leaped on to the bed and slipped under the blankets, pulling them up to her chin and fixing me with a comically suspicious eye.

'Don't think you can take advantage of me when I'm asleep.'

I promised I wouldn't but when I got into the bed she reached for me and this time it was slow and rich and indifferent to the past and what the morning might bring. And afterwards when she turned over, heavy with sleep, she said something that might have included a word like love, but her voice was heavy with sleep and I couldn't tell, so I put my arms around her and lay listening to her easy breathing until I fell asleep as well.

If there was a reserve between us in the morning, it was only that of two people who have work to attend to and know that it might not be easy for them to be together again. She sat up in bed with the blankets wrapped around her, watching me and eating toast, as I put on my heavy mountain boots and waterproof fleece, and she didn't flinch when she saw the shoulder holster, although I could tell she wanted to ask me why I was taking a can of ultraviolet paint with me on a mountain walk.

It felt good to have her there, sleepy and tousled, watching me. But then in one sudden movement she was off the bed and into the bathroom and when she emerged she was dressed. She looked good and fresh, but also distant, but there was nothing distant about the kiss she gave me before she turned for the door.

'You'll be seeing Liam?' she said. I nodded. 'He'll know where to find me,' she said, 'when you've finished whatever it is you have to do. Both of you.' Then, with a sad smile, 'Whenever that is.'

I had the feeling of being given some kind of ultimatum, though I knew she was too subtle in her thinking for that. We had been in this place before, a long time ago.

I watched from the window as she walked across the road. I think that was the moment I allowed the thought of a future to enter my head. I should have known that, in this work, there was an unspoken rule: if you loved something or someone, the best thing to do was to keep them as far as possible away from you.

6

By lunch-time, I had investigated four of the six passage graves. Three of them were unlikely. They had been open to the elements for centuries probably and their old bones had been plundered by graverobbers who were long dead themselves. However, one of them had its entrance blocked with rubble and I marked this one with the ultraviolet paint. From this height, I could see half-way across the country, and the dark edge of the weather front that had been promised for later that day was apparent. It was going to be a dirty night. As it turned out, if it had been a night with good visibility, I would probably have ended my days on that bleak mountainside, but for the time being I cursed the weather. I had to investigate the last two sites, walk back to Carlingford and prepare for a gruelling night on the mountain. I hadn't exactly been conserving my energy the night before and I was short of a few hours' sleep, but I knew how much a body could take if put to the test.

I found the other sites quickly. Only one of them could be described as suitable, although it was collapsed all along its length. I marked it and made a mental note that I was going to need a crowbar and some heavy gloves, which meant getting back into Carlingford quickly. As I walked back towards the Land Rover which I had parked at the eerie hilltop bowl they called the Long Woman's Grave, I saw two figures coming towards me. Without knowing quite why, I ducked behind a high tuft of reeds and peat and waited for them to pass. They were wearing brightly coloured all-weather gear, walking fast and in silence. Walkers weren't particularly rare in this part of the country, even at this time of year, but it was unusual for them to be heading up into the hills at this late hour of the evening, with the shadows lengthening. They had their peaked hoods pulled down, hiding their faces, and I felt a shiver going down my spine, as though I had looked upon medieval pilgrims engaged in some ghostly pilgrimage, and I found myself ducking behind the tuft of grass as though fearing that they would turn their burning eyes and skeletal faces on me.

It was fanciful, I reflected, as I was telling Liam about it afterwards, but in a way it did seem like a premonition, for there was to be death on the mountains that night, and I was going out arrayed as a graverobber. Liam said nothing, but gave me a strange look.

By eight o'clock it was dark and I was ready to go. I shivered as I hit the cold rain outside the hotel. I realized that it would probably be falling as sleet on the mountain. I ran the Land Rover without lights for the last few miles of the twisting mountain road and parked it in a small plantation of scrubby spruce, dragging a few branches across the entrance to make it look unused. With a last check on my gear, I set out.

As soon as I left the shelter of the trees, I realized the night was worse than I thought it was going to be. The wind cut like a knife and the frozen sleet cut into my eyes. I had night-vision goggles but had decided to keep them for the work on the passage tombs. I wanted to get a feel for the night. In these conditions the glasses could be more of a hindrance than a help. Besides, they were only a tool. I always thought that men relied on them too much when they were moving about in the field. They restricted your field of vision and reduced the input from your other senses. You couldn't see a man coming up behind you, no matter how good your gear was. Narrowing my eyes against the driving wind, I started to climb, seeking the lee of the hill whenever possible. It was below zero anyway and I calculated the windchill at perhaps another -15 Celsius. When I had got half-way up the hill, I had already decided to take a different route back to the Land Rover. Although it was a little further I would be able to seek the shelter of the ancient trees there and the easier walking of the forest paths that had been cut for picnickers and day-trippers.

I climbed for an hour, using compass bearings and GPS readings that I had taken during the previous two days, covering both bases with the handheld GPS unit and the brass-mounted compass I'd had since I was a teenager. At one stage, the sleet stopped and the clouds parted. I looked to the west and saw more thick clouds racing across the night sky, blotting out the stars, and this time they had the faint, yellowish tinge of snowclouds. I cursed to myself and pulled out the new binoculars, screwing on the UV-sensitive filter. Almost at once I saw the paint I had left on both graves and saw that I was closer to the one that was tumbled in. I started towards it. Once there, I quickly strapped on the night-vision goggles. I couldn't risk a light, especially since I was in full view of the distant Dromad mountain base a mile to the north-east, a place where they took strange lights on the mountain very seriously indeed. Using the crowbar, I started to lever back the large slabs that covered the tomb, with a silent apology to its inhabitants, although in some strange way I thought they might understand. They had been warriors too. It took almost forty-five minutes to work my way along it, peeling back the stone lid and verifying that it was empty, empty even of the long-dead bones of its original inhabitants. As I took off the goggles and felt sweat trickle down the inside of my thermals, a single snowflake settled on the metal of the goggles. Quickly I took a rough compass bearing on the second site and started moving. Wind and sleet were one thing, snow was another. I had about a quarter of a mile to cover and by the time I was half-way across, the snow was coming down fast. You couldn't exactly call it a blizzard, but it wouldn't have taken much to turn it into one. I felt the chill starting to seep into my bones and knew that if there was nothing in this souterrain, then the others would have to wait for another night. By the time I had covered another hundred yards, I wasn't sure if I was going to be able to find the one I was looking for. In the end, I fell over it, which says something for dead reckoning. Or fate. Or just plain luck. I set to work again.

It took about twenty minutes to lever the entrance stones away. They had sunk into the springy turf and were difficult to move. When I had finished, I saw the entrance to the tomb but felt a strange reluctance to enter. As I stared at the blackness of its entrance, the snow that had frozen on my collar as I dug chose that moment to slide down my neck. I stirred myself. Even with the best mountain gear, hypothermia is never far away in conditions like these. After all the work, my skin and inner garments were wet and clammy and I was already starting to cool. Deciding to risk a light, I turned on a small Maglite and lowered myself into the tomb.

There was a stillness inside which should have been a relief after the storm which raged outside, but somehow it wasn't. There was a strange musty smell which might have been related to the smell of death somehow, and a feeling that some ancient malice lurked here, biding its time in the dark. I told myself not to be stupid. I shone the torch along the inner walls of the tomb, which were green with lichen and had root tendrils poking through them. The place was about four feet wide and twenty feet long and completely empty except for what looked like a pile of rags at the very end of the tunnel. Strange how human remains take on the look of a pile of rags soon after death and seem to remain that way for years. I moved towards the body, knowing I had found what I was looking for.

Even before I reached the man, I could see from the angle of his head that his neck had been broken. A bundled parachute lay on the ground and as I put my hand on it, it turned to dust. The man was propped against the back of the tunnel as if he was sitting in an armchair, in an attitude of grotesque relaxation, one bony arm propped up against the wall and the empty eye sockets staring. The jumpsuit the man had been wearing was intact. It had been stripped of insignia, but something about it was familiar. A paratrooper's jumpbag had been pushed in behind him in what seemed like a pathetic attempt to hide it. As soon as I set eyes on it, I knew that this was what I was looking for. Overcoming my reluctance, I eased it out from under the dead man. The fabric was strong but age and damp had started to work on it, and the top flap tore as I tried to open it. However, inside there were several packages wrapped in some kind of black oilskin material, which looked as new as the day they had been put in there. One of them seemed to contain documents, the other, which was bigger, seemed to contain perhaps ten square objects and several other boxes. Underneath the packages, there were several weapons. An Israeli-made Starck-50 machine pistol with a distinctive long barrel for single-shot accuracy, and a pump-action shotgun with stock and barrel sawn off. I frowned at this. The Starck told me something, and the combination of the Starck and the pump-action confirmed my suspicion. It was a combination of weapons which belonged distinctively to American Special Forces and I realized that the flight overalls were exactly the same as the ones on the body of a US pilot downed over Lebanon in 1974 which had been handed over in a secret exchange three years later. They had stuck in my head because I had had occasion to study the photographs of the handover to try to identify some of the senior Mossad men in the background. Another thing struck me about the corpse. The bone of the skull was yellowed and old and the flesh had long since faded away, but the teeth were as perfect as the day the man had died. Americans are big on dental care, and I wasn't the first man in the field to use the fact of perfect teeth to identify the body of an American.

I felt uneasy. What in the name of God was the body of an American Special Forces paratrooper doing on this bleak mountainside? What mission had he been on? A gust of wind sent a flurry of snow through the entrance to the tomb and I realized with a start that I had spent far too much time in the place. I put my questions to the back of my mind. Working over puzzles like that ruined your concentration on the task in hand, and the task in hand was getting myself back to the Land Rover alive. I shoved the oilskin packages into the backpack and turned away from the body, leaving him to his lonely vigil.

I emerged into a different world. If it hadn't been a blizzard before, it was one now. Snow was starting to drift on the windward side of the grave. Visibility was only a matter of feet in the large snowflakes whirling through the air, soft and deadly. I had rough bearings for the edge of the forest and I wasn't too worried. I was bound to hit the trees at some stage unless I went badly wrong, or broke my leg in a crevice or fell into a boghole. Just a stroll, I told myself, trying to watch where I was putting my feet. In daylight and good weather, twenty minutes would take you to the edge of the forest. Move slowly, I thought, watch your feet. Forty minutes or an hour should take me there. I would never find out. I started out cautiously, picking my way along like an old man, watching my feet, so that I almost didn't see the man looming out of the snow. I was fortunate in that he was wearing night-vision goggles which were worse than useless in this weather, because of the false sense of security induced by the green-tinted world he found himself in. I saw the red all-weather gear which he had been wearing when he passed me with his companion earlier that day on his way up the mountain. However, he hadn't been carrying the Uzzi which was now slung over his shoulder. Just as he saw me and tried to swing up the Uzzi, I hit his goggles hard with the heel of my hand, driving them into the cartilage of his nose. He yelled in pain and staggered backwards, but he came back trying to lift the Uzzi and shouting something as he did so. I did what I should have done in the first place and shot him. As he went over, his finger tightened on the trigger of the Uzzi and the magazine emptied into the air, as though in celebration. Answering shouts came from several directions and I heard a sound like cloth ripping and hit the deck as bullets stitched the air above my head.

Moving on my hands and knees, I crawled towards the forest, crashing through mud and the oozing peat and heather that tore at my face and hands. When I judged that the voices had fallen a little behind me, I straightened to a crouch and began to run, heedless of the danger, tripping and falling headlong, heedless of the pain and the stitch that started in my side and the breath that came in great rasps and made me feel as if my lungs were going to burst. I heard the sound of one machine pistol behind me, a mechanical chatter, then another, laying down an overlapping field of fire. Their chances of hitting me were slim, but they were going the right way about it. I was going full tilt downhill now, my feet barely touching the ground, and if I'd run into a tree trunk instead of a low-slung branch, I would probably have done enough damage to ensure I never got off the mountain. As it was, I saw stars as the branch hit me right on top of the head, sending my feet into the air and dumping me on the forest floor.

I allowed myself to lie there for a few moments. It was quiet and dry under the trees, and the pine needles were soft and welcoming. I could hear my heart hammering in my chest and I was light-headed from the blow on my skull. What moved me was the light of torches moving through the trees at the edge of the forest. I eased myself to my feet and checked my limbs to make sure everything was still working, which it was, up to a point. I started down through the forest and saw that the torches were cutting across my path down the mountain. I knew this forest well and realized that I couldn't have entered it at a worse point. A steep finger of rock would stop me going north. It looked like the men with the torches were going to block off the route straight ahead, which left only the south, an impenetrable tangle of old-growth trees and rhododendron. Unless I went down the gully of the Ravensdale river. I groaned internally. There was nothing for it. I heard voices behind me on the mountain and hesitated no more. I turned into the forest and plunged south.

I believe now that I came as close to dying in that gully as I ever have. I was already weakened from the cold of the mountain and I was barely able to climb down into the deep, rocky culvert the river had cut for itself in the living rock. Before I climbed into the water, I took two of the amphetamine tabs from the emergency kit in my pocket, and then I lowered myself down, knowing that the combination of amphetamine rush and cold could stop the strongest heart. I had no choice, however. I wasn't going to make it without artificial stimulation. The cold of the water was unbelievable. I couldn't feel my legs or my fingers. The water constantly tried to push me off my feet. The noise of the water in the enclosed area of the gully was thunderous. At first, I tried to scan the edges of the gully for hostile faces, but in the end I was clinging to the stone like a blind man, lowering one foot after the other, fumbling, falling into the icy current, oblivious to all but the unthinking animal desire to survive.

I was lucky. The river curved south, running close to the plantation where the Land Rover was parked. I was able to clamber on to the bank as the river slowed at the bottom of the mountain. It wasn't far, but then again my body wasn't functioning as it should. I forced myself to my feet. I knew that hypothermia couldn't be far away. Swaying like a drunk, I forced myself towards the Land Rover through the snow which was falling gently at the bottom of the hill.

As I approached the Land Rover, some tiny, alert part of my brain noted that the snow around it was undisturbed. At least I wasn't going to get knocked on the head before I got to it. With agonizing slowness, I managed to get the key out of my pocket, dropping it in the snow several times, almost sobbing with cold and frustration. Finally, I got the door open, forced the key into the ignition and started the engine. It was risky but I knew I needed the heat. I was shivering uncontrollably. I dragged my saturated clothes off, struggling with fasteners and frozen fingers and then the excruciating pain as sensation returned to my frozen hands. I pulled a spare set of thermals from the back and fought my way into them. I was starting to feel that I might get through the night. I shook too hard to drive for ten minutes, so I had to sit it out. The worst thing was that as the feeling flowed back into my body, I began to feel the battering I had taken from the water and my headlong run down the mountain.

It took three or four attempts to force the Land Rover into gear and reverse into the road. Once there, I stuck it in four-wheel drive and let it take me down the mountain.

I met a Japanese four-wheel drive on the way back to Carlingford. It was the type of jeep that is designed for the city and it was struggling in the snow. In any other circumstances, I would have stopped to help, but I thought I saw a hire car decal on the back of the vehicle, and you had to wonder what a hired vehicle was doing in this place at this time of the night. Then again, I concluded that it wasn't really any of my business.

There was another thing I had to think about. The man I had shot had thrown up his arms and shouted out something when he was hit. I hadn't been able to make out the words, but I had made out the accent and it was as American as the Empire State Building. I wondered for a while what a crew of Americans were doing, hunting men on the border by night. Then I put it to the back of my mind.

I hid the oilskin packages under the floor in my bedroom. It was all that I could do, my curiosity blunted by exhaustion and trauma. I crawled between the blankets fully dressed and fell into a deep sleep. I would like to say I dreamed of the man I had killed on the mountainside earlier that night, but I didn't.

It was near noon when I woke, the spacious gleam of the sea lighting up the room. I felt all right until I tried to move. In the bathroom I stared at my body. My skin was mottled with bruises and one large black bruise started at my right elbow and enveloped my whole shoulder. My face was scratched where it had been whipped by the branches of the forest, and both elbows and knees were skinned. I sucked in my stomach and looked at myself ruefully. It seemed unfair that you could put yourself through a night like that and still realize that you needed to lose a stone. I had a bath and ran down to the kitchen to ask for breakfast. When they said it was too late, I begged and offered bribes and eventually one was sent up to me – local sausages and black pudding, soda farls and fried bread. If the girl thought anything of my scratched face, or of the pile of sodden and torn clothing in the corner, she was careful not to show it. I persuaded myself that I needed a calorie jolt to help my bruises heal. When I had finished and poured another cup of tea, I closed the curtains and placed both packages on the bed. Somerville had told me not to open anything, but he'd also told me that the job would be a piece of cake.

I opened the larger one first. I moved very carefully and when I saw what was in it, I moved very carefully indeed. Because the large, soft blocks turned out to be C3 explosive, the forerunner of modern C4. The smaller devices turned out to be a variety of very small, very well-made power timer units – detonators, effectively. Among them I also found five mercury tilt switches, the type you attach to the bottom of a car with explosive attached. The slightest movement stirs the mercury, and the driver loses his legs if he's lucky. I looked at the explosive. It appeared to be in good condition. It had been vacuum-sealed and as far as I could see the vacuum was intact, and there was no condensation to indicate sweating under the wrapper. Still, I was no expert and the explosive was over twenty years old. As far as I could see, the detonators were in perfect condition and were sophisticated for their time.

I turned to the other package. I thought about this for a few minutes. Sometimes there were things you were better off not knowing and I had a feeling that the documents inside this package were going to fall into that category. I opened it anyway.

It took a while to put the thing together. There were grainy surveillance photographs of isolated farmhouses and trim, terraced houses. There were lists of names, some of them with workplaces also indicated and details of their movements. There were detailed Ordnance Survey maps of the North Louth and South Armagh areas which were grid-referenced to the surveillance photographs. There were more photographs – ordinary-looking faces of working men and women – a predominance of rural people but some shots taken in towns as well. These were also indexed to the map and it wasn't hard to work out that they were the inhabitants of the houses marked.

I didn't know any of the names, and didn't recognize any of the places, although some of them were vaguely familiar. I turned to the second set of documents. These were detailed street maps of six or seven major Irish centres of population, from Dublin to Monaghan to Drogheda. As far as I knew, there was nobody in Ireland at that time doing such maps, so somebody had gone to a great deal of trouble. The second thing I noticed was that they were all reasonably close to the border, the furthest away, and the biggest, being Dublin, at sixty miles. That was it. I was, as they say, none the wiser.

I replaced the packages in their hiding place under the floor-boards and turned on the television. It had been quiet in the border area for a long time, but Liam was home and trouble had a habit of following him around. When the television started showing images of a bullet-riddled car outside the old Carrickcarron customs post, I turned up the volume and paid attention. The commentator described how a fire-fight had erupted between the lone occupant of a stolen black BMW and the occupants of another Dundalk-registered car. The gunman driving the BMW had abandoned it after it had been disabled and disappeared into the crowd leaving the disco at the nearby Carrickdale hotel. The other two gunmen had sped off in the direction of Jonesborough. Two things suggested that it had been Liam driving the stolen BMW. The first was that the car was a custom M3. The other thing was that the television piece included an interview with one Detective Inspector Ronnie Whitcroft from Newry, who displayed the most breathtaking cynicism as he talked about his concern for the peace of mind of the local population and the fact that they didn't need this kind of criminal activity in their midst. I turned off the television, noting that there had been no report of an American being found on the mountain with a large hole in him.

I sighed. Whatever Liam had tried to achieve, it seemed that he hadn't achieved it. It was doubtful that the men shooting at him were MRU, or any other branch of British counter-intelligence. Even in the new, supposedly peaceful world of the border, they were unlikely to choose Jonesborough as their line of retreat. That meant that his old comrades were still after Liam. I thought for a while. I had achieved what I had set out to do. I had a rendezvous with Liam that night and it would be helpful if I could arrive armed with some information.

That afternoon I drove into Dundalk by way of Greenore point. At Greenore, I walked to the tip of the point. There were swift and strong tidal currents at this point of Carlingford lough and the water ten yards beyond the dry land boiled and hissed with an evil sound. One by one, I lobbed the packets of explosive into the water. They might have evidential value, but with twenty-five-year-old explosives in the car, I was a mobile bomb. They would be carried out to sea and buried in silt along with the rest of the twentieth-century junk that had found a final resting place there.

Outside Greenore village, I stopped at a phone box and rang Somerville. In my mind's eye I could see the phone ringing on the hallstand, an old-fashioned black bakelite phone connected to several million dollars' worth of secure satellite. Somerville answered. I said nothing, waiting until he had barked hello into the phone several times. It was a minor and quite juvenile way of delivering an irritant to Somerville, but we take our pleasures where we find them.

'I found what I was looking for,' I said.

'Where is it?' he asked. I hadn't expected pleasantries.

'I ran into some unexpected company,' I said.

'Tell me about the company in a minute. Tell me about the items now.'

In careful language, I described the oilskin packages.

'I don't suppose you're going to tell me what I found?' I said.

'Certainly not,' he answered. 'And I would be very careful about drawing your own conclusions. Just bring the material to me and then forget it. Some things are more dangerous than you can imagine.' His voice was harsh, but there was an eagerness there which worried me.

'Not enough,' I said. 'There's a fair-sized mob of well-armed men on my heels and I need some information. Like how I avoid getting killed.'

Somerville spoke slowly, picking his words carefully.

'Bring the material back to me in one piece, and that is the last work you will have to endure on my behalf. You will be retired, on a suitable pension.'

'How much is suitable?' I asked, knowing what his answer would be.

'We'll discuss that when you get here,' he said cautiously, his natural penny-pinching instincts asserting themselves.

I put the phone down and stepped out of the phone box. A cold wind rattled the scrubby bushes along the side of the road. I shivered. I didn't like Somerville's attitude one bit. My experience was that people left his employ in a box. I realized now that I was embarking on a very dangerous journey, fleeing from danger into danger.

An hour later, I parked outside a small bar in Dundalk. It was a rundown part of the town, one side of which was dominated by the turreted wall of the old army barracks, and at first glance Eamon's looked almost derelict, but a second glance showed that the brass knocker on the door was highly polished and the locks on the doors were new and sturdy. Looking closer still, you could see the small, polished button of a miniature camera above the door.

There were a few pubs in the town which were known as IRA haunts but in fact the only people who haunted them were Troubles tourists and Special Branch. But Eamon's was the real thing, and the proprietor probably carried more information about the northern war in his head than any other single man. Under normal circumstances, a man in my line of work was likely to find himself in the boot of a car heading for a shallow grave before he even got as far as the bar, but Eamon and I had a link. His son had been a bad egg, getting involved in drugs and importing them from Rotterdam. Like his father, he could be charming. Unlike his father, he lacked anything that could be described as principle. When they fished him out of the harbour in Rotterdam in 1988 with most of his face removed by close proximity to a sawn-off shotgun, I was at the dockside to help identify him, thinking he was an informant who had disappeared from a Russian freighter several days earlier.

I met Eamon in the morgue. Eamon took one look at me and recognized me for what I was, and of course in the meantime I had discovered the young man's family background and knew Eamon for what he was.

'The names,' Eamon murmured to me without looking in my direction. 'Just get me the names.'

I knew that a man like Eamon would never turn informant, but I also knew that he was offering me a friendship that could only be useful. I got him the names of the men who had killed his son. I don't know what happened to them but police friends in Rotterdam told me that they were mystified by the sudden, unexplained and permanent disappearance of some of the best-known faces from the Rotterdam drug scene. Ever since then Eamon had been a valuable source of information, as long as that information didn't jeopardize the cause.

The door clicked open when I leaned against it and Eamon was standing with his hand out when I walked into the small, neat bar. A fire burned in the grate and there was racing on the television. Eamon's wife Maura was standing smiling in the doorway that led through to the kitchen.

'Well,' Eamon said, examining me shrewdly, 'you look like a man who has been getting more exercise than he's used to.'

'Leave the poor man alone and get him a drink,' Maura said, stepping forwards and taking my hand. The look she gave me was shrewder and longer.

Eamon set a Paddy and water on the bar.

'You here on pleasure or on business?'

'He's here about Liam Mellows, you know that rightly,' Maura said. There was a sharpness in her tone that suggested that Liam's fidelity had been debated more than once over this bar.

'Mellows, is it?' Eamon was watching me closely.

'Liam will wait for a while,' Maura said. 'Are you hungry?'

'Well . . . I had a fry this morning but . . .'

'This morning? Sure, what good is this morning to a man? I can see the ribs standing out of you. You look weak with the hunger.'

As Maura bustled off to the kitchen, I took a drink from

the whiskey to stave off the immediate physical collapse predicted by Maura.

'There seems to be a bit of an atmosphere around the name Mellows,' I said.

'There is,' Eamon said gruffly.

'Is it as bad as that?'

'It is, Jack. As bad as that and worse.'

'The photograph. The one of Liam and Whitcroft. It's a fake.'

'That's not all there is to it. In fact it's a minor point.'

I could see that this wasn't going to be easy.

'I've known Liam Mellows since he was a child,' Eamon said, 'and I would have trusted him completely. But people change, Jack. If you learn one thing in a life, it's that people change.'

'I can't believe that Liam has changed.'

'If you'll allow me to say, Jack, you're a little bit too close to the family to see clearly. Your judgement might be coloured by what you want to be true.'

I was surprised by how strong my reaction to this was. I fought back an unexpected tide of anger. But the colour rose in my cheeks and Eamon saw it.

'It's not a bad thing in you. Loyalty.' He said. 'It's not a bad thing at all.'

'What is it then, Eamon?' I said softly. 'What has he done?'

Eamon hesitated. He rose and went to the bar and poured a cognac from an ornate, old-looking bottle that he took from a bottom shelf. He drank it and poured another which he carried back to the counter. He sat down and sighed heavily.

'For many's a year now,' he said, 'we've been running a source inside the police. He worked his way quietly up the ladder. A Presbyterian man, one of the few who remember the Presbyterian love of liberty.'

I wasn't surprised by the fact that there was a high-ranking informer in the RUC ranks. What did surprise me was that Eamon was telling me. Eamon gave a little grin.

'I know what you're thinking. But you see, this man wasn't really an informer. He didn't help us set up operations. What he did was keep us informed on overall policy, what the thinking was at any given time, what way the wind was blowing.'

'And now the wind is blowing very cold for the RUC?'

'You were always quick, Jack. They're to be disbanded.'

'Therefore your informant isn't so important any more and you're taking the risk of telling me about him.'

'Something like that. He's a very brave man, Jack, and there's no doubt that, ceasefire and all, I'm putting his life in your hands by telling you this.'

I nodded. I knew what he was saying.

'So how is this relevant to Liam?'

'He has full and irrefutable evidence that Liam has turned. That's all I can say, Jack, and it doesn't give me any joy to say it.'

Maura interrupted us with a dish of Carlingford Bay scallops à la mode and a bottle of decent Chablis. The first time I had eaten in Eamon's, she had put up something similar. I hadn't expected it and said so. Maura asked me sweetly whether I thought revolutionaries ate gruel and dry bread. She said that friends of hers had died on hunger strike and that often when she prepared a meal she would think of them and dedicate the meal to them as a celebration of their lives, and if I had a problem with that then there was a chippy in the next street and I could take myself off to it.

I buttoned my lip and tucked into what was to be the first of many fine meals.

Eamon poured the wine and I helped Maura serve the scallops. Both of us were glad of Maura's chat, and the tension that had been in the air surrounding Liam's name dissipated a little.

'You've been seeing Deirdre,' Maura said. It wasn't a question.

'I have,' I said, 'I ran into her by accident.'

'No such thing as accident,' Maura said, 'and I'm hoping that you'll do the right thing by her.'

'I don't think Deirdre is the marrying type,' I said.

'I wouldn't be so sure about that. Anyway, that wasn't what I meant. Women like Deirdre don't come along every day, and she has a right to your full attention, not a quick squeeze in a hotel bed.' Maura's face was stern. To her, this business was every bit as important as any revolution.

'I will, Maura. I will do the right thing by her.' I surprised myself by the vehemence of my voice.

'I think you will,' she said, 'no matter how hard. And it will be hard.'

'Why do you say that?'

She smiled sadly.

'People like you have a way of making things hard for the people around them, Jack. That's not a criticism really. Fate, I suppose you would call it.'

We thought about that for a while and then I decided to take a risk and show Eamon the photographs I had found on the mountain. Eamon took them into the light and sat over them for a long time. When he came back, he gave me a searching look and I noticed that his lips were tight.

'Do you know them?' I asked.

'Where did you get these?' he asked.

'We can sit here all night and ask questions to which neither of us is going to give a straight answer or we can give each other as little or as much as we think fit, knowing that it's not going to leave this room,' I said. 'Deal?'

'Fair enough.'

'I found them under very odd circumstances in pursuit of a job,' I said. 'I took them from a dead man's hand, and as far as I could see, the man in question shouldn't have been there.'

Eamon digested that for a while, then told me about the men in the photographs.

'They're all Republicans. Or rather were Republicans.

Mostly from border areas. Not soldiers as such. More the icons of the movement. Thinkers mostly. I suppose you could have called them the soul of the movement. They were all killed in a three-week period in the early seventies. The assassination methods were very sophisticated and belonged to no known group operating in the area at the time. The booby-trap was a favourite.'

I thought about the sophisticated detonators I had found. Eamon was watching me carefully.

'Parallels with Vietnam were mentioned,' he said softly. I didn't look up at him, letting him know that I wasn't refuting the direction his thoughts were leading him in. But I wasn't giving him any more either.

'Those deaths did a lot of damage,' he said. 'The thinkers were gone and the hotheads took over. Somebody thought that if they killed the brain, they killed the organization. But they just made it stronger. And deadlier.'

'I tell you what,' I said, 'I haven't finished with this. If I get to the bottom of this, and if there's no threat involved, I'll come back and fill you in. That's all I can say.'

He nodded again.

'That'll do,' he said. 'There's a few old women around here – all they really want to know is what happened to the men they loved. Sometimes we have a duty by the dead. You understand?'

'Yes.'

We ate in silence for a while, then Eamon brought up the subject of westerns, about which he was passionate. It seemed strange, but there was something in his fascination with man's struggle with the evil in his own heart and the western theme of evil overcoming the high-minded that made me feel that there were aspects of the IRA's long war which had left this most dedicated of Republicans with an uneasy feeling. Still, he was a good talker with a good store of movie star anecdotes and when I glanced towards the window I was astonished to see that it was dark and that I was running late for my rendezvous with Liam. I thanked Maura, and Eamon walked me out into the freezing night.

'You'll be seeing Liam,' Eamon said. It wasn't a question.

'I'll be seeing him,' I said, 'and I won't have any good news for him, will I?' Eamon sighed and stared out across Dundalk Bay towards the dark mass of the mountains.

'Tell him to stay away,' he said in the end. 'Tell him to leave this country and go to one of those end-of-the-earth places he was always talking about and not come back. That's all I can do for him.'

He was telling me that if Liam got out of Ireland and out of Europe, then there was at least a chance that the pursuit might ease.

'And watch yourself,' he said. 'Once a man turns, he's dangerous and unpredictable, even to his friends.'

'Who was it,' I said, turning to him, 'who said that given the choice between betraying his country and betraying a friend, he hoped he would have the guts to betray his country?'

'There's good men dead because of Liam Mellows,' Eamon said, 'and this organization has never forgiven that sort of treachery. It's an iron law, Jack. So don't get in the way yourself.'

There was no malice in the last remark. He was merely stating a grim truth. By the time I had started the car, he had turned his back and re-entered the pub. But as I drove away, I looked up and caught a glimpse of Maura's worried face at an upstairs window.

My thoughts weren't on the road as I swung on to the new bridge out of Dundalk.

As a meeting place, Liam had chosen Faughert graveyard and I put his choice down to the strange, fey mood I detected from him. Faughert was an ancient place, lost in pre-Christian history, located right in the dark gap of the north where men had been spilling blood for millennia. The tiny, ruined Christian chapel on the site, old as it was, was only a recent addition to a place whose pagan past was felt in every stone. The ancient yew trees so close to the pre-Christian people of the area loomed over the little church as though to remind it that it was a mere interloper in their ancient pagan mystery. I parked the car close to the wall, where it couldn't be seen from any of the army observation posts, and entered the graveyard. The wind was getting up and the branches of the trees shifted and whispered as though my presence generated unease in their ancient spirits.

I felt the gun barrel on the back of my neck before I heard Liam's soft laugh.

'Well, Jack,' he said softly, 'it's good to see you.' I heard the words but I noticed that he didn't remove the gun from the back of my neck.

'Anybody with you, Jack?' I felt a small, cold shiver of fear as I stood in the graveyard, and it seemed that the spirits of some old malice stalked among the half-fallen tombstones. I knew Liam had been pushed hard in the past week or so. Perhaps everything that had been constant with him for so many years had been undermined, and he had started to see even the people who cared for him as enemies.

'Come on, Liam,' I said. 'You think that after everything I would set you up? Do you really think that?'

There was a small pause and then the gun was removed. I turned to him. His face was thinner than I remembered and from the state of his clothes I guessed that he had been living in country for at least twenty-four hours. He looked exhausted.

'Sorry, Jack,' he said ruefully, sounding more like his old self. 'I've been here for a while. You start jumping at shadows, you know? Something about this wee graveyard gets in on you – you get the feeling there's unquiet spirits here and they'd turn your mind if you gave them long enough.'

I clapped him on the shoulder. When I had started in this

business, I would have seen Liam's actions as showing a fatal loss of trust, making a working relationship impossible. But as I got older, I realized that you've got to give people room for their demons. If the trust that counted had been lost, then Liam would have put a bullet in my head and that would have been that. Nevertheless, it was time to do some talking.

'Are you ready to tell me what's going on then, Liam?' I said. He gave me a long look.

'I suppose it's about time I told somebody,' he said. A tight grin stretched his features, but he couldn't keep the haunted look at bay.

A woman was at the heart of it, and it was something I should have guessed at. A bad, beautiful English bitch, as Liam described her. Liam was attractive to women. They were drawn to his warmth, his wildness and some of them were drawn, I think, to his dark side, the stone killer in a good cause. But I'd never seen the attraction work the other way. Liam treated them all with a kind of faintly amused good nature and they seemed to accept it when they woke up in the morning and found that he was gone. This one had been different.

We walked down the graveyard to the holy well where scraps of cloth tied to the trees around it testified to the pilgrim faith of the childless and the ill. It was the kind of place where you expected a grim and primitive feeling, but as we hunkered down out of the wind, there seemed to be a certain calm in the mossy old walls. I was glad of that. It seemed to tone down the sense of danger and despair that had started to follow Liam around. It seemed as good a place as we were likely to find to get down to the truth.

Liam had met the girl in Germany, at a party held in his honour. There is a certain strand in the German character which gets misty-eyed about Ireland and is inclined to see IRA men in very idealized terms. There were more revolutionary groupies in Germany than anywhere else. They were starry-eyed and serious-minded, but when the chips were down they were middle-class girls chasing a bit of revolutionary rough, and more than one had cried for Daddy and coughed up all they knew when they got a bit of rough handling from the security services. So Liam was wary at first, and it was with some surprise that he realized she was English. She was tall and slim with black hair and a fencer's dangerous grace. She was an artist with a good reputation in Berlin, a working-class English girl with a history of delinquency and rough living who had scratched and kicked and slept her way into the rarefied atmosphere of the Slade School of Art. She told Liam that the scratching and kicking had had a small hand in her success, and that seduction had had a lot more to do with it. She made no bones about it and she made it clear that she wouldn't take any nonsense from Liam on the subject. They left the party early and made their way back to his small hotel room. That was it. Liam was mesmerized.

The next day, he went back to Berlin with her. He stayed there for three months, sleeping on the floor of her studio, watching her while she worked during the day, making love and talking at night. It was spring in post-reunification Berlin and everything seemed possible, but experienced hands will tell you that centuries of Central European intrigue and dark machinations have darkened the soul of Berlin, and nothing is ever quite as it seems.

That first night, after they had caught their breath, she got out of bed, took a bindle of heroin and a piece of tinfoil. Liam watched her as she sat naked at the dressing table and, heating the tinfoil, inhaled the opium smoke from the top of it. There was something dangerous and exotic and attractive about the image. The naked girl sitting in the half-light, the room filling with the heavy, sultry smoke of opium. Chasing the dragon, they called it. I asked him if he had tried it. A few times, he said. But he had seen things in real life that started to come back to him in the eerie, distorted images of opium dreams, and he didn't like it. 'There's a few dead faces still haunt me at noon on a midsummer's day,' he said. 'I don't need them coming to me with heroin's sweet grave-breath blowing in my face.'

I asked him if he thought the heroin had anything to do with her betrayal. Perhaps somebody was controlling her supply. Not in that way, he replied. Heroin was cheap and easy to come by in Berlin. But he thought that the drug might have had something to do with what she was doing. It made you see things in a different way, re-ordered your priorities. It was a subtle, betraying thing, and sometimes, looking back, Liam thought that she saw life as a kind of spirit world where reality did not hold sway.

He also said that she was funny, smart and worldly. They laughed a lot. That seemed to be important to him. He thought that she loved him, despite everything. Above everything, that mattered. He could live with betrayal as long as that truth existed.

He hadn't told her anything. He didn't need to. She knew his contacts, who he was meeting and where. She knew that something big was afoot. She passed on the information to her handlers and they did the rest.

As far as I could see, the scheme involved a small number of large bombs, similar to the Canary Wharf and City bombs that had played such a large part in bringing the British government to the negotiating table. It was one thing to see Belfast destroyed, it was another thing to see big business being driven away from London. Except that this would have ended the war two years earlier. It might seem a contradiction that such an attack at the very heart of your enemy should be undertaken in order to achieve peace, but the logic was impeccable.

Such a prospect would have appalled many people in the British security establishment. There wasn't one single reason for their fear of peace. For some, it was a power thing: they gathered kudos and resources to themselves by engaging in an undercover war against the IRA. Some were genuinely appalled by the prospect of having to negotiate with the IRA. Others believed that the war could still be won, and then there were the romantics, the believers in empire and the lost cause of the northern Unionist, who believed that the IRA and everybody associated with them must be eradicated at any cost. There were a lot of vested interests involved in continuing the war, and some of those interests must have been running Liam's dark, sad English girl.

Liam told me how the bombs had been concealed in four small lorries which were in place in the yard of a bomb factory in the remote Slieve Bloom mountains. Nobody knew quite what happened, but the IRA personnel at the bomb factory didn't report in. When somebody went up there to investigate, they found five dead men, all senior activists, tortured and mutilated. Liam heard that it was a professional job. That the men were tortured in order to extract as much information as possible and then killed by means of a single bullet in the back of the head. It seemed that the killers then got into the four lorries and drove them off, most likely across the border and into a barracks in Lisburn or Armagh where the contents could be examined at leisure.

There was a suspicion that some of the southern security services must at the very least have been aware of the operation. There was no love lost between the Special Branch and Republicans.

The search for the leak started immediately. IRA internal security was a fearsome matter and they usually found what they were looking for, no matter how long it took. There were no second chances and no appeals, and the contempt they felt for informers in life was often reflected in the way they died. Liam didn't know how they traced the leak to his stay in Germany. All he knew was that a friend had contacted him and told him that an interrogation squad was on its way to speak to him. The interrogation squads were better known as the 'nut squad', after the bullet in the head with which their sessions usually ended. He wouldn't tell me who the friend was, but the name of Maura Wright sprang to mind. Maura was as passionate a Republican as any of them, but she struck you as a woman who, in her younger days, would have known the value and temptations of pillow talk.

Liam faced the girl with it. She didn't deny any of it. She didn't offer excuses or get down on her knees and ask for forgiveness or mercy. They were in her studio. A gas fire spluttering, rain sweeping in from the Baltic and beating against the windows. Liam walked out into the night and spent the dark hours wandering the streets. When he came back she was gone.

'She left me this,' he said. He took a Polaroid print out of his pocket and handed it to me. The Polaroid was scuffed at the edges as though he had handled it many times.

'The original painting is in a safe place,' he said. I used the Maglite to examine it. Even in such bad light and with such a poor reproduction, you could see that it was a very good painting. Abstract colour, black mainly, with streaks of ochre applied over it. It reminded me of Rothko. I had always scorned Rothko, saying that there was no way you could respond to paintings that were merely huge squares of one colour, particularly when that colour was black. That was until I saw the actual paintings in Paris. I don't know how the man managed to get such emotion into his work, such melancholy beauty, but you understood when you saw people standing in front of them with tears running down their faces. The painting by Liam's unnamed English girl had the same power.

'Did you see her again?' He shook his head. He was staring at the ground.

'Do you know what happened to her?'

He lifted his head and turned to me. His eyes met mine and I swear it was like staring into the grave.

'Who . . .?' I said.

'Her own people,' he said. 'They gave her a terrible death, Jack.'

We sat in silence for a long, long time. The wind stirred the trees around us and the grass whispered as though all the souls interred here over millennia were speaking to each other.

After a while, Liam told me how he had bushwhacked the nut squad. He told them what had happened and his role in it. He had them covered and they had listened in silence and made no attempt to follow him when he slipped away. They had all the time in the world.

'Surely they'd recognize you made a mistake . . .' I said.

'I broke the rules, Jack, and by their own lights they have right on their side. I would have done the same thing myself a few years ago.'

'There's something else, isn't there, Liam?'

'The men who were killed? One of them was Canning's brother. He was married to a sister of Marks's.'

'But Eamon . . .' I said. Liam gave a grim laugh.

'I cost five good men their lives,' he said.

'Not Eamon as well . . .' I said.

'His younger brother,' Liam said, 'the one he always looked after.'

There was nothing more to be said. We sat there for a while longer. I coaxed Liam to his feet, but he seemed strangely reluctant to leave the graveyard. I knew I had to get him out of this mood, otherwise he wasn't going to survive long. Before we got to the car, I saw there was a more immediate problem to deal with. I don't know what it was. A flicker of movement. A shadow darker than all the others. I was in a crouch with the Glock in my hand. I started to move around the car in a flanking movement and looked up, assuming that Liam was taking the other flank. He wasn't. He was standing where I had left him, staring into the darkness. I cursed him under my breath. We had been foolish staying in the graveyard for so long with the car exposed on the road. I swore that if I got out of the next ten minutes alive, I'd make him pay for his inattention. As it was, it wasn't going to be me that would make him pay. As fast as I moved towards the car, the shadow moved faster, heading towards Liam. I levelled the Glock. Maybe the spirits in the graveyard weren't as malicious as I thought they were. Or perhaps they were solicitous of their own. Or perhaps it was their way of making the game last, of sparing you now in order to have more sport with you later. In any event, I didn't fire at the shape moving towards Liam and a minute later heard Deirdre's voice and felt myself sag in relief. Deirdre told me to put the gun down and stop making such a fool of myself.

'I nearly shot you,' I said. She gave me a look of such withering scorn that I almost threw the gun into the ditch at my feet. But Liam she took by the shoulders, her hands caressing him as she looked into his eyes, a troubled look on her face. She turned to me.

'We'll go to Edentubber,' she said, 'Liam can come in the car with me.'

Following her tail-lights down the narrow road on to the main Belfast–Dublin carriageway, I was surprised that I was able to keep up. Normally Deirdre would have left me far in her wake, even with my turbo-charged Land Rover. But this time she was taking it easy, and I realized that they were having a long talk.

At the old customs post at Carrickcarnon, we took a right-hand turn and drove up the narrow border road, past the monument to five IRA men killed by their own bomb. About a mile and a half up, we turned on to a narrower road that went straight up the mountain. Two cars in convoy made a good target for any of the various agencies engaged in surveillance on the border, but the sleety rain was heavy now, and I doubted that even the army, a mere quarter of a mile above us, could see as much as a headlight. I hadn't seen the old house at Edentubber in years and, even in the dark and rain, I could feel the memory of happy times come flooding back. There were few places that could make me feel like that, and Edentubber was one of them. A stone cottage with a few outbuildings over-looking the low hills of South Armagh. A small orchard where you could sit out, sheltered from the mountain breezes. An old hearth where you could build up a sweet-smelling fire with turf from the mountain behind and apple logs from the orchards further to the west. And an old-fashioned feather bed tucked under the eaves where, according to Deirdre, she had been conceived.

Deirdre told me that the bed had been downstairs in her grandparents' time. She had moved it upstairs and lifted the flags in the kitchen to deal with a persistently leaking water pipe. Under the flag where the bedhead would have rested, they had found a horse's skull. She was told that the skull of a horse was a symbol of luck and fertility. I suppose it made sense. The Celtic god of light was a horse. She said she had put the skull back and relaid the flags. One day I tapped my way around the flags and there was a hollow one under the window.

But those were happier times and now I was tired and strained and cold and wanted to get indoors. I reversed the Land Rover into the old garage at the back and entered the house by the side door of the garage. There were cooking smells coming from the kitchen already, and a bottle of Fleurie warming by a bright fire. I spent a desultory few minutes checking the windows and doors, dog tired as I was.

'You're as safe as you can be anywhere with the Mellows family,' Deirdre said, standing at the kitchen door. 'Probably safer.'

'He told you.'

'I had a notion there was something going on anyhow,' she said.

'I can't see how it's going to be sorted out,' I said wearily. 'It's a real mess.'

'There's a way out,' she said. 'I know there's a way out.'

'I don't see it, Deirdre.'

'No, neither do I, but there's something in all of this that's not quite right.'

'In the fact that they're coming after Liam as hard as they are?'

'No. Something else. I just can't put my finger on it.'

She wouldn't be drawn on it, and the way I looked at it, if her intuition was finding a flaw in the remorseless logic that seemed to be pointing towards a shallow grave for Liam, I didn't want my cold analysis interfering with her thinking. To change the subject, I asked her about the smells coming from the kitchen.

'*Pappardelle alla lepre*,' she said, 'Pappardelle with hare. I had it in the River Cafe, but I think I managed to improve it a bit with chanterelles.'

I opened my mouth to ask her when she had been in the River Cafe when what I really wanted to ask her was who she had been with. In the end, neither question came out and instead I asked her where she had got the hare. She jerked her thumb at the mountain behind the house and made a wringing motion with her hands, as if she was breaking a neck.

'Snare,' she said. 'This morning.' I could see the amusement in her eyes. She knew that I both admired and was appalled by her lack of sentimentality when it came to animals for the pot. She also knew that I was dying to ask her about the River Cafe. To make my confusion complete, she looked me up and down with a look that made my toes curl up and ran the pink tip of her tongue along her lips with a gesture of such lingering lasciviousness that I felt all my famed Victorian morals beat a retreat into the rainy night air. Just as she laughed and turned back into the kitchen, Liam came in towelling his hair from the shower. He looked at me, and looked at Deirdre's retreating back, and, sensing the atmosphere, gave us both a disapproving big brother's look.

'Pour Jack a whiskey,' Deirdre shouted over her retreating shoulder. 'The poor man looks like he needs one.'

As Deirdre was cooking the hare, Liam lit a fire in the big old whitewashed fireplace and I opened the wine. The fire was going well by the time the food was on the table. I found a few wax candles in a drawer and placed them on the table on saucers.

'It's not quite the River Cafe,' I said, drawing a look of lofty amusement from Deirdre which made me feel two inches high. However, a few minutes later she ruffled my hair as she passed and gave me a cheeky grin. This had the effect of making me feel like a schoolboy with a crush on his teacher, not exactly dignified for a man of my age but an improvement on the previous smallmindedness.

The hare's dark, almost oily meat fell away from the bones in succulent flakes, the chanterelles' earthy flavours adding texture to the dish. Huddled around that small table on a cold mountainside in South Armagh, you could have believed yourself in a peasant hut in Umbria, and as I soaked up the last of the juices with a piece of bread, I started to think I was subject to the aural hallucination of a cricket chirping. The noise stopped and then I heard it again. I looked at Deirdre to see if she had heard it as well.

'*Píobaire no gríosaí,*' she said, smiling gently. I looked to Liam for a translation.

'It's a cricket,' he said. 'They used to be common in Ireland. They live in the cracks of the old chimney breasts. They seem to go into suspended animation until the stone is warmed by a fire.'

'They reckon they came from Italy or Spain in the Middle Ages,' Deirdre said, 'in cargoes of grain.'

'What does the Irish mean?'

'*Píobaire no gríosaí?*' Deirdre asked. 'It means "the piper in the ashes". The poor thing is calling for a mate. But I don't think there are any other crickets left around here any more. It makes it a lonely sound, I think.'

She looked at me as she said this and there was something unfathomable in her eyes.

'Right,' Liam said, breaking the mood, 'what about his surprise?'

'I don't know,' Deirdre said, 'he's putting on a bit of weight . . .'

'Come on,' I said, 'spare me the Laurel and Hardy routine.'

'Shut your eyes,' Deirdre said.

'I . . .' I began.

'Shut them!'

When I opened my eyes, there was a bowl of tiramisu in the middle of the table. I had a guilty passion for the creamy Italian dessert and I fell on it with appropriate cries of rapture. Deirdre couldn't finish her portion, so I had that as well. I was so absorbed in it, I didn't notice that the table was quiet. As I scooped up the last, guilty mouthful, I looked up and saw that they were both looking at me intently. It was the same green-eyed appraising look that I had seen in Liam before, that seemed to look into your soul and weigh up the very stuff you were made of and it was unnerving to see the identical look in two pairs of eyes.

'What?' I said.

'Is it not about time you told us what you found up the mountain, Jack?' Liam said softly. I took a deep breath.

'Let's have some coffee,' I said, 'and I'll tell you about some dead men.'

Over thick, dark espresso, I told them what I had found on the mountain and what I had found out about the men in the photographs from Eamon.

'I mind it well,' Liam said. 'There's some say the organization never recovered from the loss of those men.'

'I don't understand,' Deirdre said. 'What would the Americans be doing here? I mean, if they were on anybody's side, they would be on ours, wouldn't they?'

'Not necessarily,' Liam said. 'There's always been popular support for the cause in America, but the State Department is a different matter altogether. There is a lot of sympathy for the Brits in the White House and the Pentagon. Langley as well. It's low key and very effective, and they have access to Special Forces.'

'It still doesn't make sense.'

'Let's start with the basics,' I said. 'It appears that American Special Forces were carrying out a specific operation in this area in the early 1970s. What were they doing here?'

'More to the point,' Liam said, 'why does it matter now? I mean, why did your boss send you to find this stuff now?'

'Not just me. I think somebody else was looking for it as well.'

I told them about my night on the mountain. I could see the look in Deirdre's eyes.

'They almost killed you,' she said. I didn't answer. She was sitting beside me and I could feel her body stiffen slightly, withdraw from me in a subtle way. I didn't know if she was disapproving of the work that led me into danger, or whether she sensed how close to death I had come, so that to her highly intuitive mind there was still something of the dead about me, some ghoulish presence.

'So somebody else wants to find this,' Liam said, 'and they're not too keen on letting the world know what they're doing.'

'You're right,' I said. 'This doesn't come from government. If this was official, they would survey the area by satellite and swamp it with personnel. No, this is somebody who has access to men and materials, but doesn't want to operate through channels.'

'It's a long time ago. Why are they worried about it now?' Deirdre said.

'American Special Forces carrying out assassinations in the territory of a friendly European state? Killing Irishmen in Ireland? Apart from the breach of sovereignty, there are forty million people of Irish descent in the States and they tend to be voters. It would go down very, very badly and anybody associated with it would find themselves in real trouble.'

'So, what then?' Liam said, 'Maybe somebody has worked themselves into a position of power and is now worried about the past coming back to haunt them?'

'I wish you wouldn't use words like "haunt",' Deirdre said, hugging her own shoulders, 'I keep thinking about that poor man left all alone on the mountain. There's something so lonely about it.'

I opened my mouth to say that he was a professional assassin, but decided that I wasn't really in a position to start impugning the dead man's occupation. Liam got up from the table to make more coffee. I started thinking about the man on the mountain. What was he doing there? It suggested an *ad hoc* operation bordering on the reckless. It wasn't the way such things were done. If you wanted to carry out a programme of assassination, you went in and cultivated fringe opposition groups. You trained their men and had them do the dirty work. That way, you didn't get your own hands dirty. Proxy war. You had maximum protection, maximum deniability. That was the mature way to go about it, in a miasma of corruption, ruined principles and ruined lives. From the jungles of Guatemala to the back alleys of Beirut. The other way was the gung-ho way. You went in with all guns blazing. Sometimes you could make a reputation with an operation like that, but more often, things went wrong. It was a young man's technique, I thought, somebody in a hurry. A high-flyer who would have command of covert forces. That would make him mid- to late-fifties now. The time of life when men take on the big jobs, acquire gravitas, solidity. But still a hint of that recklessness. The men I had met on the mountain were professional, but there was a feeling of an operation prepared in a hurry, not thought through completely. I was starting to get a feel for the man behind the hard-faced men in all-weather gear.

Somerville was another matter. It would take a cleverer

and more devious mind than mine to fathom his motivation, but I suspected that somehow he wanted to use the information I had gathered to gain influence over whoever had carried it out.

'Liam needs to decide what to do.' Deirdre's voice broke into my thoughts.

'I know,' I said.

'Will you help him?'

'I will, Deirdre. I will help him. God knows how, but I will.'

'Glad to hear it,' Liam said. He was standing behind us in the doorway holding the coffee-pot. 'But you know, I've a fair bit of experience in looking after myself.'

'You can't do it all on your own, Liam. It's different this time.'

'Let's look at it objectively,' I said, 'If there is a way out of Liam's problem, he's not going to find it while he's on the run and looking over his shoulder all the time.'

'So what have you got in mind?'

I knew that we had to get Liam out of Ireland. If I got him to Scotland, I could find him a safe house and give him time to work out his options. But I knew that if I suggested this, he would regard it as retreat and refuse to go along with it. So I tried a different tack, one that undoubtedly included my self-interest.

'Liam comes to Scotland with me. If the Americans come after me, I need somebody to cover my back. Equally, if Liam needs cover, I can provide it.'

'What about Deirdre?' Liam said. I found that every fibre of my body ached to tell her to come with us. But I would be bringing her into terrible danger, and imperilling all of us. I could work with Liam as an efficient and deadly team, but our effectiveness would be halved by having somebody to protect. We could all be killed. I shook my head.

'She can't come with us, Jack.' Liam turned to her.

'I'll be all right, Liam,' she said. 'It wouldn't be the first time I had to look out for myself, would it?'

Liam looked doubtful.

'I don't know, Jack. I'm not that contented in myself with the idea of hiding out in Scotland. On the other hand, you're going to be needing help all right. I need to think about this.'

Later, in the small bedroom under the cottage eaves, Deirdre stood silently with her back to me, staring out of the window. The wind and rain had died away and it was a cold and starry night. You could see the outline of the dark crags of South Armagh and the small houses and stony fields in the moonlight. I put my arms around her from behind.

'There's not much in the way of future in this, is there, Jack?' she said without turning round. 'Me waiting for you to get killed.' I didn't say anything. There wasn't anything to say.

'I think I'll go back to Africa,' she said. 'I've been putting off the decision. They've asked me to go back to Somalia. It gets harder and harder every time. The way people suffer. Even the soldiers, Jack. Men who have done terrible things. They have pain in their eyes as well. Pain and guilt and fear. It's the same look that I'm going to see in your eyes one day. Your eyes and Liam's eyes.'

I put my hand to her face and felt the tears.

'I'm afraid, Jack,' she said, and then, 'Hold me.'

Our lovemaking that night was the sweet and solemn coming together of two people who have lost the flush of youth and who now know each other to be beholden to dark imperatives which will make permanence impossible. We hid nothing from each other and we reached a place which was almost sorrowful in its intensity. When we were sated, Deirdre curled into my chest and fell asleep and I lay back against the pillow, my mind roaming restlessly, kept awake by an overwhelming sense of lost opportunity. I thought back to the first time I had met Deirdre, and had shared the same bed with her. Now it looked to me as if I had taken everything she had and had then got up and walked away. Looking back, I wondered if that was what she thought at the time as well.

It had been a warm July in 1980, and the weather had become gradually more humid and thundery. I flew into Belfast and drove up the motorway to Portadown with a heart full of misgivings. I had been sent in on a job to contact a rogue agent and persuade him to go back to London. Once they had him back, I was reasonably sure they would slap him into a strait-jacket and keep him in it for the next ten years. The man had been a corporal in what was nominally a signals unit but was in fact a military intelligence vehicle designed to run auxiliaries inside the Protestant paramilitary units active in the area. In the jargon of the time, they were referred to as 'assets'. The problem was that this agent, known by the pseudonym of Blackman, had gone native. He had taken part in several sectarian assassinations and had set up a headquarters in a tough estate on the outskirts of Craigavon with a gang of acolytes and a tribe of children. He had established himself as a demagogic preacher and took part in gospel tent missions in the area. He had been known to speak in voices. All in all, he was a thoroughly unstable and dangerous character and the only persuasion that was likely to work with him was the kind of persuasion that was made by Smith and Wesson, among others. However, persuasion was my mission and that was the end of the matter. I called the man from a phone box outside Craigavon. His voice was slow, gravelled, measured and carried the terrifying conviction of the truly insane. He told me to come to the house. I asked him for a guarantee that I would be safe. He said that my Saviour would be my guarantee. It wasn't very reassuring.

I parked the hire car at the entrance to the estate and walked up. I had the feeling that I was being watched from every window, that my footfalls were being counted and weighed up in some scales that were going to count against me in some deadly endgame. As I approached the house, men began to appear, standing in doorways and scrappy gardens, watching me. There were four or five of them outside Blackman's house. Older men in Wrangler jackets with three-day stubble and a look of old trouble about them. One of them opened the door and I stepped into an ordinary council house hallway and then into an ordinary council house living-room complete with brass ornaments on the mantelpiece and chintzy furniture. There was nothing ordinary about Blackman, though. He was an intense, brooding presence in the room. Nothing in particular was said during the interview. I asked him to come back to London. He refused politely and said that he was happy where he was and had discovered a new sense of purpose in his life. Despite this, when I finally got out of the room the atmosphere of malevolence was so strong I thought it would choke me. One of the men outside smiled at me as I went past. It wasn't a friendly smile.

Things were all right until I got to the car. Then they went wrong very quickly. I got into the car and started it. I rounded the first corner to find the road blocked by a coal lorry parked longways across it. I threw the car into reverse and careered wildly backwards. I was fast but not fast enough. A Post Office van blocked the road behind me. I decided the car was a liability and got out, looking for an escape route. The odd thing was that I couldn't really see my attackers. Shadowy figures behind the wheels of both vehicles but otherwise an eerie calm. Nor did I really get a fix on the youth who ghosted out of a garden with a brick in one hand and a petrol bomb in the other. The brick went through the windscreen of my car first, followed by the petrol bomb.

If people knew how quickly a car goes up in flames once fire catches, they would wear a flameproof suit in the driving seat. Within seconds, it seemed that I was enveloped in toxic smoke, which was what was intended, it seemed, because the man who appeared behind me with an old-fashioned Luger in his hand had used the smoke as cover to get close to me. I recognized him as one of the men from outside Blackman's house. As I turned towards him, he raised the gun. He looked like a mechanic and he was studying me as if I was some kind of minor mechanical problem. He raised the gun and aimed it downwards. I think the fact that I was turning saved my leg. The bullet that was aimed at the knee joint passed behind the joint and in front of the knee tendons. But there is nothing minor about any gunshot. Trauma, blood loss, bits of cloth and foreign matter driven into the wound. It is like films when someone is hit and slumps to the ground. Being hit by a bullet is like being hit by a sixty-pound sledge. You are dazed, disorientated, unable to get your bearings. I found myself on the ground, not really knowing how long I'd been there. I scrambled to the cover of a wall and huddled against it. It was a bit pointless. If they had wanted to kill me, I would be dead. In fact, the place was deserted.

In front of me was a patch of grass, perhaps two acres, and on the other side was a phone box. There was a playground but there were no children in it. There were park benches but there were no pensioners sitting on them. I forced myself to look at the leg. The blood loss was light to medium, but it didn't show any sign of stopping. I knew I didn't have much time. The pain was starting and the blood loss would weaken me progressively. I wondered if somebody would call an ambulance. Even posing the question made me realize I was lightheaded. There was no ambulance.

It took an eternity to get across that grass, aware that I was leaving a trail of blood behind me. I prayed that the phone would be working. I knew that I couldn't call an ambulance. That would mean police. My MRU affiliation was no good to me with the RUC. For a start, it would compromise my identity. Secondly, it wouldn't be unlike Somerville to deny all knowledge of me. And if that wasn't enough, the police there were major players in a deadly multi-faceted game involving paramilitaries and anything up to half a dozen covert agencies. There were no guarantees that my body wouldn't turn up on a border road with a bullet in the back of my head. No. That wouldn't do. I only had one option. Liam had given me a number and made me memorize it. 'If you're ever in real trouble in Ireland, ring that number,' he said. 'You'll get help from the man who answers it.'

The phone was working. I hauled myself upright and felt in my pocket for a coin. I pulled out a bloodsoaked tenpence piece and fed it into the slot. I was feeling curiously detached from my body. I could feel the breath coming in great shuddering rasps, but it seemed to be somebody else's breath. The phone answered on the second ring.

'Yes?' It was a countryman's voice. Simple cadences disguising the shrewdness in the tone.

'Liam Mellows gave me this number. I'm shot. He said you would help me.'

There was a long pause, then the voice spoke again. This time there was a definite air of command to it.

'Where are you? Exactly.' I told him. I didn't know if he said anything more. I felt the phone fall from my hand. I was conscious for long enough to ensure that I slid down the inside of the phone box without spilling on to the street. Then the lights went out.

7

Apparently the rescue was dramatic enough to make me wish I'd stayed awake for it. Two men came for me and were lucky to make it out, their van peppered with small arms fire. It was a measure of Liam's prestige that they came. I was aware of how much I owed him but it was a long time before I could hear the details. I had lost a lot of blood and I was very weak. Liam brought a friendly doctor to see me. The man sensibly wanted to hospitalize me but Liam apparently refused. The wound itself wasn't bad, but an infection had set in. I was on the wrong side of consciousness for almost two weeks, tossing in a fever which brought strange faces from the past floating into my mind; strange, dead faces. The mother and her children from Swartzhoek, and other, less innocent spectres. Until one bright August morning I awoke, weak as a baby and thin as a rake, but alive and faced with the welcome spectacle of Liam Mellows carrying a sleek Hardy fly rod in one hand and an equally sleek eight-pound sea trout in the other.

'Dinner,' he said, nodding at the fish. 'Spate fishing in the Whitewater. How's the boy?'

'The boy is good,' I said, noting that he had probably negotiated at least three heavily armed checkpoints to get to his little spate river in the Mournes.

'We nearly lost you,' he said. I could smell bacon frying somewhere close by.

'I'm hungry,' I said.

'You know something?' he said thoughtfully, 'The new slimline you is a definite improvement.'

'Feed me, Mellows,' I growled.

Ten minutes later, Deirdre came in with a tray of food. She

was seventeen, I learned later, and she had a shy, coltish grace that swamped you with a boyish lust, then made you ashamed of yourself for entertaining base thoughts. She had a way of letting her fringe fall forwards over her eyes and looking at you through it while biting her lip thoughtfully, which would have drawn sighs of longing from the driest of bishops. Only one thing could have distracted me. She put the tray down on the bed. There were creamy scrambled eggs laced with shreds of smoked salmon, Isle of Man kippers, the good oak-smoked ones, and a dish of crisp bacon. The coffee was Columbian. The good, white bread was fresh-made that morning but its spiritual home was Spain. I sighed happily.

'Thank the cook for me,' I said.

'Thank her yourself,' Liam said. 'She's standing in front of you.'

There must have been some disbelief in my eyes that a seemingly young, unsophisticated girl could come up with such a spread. The colour spread across her face. She turned on her heel and walked out of the room.

'She looked after you, you know,' Liam said thoughtfully. 'Cleaned you up, sat by you at night when you were bad.'

He followed her out of the room, leaving me with my delicious breakfast and a bad conscience.

She came in for the tray an hour later, keeping her head down so that her hair was covering her eyes.

'Deirdre,' I said, meaning it, 'it was extremely bad-mannered and ungracious of me to come into your house and cast doubt on the abilities of my hostess and carer. I really am sorry.'

There was a pause, then she flicked her hair back and turned to me with flashing eyes.

'Go to hell,' she said, but there was a flicker of amusement in the eyes and I knew from that very minute that if Deirdre Mellows did indeed require me to go to hell, I would freely do it for her. It was a vertiginous, heart-stopping moment and I had never experienced anything like it in my life before.

Her own expression softened to a quizzical one as though she had seen something in my eyes or in my heart.

'Liam said you would apologize. He also said I had to be friends with you.'

'Will you?'

'Maybe,' she said, as she lifted the tray and walked out of the room with her strong, graceful, dancer's stride. 'Maybe.'

It took me a month to recover. It was a good summer, hot during the day, mellow and warm at night. I spent the first days sitting in the garden in front of the house, listening to the bees buzzing in the apple trees and looking at the bog cotton and yellow flag irises that inhabited the boggy ground. Liam wasn't there very much. I assumed he was on active service and I didn't ask questions. Deirdre cooked in the evening and when we had finished, we cleared the table and sat and talked long into the night. Intense conversations, absorbed in each other, our heads almost touching in the candlelight. One night I reached across the table and took her hand. She looked down at our joined hands as if I had placed some wondrous object on the table between us. Then smiled gently at me and picked up our conversation where we had momentarily stopped. That was as far as it went. Perhaps it was because we were alone in the house and we felt that greater intimacy would have been a betrayal of Liam. But I think it was because the relationship was suffused with an idea of old-fashioned courtship.

During the day, she showed me around her country. It was a subtle and beautiful place and she was of it and steeped in its history and tradition. She was good at avoiding the military checkpoints but several times we were stopped. She violently resented their presence in her country to the point that she was almost ashamed of herself for inhabiting the same space as them. She refused to talk to them and I had to do the talking. I resented them almost as much as she did, but for different reasons – my resentment was at the way they stared at her, their gaze lingering on her, aware of the power their guns conferred on them. I fought back by inventing ever more ridiculous identities for myself from a variety of fake identity documents that I carried with me. It lessened her sense of humiliation to feel that we were secretly making fools of them.

The first signs of autumn came, blackberries and haws growing thickly in the valley below the house, and still the weather held. We were uneasy with each other. Deirdre was starting college in Belfast. My own work held me with, if I had known it, an iron and amoral grip. That wasn't the only reason for our unease. One night, she took me to the Mountain Inn in Forkhill. The locals heard my accent with a little curiosity, but the fact that I was with Deirdre was good enough for them. An old woman came over to sit beside us. She was a wiry woman in her seventies with shrewd, humorous eyes in her gnarled old face. We talked to her for several hours about local events going far back into the past. I was lost at times but knew enough to realize then that the war had barely grazed the surface of this place. As she was getting up to leave, she looked us both in the eye and smiled.

'Man and woman wasn't put on this earth to hold hands,' she said, 'and you're doing this girl no kindness, sir, a man of the world like yourself.'

We drove home in silence, moonlight casting long shadows across the interior of the car. She was quiet as we let ourselves into the house. I tried a light switch but the power was gone. The cross-border electricity interconnector was often bombed in those days. I felt the old woman's words keenly and I took Deirdre by the wrist and drew her towards me, a little too roughly perhaps. She put her hand on my chest and pushed me away.

'Wait,' she said. She turned swiftly and left the room. There was something mesmeric about the moonlight and I felt myself in a kind of fury as I stood there, not knowing whether to go after her or not. Then she came back, stepping silently into the room, naked, her hair about her shoulders. She was more beautiful, I think, than anything I had ever seen, and her look was direct and calm. I had never seen anyone strip themself so completely of barriers, expose themselves to another in the way she did that night. I knew then that I was the first and I understood the privilege that was being conferred upon me.

'Come here,' I said gently. 'Come here, Deirdre.'

8

It would be pointless to talk about regrets, because neither of us had any regrets about anything to do with that time. But circumstances were not with us, and we both knew the folly of trying to force the bond that existed between us. As I lay in the small bedroom under the eaves, trying to work out what went wrong and how to put it right, I must have fallen asleep. When I woke, the wind had got up again and the branch of an apple tree was tapping against the window. It wasn't the branch that woke me, but the small metallic click that came from somewhere outside. It was the click of a safety catch being taken off or a pistol slide being pulled back. The tiny metallic sound of men readying themselves for killing. I was out of bed in an instant and Deirdre was beside me, her eyes watchful but unafraid.

'I'll wake Liam,' she said.

'I'm going out the window,' I whispered, 'I'll try to get to the Land Rover and meet you at the front door.'

I grabbed the bag containing the documents, my boots, trousers and gun. I slid open the sash window and swung myself out of the window, lowering myself by one hand, the Glock in the other, until I was close enough to the ground to let go. I hit the ground hard. The wind whipped the bushes around me and I was soaked through straight away, the driving rain almost blinding me. When you're being hunted, you need the use of as many senses as you can possibly bring to bear, sometimes a few extra, and I knew I wasn't in a good spot. How bad a spot I was in became clear to me a few seconds later when I felt the long barrel of a Mauser being placed carefully against the side of my head. I should have known they would cover the window. If you're not trained for it, the cold feel of a gun barrel might as well be a blast freezer, for it turns your limbs to ice and it freezes your thought processes. Even the bravest take four or five seconds to react and by then it's probably too late. What they tell you is not to think. Just to act. As soon as the gun barrel touched my head, my hand swept up, pushing it out of the way, and my leg swept in under the unseen assailant's leg as I went down. Drop and hit. I kept turning with the momentum of my fall. I went the whole way round and drove for the base of his spine with the same foot that had swept his legs from under him. If I had connected, he would have spent the rest of his days in a wheelchair, but I missed by an inch. Still, I heard a gasp of agony and knew he wouldn't be going anywhere in a hurry for some weeks to come. I ran for the small wooden garage. I didn't know how many of them were there. A small team, I reckoned. Perhaps even Marks and Canning alone. But I couldn't discount the Americans. Or perhaps even Somerville had got tired of waiting for me.

I slipped into the garage and pulled on my trousers and boots. I had no intention of being shot without my trousers on. As quietly as I could, I opened the garage doors. The rutted wheeltracks from the garage ran steeply downhill alongside the house, then turned sharply along the front of the house. The floor of the garage itself sloped steeply, being built on the side of the hill. I got into the Land Rover and put the Glock on the dash in front of me. I slipped off the handbrake and the Land Rover started to roll. Before it had gone fifteen yards, it had picked up momentum. With the engine turned off, I had no power steering and I had to battle with the wheel. When I hit the sharp turn at the corner of the house, I nearly rolled it as I wrestled the steering round the bend. I peered through the windscreen and saw a shadowy figure at the front door of the house. It looked as if they were working on the lock of the front door. The sinister figure in dark clothes at the door looked like some hunchback spewed out of a pit to visit evil on us. With a degree of coordination which surprised me, I turned on the engine, hit the lights, scooped up the Glock and forgot to hold on to the steering wheel. As I held the Glock out of the window and fired a few speculative shots at God knows what, the front wing of the Land Rover dug a furrow of plaster out of the wall of the house. Cursing, I pulled it back into line as the dark figure at the door straightened up and threw himself away from the careering Land Rover, executing a practised roll over the wall and into the orchard. It was probably in his own interests, as Liam burst through the front door with his automatic in one hand and waving a shotgun like a toy gun in the other. Deirdre followed him, scrambling into the Land Rover as Liam let go with both barrels into the orchard and then jumped in beside her as I put the pedal to the floor. Liam scrambled into the back and flung open the rear door in time to catch the muzzle flash of automatic fire coming from the orchard. He emptied the magazine of his own pistol in that direction with no discernible effect, although the Land Rover was bouncing enough to present a poor target. Rounding the corner at the bottom of the lane, I thought we were home and dry. Of course we weren't. The attackers had left their car in the gateway at the end, a big old petrol Opel with Armagh plates. There was nothing I could do.

'Hold on,' I yelled and aimed the front bumper of the Land Rover at the side of the car. There was an almighty impact and grinding of metal as the Opel was driven back out of the gap. The steering wheel bucked like a live thing in my hand. Liam cursed in the back, the Land Rover broke free from the wreckage of the Opel and careered into the ditch. There was more bad news. Someone was firing at us from the front of the house and his aim was better this time. Liam was muttering something in the back to the effect that my poor driving had resulted in him dropping his gun and being unable to find it in the dark. I threw the gear lever in reverse but the wheels could find no purchase. A bullet shattered the side window and I was beginning to feel glad I'd taken the time to put my trousers on when a burst of fire from beside me startled me even more, apart from almost searing my ear off with muzzle flash. When I turned to look, Deirdre was taking aim again, letting off another long burst and emptying the magazine. It was a classic case of not knowing what friendly fire might do to the enemy but knowing that it sure as hell scared the living daylights out of you.

'Where do you keep the things for this . . . the bullets?' Deirdre asked, a look of mild annoyance on her face that the weapon had run out so easily. A burst of fire from the back told me that Liam had located his weapon. I took a deep breath and engaged the four-wheel-drive's lowest gear. I eased out the clutch and the Land Rover began to move very slowly, the front emerging dripping and battered from the water-filled ditch. I realized then that we had another problem. The wreckage of the Opel had blocked the road south. I had intended to flee that way but it looked as if I would have to go north, at the mercy of whatever army patrols might have been attracted by the gunfire. There was nothing for it. With a roar which told me the exhaust hadn't survived the encounter with the Opel, I swung the Land Rover north towards Killeen, hoping either to chance the main road across the border or cut across it towards Kilnasaggart and make for the south that way.

When the chatter of the Glock from the back had stopped, I listened for noises which would tell me that the Land Rover had been mortally damaged in the collision. Over the noise of the exhaust there were a few other noises which suggested tyres rubbing against bodywork, but nothing worse. I wondered if Paddy Regan had reinforced the bodywork in some way. Liam draped himself over the front seats, looking through the windscreen anxiously. He was in a bad position. If the army caught up with him, he was looking at the rest of his life in jail, if he was lucky enough to escape a bullet in the head by the side of the road. We travelled about a mile and I was beginning to think our luck might be in. But our night wasn't over yet, not by a long shot. I had just decided that I would chance my luck with the main road when all of a sudden the dark, sodden landscape around me burst into sudden blazing light. Deirdre gasped and shielded her eyes and Liam cursed bitterly. I stood on the brakes.

'Nitesun,' Liam said. 'We're in trouble.'

The Nitesun was an immensely powerful searchlight attached to the bottom of a Lynx helicopter. From ten thousand feet, the beam was powerful enough to light up three or four acres. No matter where we went, the chopper could follow us. I suddenly started to feel very tired. Liam pounded my shoulder.

'Get moving, get moving,' he shouted urgently. I suddenly realized the cause of his urgency. The choppers normally travelled in twos. One held the light on us, the other was probably circling around to land troops in front of us. We hadn't much of a chance of making the border, but what chance we had was lessened every second we sat there. I took off.

It was a strange sensation, careering down the narrow roads in the centre of a huge pool of light, moving and keeping us dead centre in a leisurely progression. The cab of the Land Rover was lit with an eerie, yellow glare which made our faces look sickly and strange. It was a nightmarish pursuit, something that seemed to be taking place in another dimension. We had almost reached the main road when Liam looked up and saw the rotors of another helicopter swooping above the trees like a malicious prehistoric bird.

'They've landed troops,' he said quietly. 'Stop the jeep.' I pulled up.

'Let me out,' Liam said. I knew that he was thinking of fighting his way out of it.

'I can't let you do this, Liam,' I said. He would be pinned down under the searchlight and despatched within minutes.

'Wait,' Deirdre said. 'We can try The Cadgers.'

'What's that?' I said.

'The Cadgers Pad,' Liam said. 'It's a path that leads across the mountains from Carlingford. Fish merchants used to take fish over the mountain on donkeys. It runs across the bog on a causeway here. You can't see it, but Deirdre knows where it is.'

'I don't know what you're talking about,' I said, 'but let's get moving.'

'That field, there,' Deirdre said. I put the Land Rover through the rusted metal gate and half-drove, half-slid down the field beyond. At the bottom of the field, we splashed through a small drainage channel and found ourselves at the edge of a bog which was perhaps a quarter of a mile across.

'The border runs across the middle of it,' Liam said.

'There,' Deirdre said. 'It starts there,' pointing to an area of bog which was indistinguishable from any other. I knew better than to say anything. I put the Land Rover into gear and trundled into the morass.

Straight away, the Land Rover sank to its axles, then a little more. But then the wheels started to bite, to get purchase on something solid beneath the mass of the bog. Prehistoric peoples laid roads of wattle across the bogs and travelled across them, and later I wondered if some ancient roadway lay beneath the surface of this bog.

'Keep right, keep right,' Deirdre said, her face strained with the effort of trying to remember the location of a path she hadn't walked since childhood. The Land Rover suddenly lurched to one side and I fought the wheel to stop it burying itself in the turgid bog.

'Straighten it up,' Liam said, a bit unnecessarily.

'Sorry,' Deirdre said. 'It looks different in this light.'

The Lynx was still above us. I could hear the rotors above the Land Rover's engine. I risked a glance back. Soldiers were running towards the edge of the bog. Some of them were already taking up firing positions.

'We're going to have to do this faster,' I said. 'We're sitting ducks out here.'

'Let Deirdre drive,' Liam said urgently.

'I can't do it,' she said. 'I can't remember.'

'Move,' he said. 'Now!' She gave him a strange, little girl's look and moved obediently into the driving seat. She closed her eyes momentarily and when she opened them there was an odd light in them. The Land Rover took off with a jolt, building up speed, Deirdre driving it smoothly despite the roughness of the terrain, but in a way which seemed automatic, as if someone else were dictating her route across the ancient bogland.

Liam threw me a couple of clips for the Glock.

'Come on,' he said. We threw the back doors open. We could see men aiming weapons at us but with the roar of the chopper and the engine, we could hear nothing. I aimed high, hoping to put them off rather than hit anyone. Putting a bullet in one of Her Majesty's armed forces wasn't really on my job description, even if they were doing their level best to put one in me. Liam wasn't bothered by any such scruples, but the bucking of the Land Rover meant that he wasn't likely to hit anyone in any case. It took less than a minute to cross the bog, bathed in the full glare of the Nitesun. I had forgotten about the other chopper but when it looked as if we were home free, it suddenly appeared in front of us, hovering low, filled with menace. But it was a menace with no way of expressing itself. The Lynx carried no weapons. Liam climbed into the front passenger seat and opened the window, hoping to get a shot at the chopper. Visions of Namibia filled my mind. But before he could shoot, Deirdre wrenched the steering wheel sideways. The wheels bit on dry land and the vehicle slewed towards the undercarriage of the chopper. The pilot reacted swiftly, and the Land Rover went under the chopper with feet to spare. Almost reluctantly, like a predator slow to leave its prey, he rose into the air. He knew he couldn't follow us any further.

As it was, he had already crossed the frontier into the south. The chopper joined the other Lynx. The spotlight continued to follow us, but impotently now, and within a minute, as we crossed a field towards the main road, it changed its focus, moving across the field towards where the soldiers had stopped firing. Just before it went out I saw a figure standing behind the soldiers. I had thought that the helicopter finding us was a reaction to the firing at the house, or just plain bad luck that we came across an aerial patrol. I wasn't so sure now. It was too dark to see, but the shadowy figure in the raincoat bore a striking resemblance to the detective Whitcroft.

We drove a few miles south and pulled into the grounds of Ballymascanlon. Deirdre drove off the road and under the trees. She turned off the engine. None of us spoke. I felt weary, bone-tired. Deirdre had dark shadows under her eyes. Liam was alert, fidgeting restlessly with the butt of his pistol. After a while, Deirdre got out of the Land Rover and walked a few yards away. She sat down under one of the trees. I waited a few minutes and joined her. She took my hand and leaned her head against my shoulder. We sat like that for a while. She sighed.

'I help people, Jack,' she said softly. 'At least that's the way I like to think of myself. Trying to do good. You know when you're little you think you're going to grow up and put the world to rights? I never grew out of that. It sounds a bit silly and I know that the world doesn't really work like that and most of the time good intentions aren't enough. But I have to think of myself like that.'

I kept silent. I knew the meaning behind her words and I had no real answer.

'I don't make judgements, Jack, you know that, but this is not living to me.'

I wanted to say that being hunted like an animal wasn't my idea of a life either, but knew at the same time that too much of my life was given up to deadly games.

'I don't want it to end this time,' I said.

'Neither do I,' she said, and I could sense that she was crying. 'Neither do I.'

Liam came over to us then and there was time for no more. He had a sleeping bag and an old blanket with him. They were both covered with gunpowder residue from the back of the Land Rover, but they were better than nothing. Liam wrapped himself in the blanket. I shared the sleeping bag with Deirdre. We crawled into the back and slept.

It was eight o'clock before we woke. I could barely move, being the wrong age and wrong poundage for sleeping anywhere other than a warm feather bed. We all sat up, looking and feeling miserable.

'The hell with this,' Liam said as we stomped around, trying to get some life back into our limbs. 'I'm hungry.'

If the manager of the plush dining room in the Ballymascanlon Hotel felt any surprise at the sight of three people covered in mud and oil and faces black from muzzle residue, he didn't show it. I suppose his hotel was close to the border and you learned not to ask any questions. He showed us to an empty table, delivered a large pot of coffee and shortly afterwards a platter piled high with back rashers, Clonakilty black pudding, potato bread and pan-fried soda bread.

We finished the first platter and ordered another and by the time we had finished that, things were starting to look a little brighter. We brought our coffee into the lounge. Liam and I sat down to work out a strategy.

'I'm going to get cleaned up,' Deirdre said. I started to push Liam about coming with me, when, to my surprise, he agreed immediately. Perhaps the previous night had given him an idea of the forces ranged against him. We argued about Deirdre. Liam wanted her to come with us. I agreed that she wasn't safe as long as we were both being pursued.

But I felt she had to be allowed to go her own way, despite the risks. After ten minutes, Deirdre returned. Liam turned to her.

'I want you to come to Scotland with us.'

'I am coming to Scotland,' she said. Something in her expression told me I was going to hear something I didn't want to hear.

'When I was out in the foyer I rang the agency in London,' she said. 'They've booked me on a flight to Addis Ababa next week. I can come to Scotland with you and fly down to London from Edinburgh.'

I'm not sure what I expected from her. As I looked at her, I had a sudden vision of the rest of my life and it seemed small and bleak and lonely, a mean, morally compromised existence. I looked at her and saw those green eyes looking back at me and I was afraid I would see pity. But she was too big for that. I held her steady gaze and heard myself say that it was a good idea, that it would take her out of danger until Liam and I could get sorted out. I didn't think of what danger might await us, or of the dark shadow that could fall on Deirdre.

We made our way back to the Land Rover. I was eager to get back to the *Castledawn* and its technology. I intended to send out a few feelers to see if anyone had any idea of who in the American intelligence community would have had an interest in Ireland in the early seventies. I had one good contact who had been a CIA operative in the Dublin embassy with particular responsibility for the war in the north. He was retired now, but his contacts were impeccable. The problem was to pick his brains without telling him about what I had found.

In the daylight, the Land Rover was a sorry sight. I tried to straighten out its twisted panelling but only succeeded in pulling the front wing off. I also found a bullet hole which had been fired downwards through the roof and had buried itself in the dash. We had been lucky. I showed the hole to

Liam. Coming from above, I assumed it had been one of the shots aimed at us from the orchard.

'Do you know who they were?' I asked.

'Canning and Marks, I think,' he said. 'Anybody else would have brought a bigger team.'

You saw some fairly battered vehicles in the border area, but the Land Rover drew a few glances as we drove through Dundalk and headed for the coast, especially when I floored the accelerator and put the big engine through its paces. We stopped at a phone box and called ahead to Paddy Regan. He said he would be waiting for us. He also said that he had some interesting news for Liam. Liam took on a brighter mood when he heard that. I knew that he was maddened by the uncertainty of the past few weeks more than anything. Liam needed a visible enemy.

Regan was waiting at the entrance to his famine dock when we arrived. He raised an eyebrow at the condition of the Land Rover, then pocketed the keys without a word when I threw them to him.

'Thanks,' I said. He nodded.

'I need some diesel,' I said. He frowned.

'There's no time to be going getting some,' he said. 'I have some here, but I wouldn't stand over the quality of it.'

There was a lot of diesel laundering going on in the border region at the time. Agricultural and domestic diesel was sold with a red marker dye in it to indicate that a lower duty was paid on it. It was an immensely profitable operation to remove that dye and sell the clean fuel on. It was a complex process, involving washing with acids, and I had no doubt that Regan had a shed somewhere in the border region with a plant in it and a few tankers parked discreetly out the back. The problem was that sometimes the job was botched and the diesel would wreck an engine. I knew it was a risk, but I didn't have any choice.

'If I'd washed it myself, it would be all right,' he said.

'I know,' I said, 'and I'm grateful.'

We went down to the dock and filled the main tank using a handpump. Then Regan brought us into his office.

'Time to eat,' he said. To my surprise he opened a cabinet on the wall to reveal a small gas-powered grill. He took four steaks from a brown paper bag in his pocket and threw them on the grill.

'Mellows is always hungry,' he said by way of explanation.

'I was born hungry,' Liam said.

While the steaks were grilling I went on board the *Castledawn* and came back with a bottle of Bordeaux. We ate the steaks with lumps of bread torn from a loaf and washed it down with the Bordeaux. When we were finished Regan cleared the table. We waited. He had an ability to remain still, almost a Zen knack, suggesting mental stillness and poise.

'Well?' Liam said.

'I did a bit of looking into your problem,' he said, 'and I found out a funny thing.'

'What's that?' Liam said.

'Well, the two boys that are after you, Canning and Marks, they're not sanctioned by the leadership.'

'How do you work that out?' I said. 'We all know the word is out on Liam.'

'The word is out all right,' Regan said, 'but they hadn't named a team yet. Canning and Marks just took it into their own heads to do the job themselves. They're freelancing and the leadership isn't too happy about it. They tried to call the two boys in to find out what they're up to but let's just say the boys aren't returning their phone calls.'

'I don't understand it,' Liam said.

'Do they have anything personal against you, Liam?' I asked.

'Not that I know of,' he said.

'For God's sake,' Deirdre said. 'Does it matter who kills you, them or somebody else? How can you just sit here and talk about it like that?' She looked close to tears.

'We're looking for a way out, Deirdre,' I said. 'This could be important.'

I sensed a certain relief from Liam. Regan's information might lead nowhere, but at least it was a chink of light in the gloom that had been surrounding Liam. I left them to talk it over. I had another puzzle to tease out.

I had met John Stone at a party in London. He had been the Intelligence attaché in the American embassy in Ireland during the worst of the war. He was semi-retired when I met him, and I took him for a pleasant but ageing functionary who had been put out to grass in what was regarded as an easy, sociable embassy setting. He was a soft-spoken man who had, I discovered, a passionate interest in Mexican art, particularly the painter Frida Kahlo and her treacherous lover, the muralist Diego Rivera. Kahlo was showing at the Tate the following day and we agreed to meet for lunch. I had never seen the paintings before and found Stone fascinating in his descriptions of the savage power of the work and Kahlo's links to Leon Trotsky on the one hand and, through Rivera, to Rockefeller on the other. In later years, I think I could see why Stone was attracted to Kahlo, the beautiful, maimed visionary, with her uncanny ability to extract beauty from her own pain.

He liked to think that the terrible things he himself had been involved in had produced a better, more beautiful world in the end. But I don't think he really believed it. He had fought covert war for American interests in many dark corners of the world, and had called it a struggle for freedom, democracy, whatever. Now he was getting old and afraid of the dark. He told me one night in drink that he had ordered a bombing raid on a small Communist cell in Laos during the Vietnam war. He had been taken to see the devastation that had been wrought. Whole villages wiped out, corpses of women and children already bloating in the heat. He said that the smell of their deaths had never left him.

That when he walked into a room the odour of corruption seemed to follow him and he was continually surprised that no one else could detect it. He was a sad, dangerous, cultured man and he was exactly the person I needed to talk to in order to shed some light on the man now keeping lonely vigil in his mountain grave. The problem was that I was going to have to tell him more than I wanted to in order to be able to extract any information from him. I wondered if he already knew about the involvement of US Special Forces in the north. I doubted it. He had an ironic disdain for what he saw as the military mind's one-dimensional thinking, and he was certainly powerful enough during his stint in Ireland to keep the soldiers out of what he regarded as his patch.

I got into the stateroom of the *Castledawn* and cranked up the satphone and dialled Stone's direct line. His soft, lightly gravelled voice answered almost immediately. We exchanged pleasantries. He had been in Ireland in September, salmon fishing on the Moy and Ballisodare systems. He'd been in Brazil and had bought a painting by Aña Maria Pacheco – beautiful grotesques that I knew would appeal to his dark view of the human condition. He sensed from my tone, though, as I had intended, that this wasn't a social call. There was a pause in our talk. The satellite line hummed and crackled.

'What can I do for you, Jack?' Stone said quietly.

'I made an odd discovery regarding some of your countryfolk,' I said.

'Yes?'

'I found one of them, a dead one, in Ireland.'

'Can you be a little more precise, please, Jack?' Stone's tone was even softer now, watchful. I took a deep breath.

'He was operating in your area of authority, circa early seventies,' I said.' He was in military mode.'

'We didn't have any unaccounted-for casualties during that period.'

I wondered what that 'unaccounted-for' meant. Had the

Americans lost men during the northern conflict? I let it go.

'Something about it suggested that full sanction wasn't necessarily obtained for their activity.'

'Their activity? Plural?'

'The body was concealed. Local knowledge suggests that the tools of the trade were employed in the area.'

'This is extremely serious, Jack. I wouldn't want you to be coy with me.'

'Coy isn't my intention, John, but knowledge is self-preservation, so you can understand my not being overly frank.'

'I don't need to exaggerate the sensitivity, Jack.'

I knew he didn't need to exaggerate. He knew as well as I did that, depending on how high this went, it could rival major foreign policy scandals. The problem with these operations carried out many years ago was that the participants tended by now to have climbed the ladder and reached high positions. It would be easy to think that time took the sting out of the implications of these events once the operational necessity was long gone. But in fact the real sting was in the threat to the people involved in them, and that only increased as time went on.

'I repeat, then,' he said, 'what do you want from me?'

'Your full backing would be nice.' By which I meant help if I needed it.

'Within my limitations, you have it.' That was as good as I would get.

'Well, within the limitations of my own security, I'll tell you what I know,' I said.

He chuckled. It was an oddly melancholy sound.

'Fair enough. Can you tell me how you identified them as Americans?'

'Equipment was unmistakable.'

'Any idea as to their origin?'

'Special Forces of some kind. You'd have a better idea than I would.'

'What about their mission?'

'Direct political assassination. No local proxies.' I could sense his disapproval. He knew the risks associated with such actions. More importantly, he knew the political costs of clearing up after them.

'How do you know they fulfilled their mission if you turned up a corpse? Maybe the other one aborted, headed home?'

The last sentence shook me a little. The other one. That was what he had said. That meant there had definitely been two operatives. More importantly, it meant that Stone did in fact know something about what had been going on. He wasn't the type to let such dangerous knowledge slip by accident. It was deliberate and it was done to tell me there was a bigger picture here. The implications didn't reassure me. As far as I could see, I was the only person who was able to confirm or deny the operation. Imagine Iran Contra. Imagine Watergate. Imagine you were the only person to have evidence of the existence of either, then start calculating how far and how fast you would have to run before they caught up with you. I tried to clear my head. What had he asked me? Had the other operative carried on?

'Yes. The operation was pursued. Targets were engaged.'

'I take it you have evidence of this?' I realized that, in spite of the fact that I had known Stone for a long time, I had allowed my estimation of him to follow him into retirement. This was no old man, looking back from retirement over past regrets and trying to reconcile his soul to whatever God had in store for him. The voice coming over the satellite line was shrewd, merciless, the voice of an *éminence grise* at the height of his power and cunning. I hesitated, realizing that I should have put the evidence in safe hands. There were protocols for doing so, ways of safeguarding your information and, by implication, your life. He allowed a few seconds to lapse.

'Remember Frida,' he said softly. 'I'm no Diego, Jack.' Implying that he wouldn't betray me. There was some reassurance there, but we both knew that the moral rules of the ordinary world didn't apply to ours.

'So far, I've been doing all the talking,' I said.

'What do you want to know, Jack?'

'Everything you're prepared to tell me.'

'Let me see. How do I put this? A man toils and scrapes all his life in the service of his country, as he sees it, sometimes doing things he would rather not do. Sometimes he has a different moral compass to those he serves and acts without their knowledge. He's an impulsive man and sometimes these operations are carried out on impulse, or at the behest of a friend. Sometimes he even goes on one of these operations himself. The years go on. Now this man is older. He finds his patriotism rewarded and finds himself being appointed to a post close to the seat of government. Very close.

'He decides to tidy up a few things that he has done in his past in case they come back to haunt him. He organizes a small unit within a certain service to take care of it. Unfortunately for him, this is a misjudgement. Somebody else gets wind of his involvement, another cat smells the cream . . . things suddenly become urgent . . . I think I've fulfilled our bargain here Jack.'

I thought for a moment. A high-ranking American official or politician. Somebody with a dark secret that was threatening to ruin him. Another cat smells the cream. That must be Somerville. I must have got in just ahead of them. The question of why was still left hanging. Why would an American take such a terrible risk? Perhaps the clue lay in the use of the word 'impulsive'. However, all that was for another time. The point here was that this man had invested everything he had in this particular game and I seemed to be in the uncomfortable position of riding point on it.

'A penny for them, Jack.' Stone's voice cut in on my reverie. 'You were saying about the material?' Even Stone couldn't keep the smallest tone of eagerness out of his voice.

'I'm not sure what I have,' I told him, 'but I have something.'

'Then be very careful, Jack, be very careful indeed.' I had an uncomfortable feeling that this was a case of the fox telling the chicken to be careful, but I didn't say anything.

'I'll keep in touch, John,' I said.

'Do that,' he said. 'I know you have your professional responsibilities, but bear in mind that I'm a safe pair of hands in this.'

'To be perfectly honest,' I said, 'I have no guarantee of that.'

'There might well come a time when you will have no choice but to trust me,' he said. I wasn't sure if I was being threatened or offered a window of opportunity in the future.

'I don't suppose he has a name, this prominent man?' I asked hopefully. Stone laughed softly.

'No,' he said, 'he hasn't got a name. Not in our world anyway. I suppose we should give him one.' There was a long silence, then Stone continued. 'I'm looking out of the window here, Jack. It's one of those very cold, very still nights and the sky is full of stars. Can you picture it? I'm looking directly at Sirius, the dog star. Let's call him that.'

When I put down the phone, I tried to get a mental picture of Stone. He had told me that he lived alone in a ranch house in the Virginia mountains, close to Monticello, Jefferson's mansion, in a house he had designed himself that was dominated by his paintings. It seemed a strange, tortured existence to me, but somehow I took a little comfort in it. This was a man who turned over the moral issues in his mind before he took action. It was cold comfort to be sure, but at least it was there. I started to bring up Paolo's number on the laptop. I thought there were elements of this business where Paolo might be able to enlighten me. But I didn't have time to contact him. I heard the sound of running feet on the deck above my head. I shut down the laptop and moved swiftly as Liam appeared in the doorway. But I didn't need to see him to know that the pursuit was on again. He didn't say anything, just nodded his head to get me topside, then disappeared again. I followed him quickly.

9

I got up on deck quickly. There was no one in Paddy Regan's office. I moved outside. I saw them behind the low stone wall about ten yards beyond the door. Regan motioned to me to keep my head down. I completed the distance on my hands and knees. The proper way to do it was to wriggle on your belly, but I figured my belly wasn't really up to it. I put my back to the low wall. Liam was watchful, as was Regan. Deirdre looked exasperated.

'This is getting ridiculous,' she said. She took out a small mirror and a lipstick, as if to say that she wanted no further part in the proceedings. It seemed as rational a response as any.

'Who is it this time?' I asked.

'Stick your head over the wall and take a look,' Liam said. It took a moment or two to find them against the landscape. There was a piece of flat marshy land in front of us, then the road, then a low hill. There was a battered white Opel at the bottom of the hill and at the top a heavy-set man with binoculars, and some kind of automatic rifle leaning against his knee.

'I've never seen either of them before,' I said, 'but I'll take a guess that's either Canning or Marks.'

'Canning,' Regan said, 'Marks is smaller.' As I watched, Canning put down the binoculars. He lifted a flask from the ground and poured himself a cup of tea or coffee. He seemed very relaxed, even though he knew we were watching him. I started thinking about the Belgian-made FN sniper's rifle I had hidden in the bilges. As if he knew what I was thinking, Regan put his hand on my arm.

'Not on my patch,' he said. He was right. There was an atmosphere of mutual respect between Regan and the paramilitaries here. They left each other alone. But they wouldn't be able to ignore somebody putting a bullet in one of their men, even if he was out of control.

'In that case,' I said, 'I think we should get out of here. The sooner the better. I don't know what they're planning, but I don't like the look of it.'

'I think I'll come with you,' Regan said. 'Can you drop me off up the coast somewhere?' I knew what he was thinking. It wasn't that he was afraid of Canning and Marks, but confrontation would be bad for business.

'All right,' I said, 'let's go.'

As the *Castledawn* sailed out of the little famine harbour, I could still see Canning sitting on the little hill. He didn't seem particularly concerned, which worried me. I shrugged to myself. We'd have to handle whatever they had to throw at us when it happened. I had some fairly formidable forces on my own side. As we'd readied the *Castledawn* for cast off, Regan had run into his office and come back with a travel bag and a small black case. When I looked into the galley, he had removed a Czech-made Steg automatic pistol from the black case and was cleaning it. He looked up when he saw me, then went back to his work without comment. I went back to the wheelhouse where Deirdre had the wheel.

'A life on the ocean wave,' she said cheerfully as I entered, then 'Aye, aye, Captain' as I asked her to keep the wheel. At least somebody was enjoying themselves. There was a light swell from the north-east but otherwise it was calm and visibility was good. I checked the weather reports. The next twenty-four hours were reasonably good, with weather building after that. There was a strong front off the coast of Iceland with isobars packed tight, but it shouldn't worry us as long as we kept up a reasonable pace. I went out on deck. It was almost dusk and the mountains appeared against the winter sky as dark monoliths. I felt a shiver down my spine. Liam was sitting on the old winch mounting.

'A fine evening,' he said.

'You sound cheerful,' I said.

'Ah, I suppose there's a chink of light, that and the fact there's a fight ahead.'

'You think so?'

'Certain. Canning just looked too sure of himself. They'll be coming at us.'

The prospect didn't exactly fill me with the same joy as it did Liam. Apart from anything else, I had a lot tied up in this boat. But there was nothing I could do about it. I went back into the wheelhouse and started to plot a course for Scotland. From the wheelhouse window, you could see Liam in silhouette on the deck.

'Her name was Eva,' Deirdre said.

'Who?' I asked.

'The girl in Berlin. The English girl. He told me about it,' she said. 'It's eating away at him, Jack.'

'The fact that she betrayed him?'

'That? For Christ's sakes, no, Jack.' She gave me a disappointed look. 'Did he tell you what they did to her?'

'Not in detail.'

'He told me. They dumped her body in the river. She was hauled out a few days later. He had to identify her. They had beaten her, mutilated her. There were cigarette burns on her breasts. She had been raped.'

The wheelhouse was silent, except for the steady throb of the diesels beneath our feet. There wasn't anything to say. Such things happened in the world every day. Sometimes it's just not enough for them to kill you, they have to embroider your passage to the other world with pain and humiliation. You wonder to yourself, are these people evil, or is there some deep sickness within them, something that happened in their childhood, some perversion of the very material that makes you human, some delicate writhing pain? I had been on holiday in South Africa during the peace and reconciliation hearings and had decided to go along one day, just to see how a society heals itself. I had expected uplift. Inside, I witnessed a torturer forcing his victim to re-enact the torture he had been put through. The humiliation involved made me feel ill, although the brave man who went through it seemed to shrug it off. I thought it would be better to take out a gun and put a bullet through the head of that cruel, unrepentant man. But perhaps that showed that I suffered from the same sickness as he did.

I went up to Deirdre and put my arms around her from behind.

'Can a man get over that?' she asked, 'I don't think I could.'

The only way I could tackle that question was by putting Deirdre in the same position as the English girl. I wasn't prepared to picture it, and I think she understood.

'How come you didn't tell me you'd decided to go away?' I asked. 'Were you afraid that I'd try to stop you? Do you think I could?'

She turned to me with a wry grin. It had happened before and I hadn't been able to stop her then.

It was the last two weeks of the summer we'd first met. We had been talking the night before about Italy, Deirdre a little wistfully, since she had never been abroad before. I had been to Florence several times, spending long hours in the Uffizi and in the churches in the streets surrounding the Duomo, but I think Deirdre craved the feel of the sun and the crowds and the rich Italian food, the sensuality of the place. That morning, I got up early and slipped into Newry and booked two flights to Florence for the same night. Deirdre was furious. Firstly because I hadn't allowed her to pay for it, secondly because I hadn't given her time to shop and pack. But she calmed down and agreed to it on the basis that she would pay for the accommodation. I agreed and she went upstairs, returning with two rucksacks and an extremely weathered canvas tent. I tried to protest, but she reminded me of my promise. Camping it was, and later that night we flew out, arriving in Florence at first light. We wandered around the early morning streets, slaked with water to keep the dust down. Deirdre was filled with delight. We found a small café which was open and drank espressos. Deirdre bought some bread and we ate it with peach preserve, sitting on the steps of the Duomo. When the crowds started to appear, we found a campsite on the edge of town and lazed around there, coming back into town in the evening. I bought Deirdre a small silver pendant and got another telling-off for spending money, then a kiss.

We spent several of our five days like this; then Deirdre announced that she wanted to go to Assisi. I would never have thought of her as being particularly religious, although I knew she did go to mass sometimes, but she explained that as a child she had always loved the story of St Francis. I was delighted. I had always wanted to see the Giotto frescos in the Basilica of St Francis. In the pre-dawn dark of the following morning, we pulled out of Florence's Bellosguardo station, heading for Assisi. Once again, we arrived there in the early morning. We found a good campsite above the town and slept for a few hours. That afternoon, we wandered through the town, just taking it in. It was quiet, dusty, heat-stunned. The Basilica was closed and would not open for tourists until the Saturday, but we discovered something else. Assisi was to be the setting for a choral festival that weekend and the strains of great liturgical music being practised drifted out of church windows everywhere.

The following evening, we attended a performance of a Bach choral mass in the Church of the Sacred Heart. At one stage during the mass, I looked at Deirdre and saw her moved beyond tears. The music blazed and beguiled and in the end we walked out into the night and back to our campsite, holding hands and not speaking. Deirdre pulled the sleeping bags out of the tent and laid them on the ground and we slept there, side by side. Or I should say that I slept, for I woke some time during the night and looked across at Deirdre. Her eyes were open and she was staring at the stars.

The following day, we went down to see the frescos. Deirdre had covered her hair but had forgotten the requirement that a woman's shoulders be covered. Rather than climb back to the campsite, I gave her my shirt, which meant, of course, that I was unable to enter bare-chested. I waited outside as she went in. She was gone for a long time and she was very quiet when she came out, drifting out of the old doors with a scarf covering her hair and half-covering her face, like a medieval penitent. I asked her what she had seen but she shook her head, slipped my shirt off her shoulders, and walked past me up the hill.

The centuries slip away when you descend into the Basilica. Contributions are accepted from behind a screen by an unseen nun, an enclosed Benedictine who seems to have been entombed in that sombre vault for generations. And the frescos. They were painted at a time when the colours, the very pigments had to be invented and mixed and imbued with prayer, and the spirituality of them breathes out from the walls and you feel all around you the hand of the cunning old master and his pupils.

Later that day, Deirdre sat me down in the shade of an old wall and explained to me that we could not go on. That the things I found myself doing almost every day had no place in her life. That this was not judgement, but a question of survival for her. That she would rue every day we spent apart but that it must be this way. I think I knew what was coming from the moment I saw her leave the Basilica. I could appreciate the genius of the frescos, even feel their spiritual power. But they did not speak to me as they did to Deirdre, of belief and fear, of damnation and redemption. She understood the old, true message that the builders of the church intended to convey when they commissioned the frescos. I can still see her there, her face serious, the sunlight falling across her and the finality in her voice which seemed to dim the sun and show me the world I lived in as a minor hell of my own making.

But that was a long time ago and I had my arms around her now. I buried my face in her hair and imagined I could smell the golden warmth of Assisi. I heard the wheelhouse door as Regan came in. He looked at us with what could only be described as a paternal smile and pointed out that if one of us didn't attend to the wheel, we would end up on that big rock to starboard. Deirdre cursed like a true sailor and grabbed the wheel. However as she corrected the course, Regan led me grim-faced to the port side of the bridge. He pointed back the way we had come. Against the darkening sky you could just see a thick column of oily smoke, and at its base a mass of heavy orange flame. Regan wouldn't be using his famine dock again.

I spent the next hour attending to the boat, checking the self-inflating lifeboat, running an eye over the engines, checking the pumps were functioning properly, checking the Kent Clearview screens, the flares, the auxiliary Mercury outboard, everything on a boat that you put in place and maintained and hoped you would never need. I checked the fire extinguishers and the first-aid kit, which was extensive and included a few things you wouldn't find on the average trawler. When I had done all that, I started to break out the arms. It was risky. We had to cross the mouth of Carlingford lough and there was always a risk of a patrol in a Sea Otter pulling you in. But, the way I looked at it, I already had two men on board who were wanted by half the law enforcement agencies in Europe. Either we could bluff our way through or we could fight our way through. A weapon or two wasn't going to make any difference one way or another. I went down to the engine room and used a socket wrench with a ridiculous-looking thirty-inch extension to reach in under the engine block and detach an innocent-looking pipe. It was my own invention. An insulated pipe with four stun grenades and four mace grenades in it. I actually had no idea whether the heat of the engine might set them off. I'd put a layer of 3mm insulation in the pipe and it seemed to have worked. I thought about taking the grenades topside, but decided in the end to loosen the pipe and leave it ready to lift out. The FN sniper rifle was laid along the keel so that the metal of the keel would go some way towards preventing discovery by a metal detector. I probably wouldn't need it, but there was something about its lean, well-machined contours that reassured me. The Glock was there for automatic fire and underneath the map desk in the wheelhouse I had what amounted to an old-fashioned Derringer pistol, except that this one had been made of some kind of advanced plastic in Russia in the seventies. There were three shells in it, hollowed out and filled with mercury. They would make a tiny entry hole and a hole the size of a dinner plate on exit. That was it for the armoury. I went out on deck and checked that Liam was keeping watch. I checked the wheelhouse. Regan had taken over the wheel and he told me that Deirdre had gone to the galley. I went down to see what was going on but she pointed a wooden spoon at me and ordered me out with an authority that I didn't dare defy. I hung around the door of the galley, smelling the delicious smells like a dog outside a butcher's shop, then decided to go and start some serious work.

It was a good time to call Paolo and he answered the phone immediately. I knew it was payback time, so I gave him what I knew about Sirius on condition that any further information he acquired would be conveyed to me. Information was Paolo's business and he was suitably grateful. He knew the worth of the information I was giving him.

'There's another matter,' I said.

'There always is, my friend,' he said. I outlined what I wanted to know. He listened quietly.

'I will do what I can,' he said. The normal playful tone had left his voice, 'I do not like this kind of business and I do not like to hear of it. This one is for free, *caro*,' he said.

We had dinner in the wheelhouse. Deirdre had found a bag of frozen scallops and had fried them in bacon fat and covered them with a balsamic *jus*. She'd done some fried potatoes and served it all with bread that she'd defrosted from the freezer. We had a crisp Pouilly Fumé, and as the smell of espresso filled the wheelhouse, things started to look a little brighter. At least, that was the way I saw it, but Deirdre reckoned that good food always brought an outburst of unjustifiable optimism from me. As we were having our coffee, I outlined my plans. They were simple really. Beat up the coast and land Regan at one of the little fishing ports, Annalong or Ardglass, then steam up as far as Rathlin Island and beat across the North Channel. We organized watches. I wanted one man in the wheelhouse doing the normal nautical duties, and another on deck watching out for trouble. I wanted to be prepared for the unexpected, though I didn't exactly think the Americans were going to appear alongside in a submarine.

Deirdre took the wheel and Regan took the watch on deck. I checked the weather report. The depression to the north was deepening but we were well ahead of it. I went below again and got on the internet. I called up American news sites, the Pentagon, the National Security Council, familiarizing myself with the names and new appointments. I'm not sure what I expected – that somehow a name would jump out that would make sense to me, that a name would somehow have Sirius written all over it. Of course, I found nothing of the sort. As I was about to shut the whole thing down, I saw the green light flashing that indicated an incoming call. I frowned to myself. A few people had this number, but only a few, and I had a feeling I knew where this one was coming from. I lifted the receiver.

'Jack,' Somerville said, 'how good to find you at home. We

were starting to get worried about you. Where are you, by the way?'

'On the sea,' I said.

'You sound a little brusque Jack, a little displeased.'

'You could say that. I don't mind there being a hidden agenda, but I think I was left a little in the dark as to my survival chances in this one.'

'Just get the material to me Jack, and everything will be all right.'

'And what if I don't make it?'

'If you don't make it, then none of your friends make it either.' Somerville's voice was cold. 'My reach is long, Jack, don't forget that.'

Before I could respond, he rang off. The threat didn't bother me in the sense that there was always a threat there, but it struck me that Somerville was rattled. I went topside. It was fully dark now, and the swell was getting heavier. Still, I thought, we were well ahead of the weather. We would be level with Ardglass in about two hours. We could drop Regan off and head out to sea. I reckoned we'd lost the Americans. I'd ring Somerville and arrange for somebody to be there to pick up the Sirius material, then there was only the matter of Liam to be dealt with. As I comforted myself with these thoughts, I felt a slight stutter in the engine note under my feet. I wondered if I had imagined it. I looked up and saw Regan had noticed it too. As we exchanged glances, it happened again, both engines this time, a longer stutter. I turned and ran as fast as I could towards the engine room. I fell on the slippery companionway and left skin on the handrail before diving across the engine room and hitting the emergency stop button. It wouldn't have mattered. Another few seconds and the engines would have died anyway. I couldn't be a hundred per cent sure about it, but I'd heard an engine kick out on dirty fuel before and by the look on his face so had Regan. The laundered diesel we had pumped into the tank had been dirty.

The *Castledawn* drifted gently in a following sea, the swell still small enough to maintain a gentle motion, but I noticed that the wind was starting to knock the crests off the waves. There was a deceptive sense of peace. I broke out an anchor. It would drag, but at least our drift would be controlled. We gathered in the wheelhouse and reviewed our options before coming to the conclusion that we hadn't any. We had to carry out a partial strip of the engines or take to the liferaft.

'I know engines,' Regan said. 'I'll help you.' You could tell he felt partially responsible for our predicament, even though he had warned us that the diesel might be bad. I calculated. If the damage wasn't too bad, four hours with the two of us working hard might get one engine going. It would be enough for us to limp on, but not enough for an Irish Sea crossing in bad weather. Still, if we were under way we could work on the other one. It just depended on the damage. I worked out a mechanical plan with Regan. Strip down the engine and clean the jets. Have a look at the ports, make sure they weren't blocked with carbon. Clean the fuel filters, all the lines with paraffin, put it all back together and hope to hell that it started again.

The two great fears at sea are fire and engine failure and I knew I wouldn't rest until we were under way again. I went down to the engine room and hauled out the toolbox. Regan appeared from the galley with tea towels. He set the tools out carefully on them. He saw my quizzical look.

'Saves time in the long run,' he said. 'You realize how much time you spend looking for lost tools? All the more when there's the two of you. Just make sure you put each tool back in place when you finish with it.'

He was proved right but at the time I did wonder what I was doing crouched in a cramped engine room with a South Armagh smuggler, laying out tools as if he was about to perform open heart surgery with them.

The first job was to check the fuel filters. My heart sank when I saw them. They were filled with a filthy jelly, some slurry from the bottom of an old fuel tank. I wondered how much of it had got into the engine. There was only one way to find out.

We worked steadily. As I stripped down each piece, Regan cleaned it in meths and set it out on yet another tea towel. It was hot work in the confined space. Once again, I noticed that quality of stillness that Regan had. When he was waiting for another piece, he simply sat there, not idle, not busy, just intently there and in the moment. As I started on the jets, he sat up.

'You're going to need something to clean those jets with.' I thought about it.

'There's a compressor in the forecastle,' I said, 'but you'd need to rig a line.' He took off. When he was gone Deirdre came down with tea and sandwiches.

'You look tired,' she said, pushing my hair back out of my eyes.

'I'm done,' I said truthfully.

'I've got a very bad feeling about this trip, Jack. I wasn't going to say anything, but I can't help it. I'm worried about you.' She didn't know it, but her worry was misplaced. The shadow didn't hang over me. She stayed there until Regan came back, sitting in companionable silence. Once Regan returned with the air line, there wasn't room for three of us and she left. As the night wore on I could feel the increased movement of the boat. The weather was getting worse. It wasn't particularly pleasant in the engine room as Regan connected the jets to the air hose and started to blow compressed air through to clear them. About dawn, I decided to get a weather report.

I had felt the increased swell down below, but I wasn't ready for the scene that met me. The sky was slate-grey, shading to an ominous black towards the north. The wind was cold and biting and on top of the swell the sea was choppy and confused. I realized we were in trouble if the engines wouldn't start. I called Liam and we took the

Mercury outboard out of the forecastle. I hadn't really intended the Mercury as an auxiliary, but I had taken it off a boat I had owned several years before and was looking for a use for it. One day, on an impulse, I had fitted a duckboard to it and had drilled the stern for bolts to fit it. Even with a long shaft the prop barely reached the water, and, even though it was a forty-HP unit, it was barely able to move the *Castledawn* forward. However, it was better than nothing, and it might serve to keep some way on the *Castledawn* and keep her from broaching to. I showed Liam how to use the control cable I had rigged up and told him to keep her pointed into the waves as much as possible. I went into the wheelhouse. Deirdre had dark shadows under her eyes and greeted me with a wan smile. I tuned in the VHF for the weather forecast. It made grim listening. Storm-force winds imminent and the depression still deepening. As if to underline that things were getting worse, a handful of sleet flung itself against the windows. I realized we were going to have to put in at port and wait out the weather. I wasn't happy. It seemed to me that we were vulnerable at sea, but at least we could hide ourselves among the busy east-coast radar clutter. In harbour, however, we were very vulnerable. Apart from anything else, the ports along here were working harbours and the crew of the *Castledawn* didn't look like any trawler crew I had ever seen. These were watchful loyalist areas and it wouldn't be long before the RUC started taking an interest, and, to put it mildly, the *Castledawn* crew represented a law-enforcement nightmare.

I went below again. Regan had finished the jets and had started on the fuel lines, so I started to reinstall the jets. The Perkins is a well-designed engine and the *Castledawn* was a well-designed boat, but in the best of worlds a boat engine room is a tight space to work in, and the work was frustrating. It took another two hours before we got the fuel lines cleaned and installed. Then I had to disconnect the ignition from the second engine. It was mid-morning before I was ready to hit the pre-heater. But first I switched over to the auxiliary fuel tank, where I knew I had clean diesel. There was more diesel in it than I had thought and I realized that I hadn't needed Regan's diesel. It was irrelevant now, I realized, since we had to put in.

Regan sat back wearily while I waited for the pre-heat to warm the engine before I hit the start button. The engine turned over but didn't catch. I looked at Regan. I hit it again with the same effect.

'Fuel's not coming through,' he said. 'Leave it for a minute.'

I waited. Regan nodded and I hit the pre-heat again and then the start. The engine coughed, kicked, coughed again and then started. I leaned over it, suddenly starting to feel weary, when a sudden, large wave almost threw me into the bilge. I left Regan to keep an eye on the dials and I went topside.

I took the wheel from Deirdre and told her to go below and get some sleep. The boat was sluggish and slow on one engine, but I was glad finally to have some control. I spread a chart over the Decca so that I could look at it and keep one eye on the wheel. We could make Strangford lough in a couple of hours. It might take another hour beating up the lough before we could tie up, but at least we would be sheltered from the wind. On two engines I might have taken my chances as far as Rathlin by hugging the coast, but I had no margin for error with one engine, and insufficient power to haul myself out of trouble. After about twenty minutes, Regan appeared beside me with a toasted soda farl dripping with butter and a mug of tea. I took it gratefully. He waved Liam in off the deck and brought him up another farl. I explained my decision to them. We decided we could anchor off Strangford harbour and one of us could go ashore to organize fuel while the others lay low on board.

'I'll get to work on the other engine,' Regan said. His red-rimmed eyes looked out from an oily face.

'You've done a great job,' I said. 'You should get a bit of

rest.' But I could see the fact that he had provided the dirty fuel still bit deep and he refused the offer of a bed.

'What about you?' I said to Liam.

'I'm all right,' he said. I realized that neither of us had slept from the moment I had heard that little click outside the bedroom window. It had been less than thirty-six hours ago, but it felt like a year. I felt a sudden craving for a Redbreast, but I resisted the temptation. A warming glass of whiskey would dissolve the tension that was holding me together. I would fall into a long and pleasant doze over the wheel. I pushed the thought to one side. I looked outside and shivered. The sleet was blowing almost horizontally across the water now. I got Liam to take the wheel. It was a risk with only one man on watch, but I needed to talk to Paolo sooner rather than later.

Down below, I was even more aware of the roll that the following sea was imparting to the boat, particularly at its slow speed. I got the satphone rigged up as quickly as possible. Liam had some experience of boats, but he was no seaman. Paolo was there and he didn't waste any time. He gave me three names. I recognized two of them from the little bit of research I had done. One was National Security Council, the other was, as far as I remembered, State Department.

'All three fit the profile you have given,' Paolo said. 'The right age, background in covert affairs. They've all been involved in actions which have been – how to say this? – actions which have been not in the rule book. And they are all very ambitious. I think if I look very closely I shall discover some . . . turbulence around one of these men, no?' He laughed and told me he had background which he would e-mail to me. Then I asked him about the other matter.

Ten minutes later, I emerged from the stateroom. I had been given a lot to think about and urgently needed to talk to Liam. Going up towards the wheelhouse, I thought it might be a good idea to seek Deirdre's advice before talking to Liam. When I went into the wheelhouse, Liam was standing at the wheel, holding his balance lightly as he peered out into the sleet. He sensed me looking at him and turned with a grin, looking like a Viking. He opened his mouth to say something but he never got a chance to speak. I looked past him, out of the corner wheelhouse window. A shape loomed out of the sleet, a black hull cutting its way towards the wooden hull of the *Castledawn*. I dived across the wheelhouse and grabbed the wheel out of Liam's hand, yanking it frantically to port as the black shape seemed to tower above the *Castledawn*, then there was a rending crash as I was thrown to one side.

I jumped to my feet and grabbed the wheel. Liam was up already, the Glock in his hand. Without speaking, he was out of the wheelhouse door. I desperately tried to get a feel for the boat. Was she starting to handle heavier as water poured in through a breached hull? Looking across the deck I could see that a ten-foot section of the gunwhale was gone and the decking was splintered and pushed inwards, but it was the possibility of unseen damage below it that worried me. The door opened and Deirdre came in, her eyes still half-dazed with sleep.

'What happened?'

'Somebody tried to sink us,' I said. I tried to replay the incident in my mind. A steel-hulled vessel with a sharp, sleek bow, bigger than the *Castledawn*, but not by much. I realized that the way the vessel had loomed above us was due to the fact that it had caught a swell just before it hit us. It had been coming slightly from behind to avoid detection until the last possible minute, but they had timed their attack wrongly. Instead of coming in hard and punching a massive hole in the trawler's wooden side, the swell had lifted their bow so that it rose above the deck of the *Castledawn* and came crashing down like a giant axe, but only in a glancing blow before it slipped off the *Castledawn*'s wooden deck. There was damage, but I hoped it was superficial. I reckoned the attacker was some sort of ocean-going working boat, not a trawler but perhaps a small rig supply vessel.

Liam appeared below me on the deck. He looked up and shrugged. He couldn't see her anywhere. I handed the wheel to Deirdre and took the sniper rifle out from under the map table. An uneasy silence fell over the boat. A feral, hunted silence. I heard footsteps above me as Liam climbed on top of the wheelhouse for maximum visibility. There was no sign of Regan. I hoped he hadn't been thrown against the engines by the impact, but I didn't dare check on him. I caught a movement out of the corner of my eye on the port side and a moment later heard the chatter of Liam's Glock. I rolled into the corner of the wheelhouse. Deirdre looked at me, and I could see the whites of her lovely eyes as they widened in fear, but I hadn't time to tell her what to do and she held the wheel steady and true as the same black hull came cutting through the water towards us from the other side, this time like some fearsome and ravenous sea beast. I saw now that she was a small ocean-going tug with a re-inforced bow and realized she could easily cut us in half. I tried to get the FN scope to my eye, but there was too much motion, so I started to squeeze off shots from the hip, knowing that it wasn't going to be enough, hitting the heavy rifle bolt back with the heel of my hand. It was Liam and Deirdre Mellows who saved the *Castledawn*, acting as though some intuitive thread connected them. Deirdre swung the wheel sharply to starboard at the same time as Liam emptied the magazine of the Glock into the middle window of the tug's wheelhouse. The side of the tug crashed into the side of the *Castledawn* as her skipper instinctively swung her away from us. I could feel the *Castledawn*'s old timbers groaning. The tug's low metal gunnel caught in the *Castledawn*'s anchor port and for a few moments it dragged us through the water, although it seemed that we were racing side by side towards some great prize. Then, with a rending of timber, she tore free, the *Castledawn* wheeled to port, but just before she did so, I found myself almost eye to eye, ten feet apart, with a man on the bridge of the tug; the last time I had seen him, he had been sitting on a small hill in County Louth watching the *Castledawn* set sail. Surprised as I was to see him, he seemed even more surprised as I squeezed off another shot from hip level and sent sparks shooting from the metal frame of the wheelhouse roof over his head. He ducked out of sight as the low stern of the tug disappeared into the sleet.

The next ten minutes were nerve-racking. Liam stayed on the roof of the wheelhouse. I told Deirdre to zig-zag as much as she could, but it was next to impossible at the snail's pace that was forced on us. If they came at us again, it might slightly alter the angle of impact, but it was unlikely that they would be unlucky three times in a row. There was still no sign of Regan. I had a nightmarish vision of him lying unconscious across the hot engine exhaust. I was frustrated by the arms I had at my disposal. The FN was anything but a close-quarter weapon, and I had left the Glock in the engine room. Deirdre kept glancing at me and I could feel her fear. She was brave and capable of taking her own counsel, but I knew that somewhere at the core of her she feared uncertainty and this strange limbo was not to her liking.

'Who are they?' she said.

'I saw Canning,' I said. I had a feeling there was more to it than that. The minutes ticked past. The single engine beat smoothly beneath us. I wondered, though, even with two engines, if we were capable of outrunning the tug. Ocean-going tugs were designed with plenty of speed so that they could get to a crippled ship quickly in all sorts of weather. Salvage fees went to the first boat to arrive.

The bow of the *Castledawn* rose and plunged. The sleet seemed heavier if anything. The water seemed to boil and hiss as the sleet hit it, and it drummed off the roof of the wheelhouse. Liam would be frozen up there. The short-wave radio crackled into life occasionally as skippers swapped weather information. All of them were heading for port and from the ones who had left it late there was a note of anxiety in their voices. But it was a normal sound, the familiar mixture of gossip, banter and information that you heard any time you tuned into the seaman's channel. Under other circumstances it was a comforting sound, reminding you that you weren't alone out there. However bad the weather got, the tone of the conversation never really changed, although I'd listened in on a couple of occasions when a trawler had gone down. Both incidents had taken place many miles away, and I had been unable to help, and had felt it indecent even to break in as the calm voices of the skippers mapped out search areas and reported signs of debris. Under those conditions, you felt as if you were listening to a communal act of mourning. These men could picture a trawler going down. They knew that it was most often the victim of some sudden unforseeable calamity and that there would be few survivors. And even if they didn't know the lost men, they could visualize the small houses, the wives and girlfriends.

I had drifted into this mournful strain of thought when I saw a change in the quality of the sleet. In one of those sudden changes which often accompanies really bad weather, the sleet stopped and blue sky appeared overhead. It revealed a broken, chaotic sea, streaked with green and flecked everywhere with white. And it revealed, riding less than forty yards from the *Castledawn*'s port beam, the sleek gun-metal lines of an ocean-going tug, taking the seas easily and keeping precise station with the slow-moving *Castledawn*. She was a fine vessel, sixty-five to seventy feet, and in any other circumstances would have looked wonderful as she sliced forty-foot sheets of water to either side of her graceful bow as she cut through the waves. There was no flag on her stern and her registration number and port of registration had been painted out, but the nameplate on her bow read *Quo Vadis*. Whither Goest Thou? At that moment, it seemed less a Latin epigram than a direct and brutal question asked by a lethal and unforgiving high-seas functionary. I barely had time to take in the scene before I heard the *Castledawn*'s name given and repeated on the short-wave. Without taking my eyes off the *Quo Vadis*, I reached for the mike.

Before I could speak, a low voice with a Castleblaney accent spoke my name and I realized that somebody had binoculars trained on the wheelhouse.

'Mr Valentine,' it said, 'or maybe I should be calling you Captain Valentine since we're on the ocean wave.' It was the voice of a man who, I thought, never raised his voice or altered his tone. A voice that had heard men pleading for their lives and had told them to say their prayers with the same equanimity, like a kindly young curate dispensing a none too rigorous penance. I had seen Canning and recognized him for a cold and deadly killer, but this was a different class of a man. Given a choice, I would have taken Canning. I hoped I would never be given the choice.

'What do you want, Marks?' I said. The tone of the exchange would prick a few ears among the other skippers on the open channel, assuming they weren't too busy making maximum knots for home. That would work slightly to my advantage, since Marks wouldn't want to draw attention to himself. And I needed all the advantage I could get, for as Marks started to speak again, I saw two figures appear at the rail of the *Quo Vadis*. It seemed that the worst-case scenario I had worked out in my head had come through. I couldn't be sure, of course, but the colourful all-weather gear that the two men were wearing looked very like the gear that the men on the mountain had worn. The pair on the deck of the *Quo Vadis* were the same men I had seen there. Canning and Marks had made common cause with the shadowy men who had been pursuing me.

'You know what I want, Jack,' Marks said, 'I'd like to take one of your crewmen on board. And some of my crew reckon that a part of your catch might belong to them.'

The first part referred to Liam. The second part referred to the Sirius material I had taken off the mountain.

'Let me talk to the Americans,' I said. I wanted to make sure that I had guessed right and perhaps get some feel for what I was up against. It was a thin enough proposition, but it was a case of playing the hand I had. If I could string it out enough, we might hit a group of fishing boats heading for cover, or even a military patrol that we could tag along with. Anything to delay the possibility of seeing that lethal steel prow slicing through the water towards the *Castledawn*'s slender hull.

'Quickly, Jack,' Marks said. He hadn't denied that he had the Americans on board, and the brusqueness of his tone suggested that he knew I was trying out my hypothesis and, worryingly, that he didn't care if I knew about his alliance with the Americans or not. Marks didn't intend such information to be shared with anyone when this was over, and that meant that my position in dealing with the Americans was very limited.

'Valentine,' an American voice said, 'you're a hard man to catch up with. But now that we're all here. I'd like that little package back.' The accent sounded like Boston. That Kennedy way of slurring the 'r'.

'I can't see any reason to do that,' I said.

'I can,' he said sharply. 'There's a crewman I brought from the States with me who isn't a crewman any more, if you follow me. Now, if we have to discuss this matter on dry land or anywhere else, I'm going to take a very strong view of it.'

He was referring to the man I had shot on the mountain, and he sounded as if he was taking it personally. He sounded vengeful, in fact, and his response to my offer confirmed this.

'I think we can do a deal here,' I said.

'Sure we can. This is the deal. We're prepared to land the girl and the little guy. You and Mellows are going to join our crew. I'm sure we can find something for you to do, although

I'm not promising a long trip.'

I hadn't expected a long trip with the Americans and Liam sure as hell wasn't going to get one with Canning and Marks. I tried another tack.

'Your boss isn't going to be happy with you getting involved with local politics.'

'My boss will be happy with the cargo I bring back to him and he doesn't care about the rest,' the American snapped. Another piece of information. The Americans were reporting to one man. Marks came back on. The American's tone and thinly disguised threats would have drawn attention to our conversation on the open channel, and Marks was careful to put up a pretence of a seafarer's conversation. I wasn't sure if the American's lack of discretion was due to the fact that he was under pressure for results, or if it suggested a poor temperament under pressure. Either factor was something which could be exploited in the future.

'I think we can talk about this crew situation later,' Marks said, 'I'm sure something can be worked out.'

'I don't think so,' I said, 'I think I'll hold on to the hands we have.'

'Fair enough,' Marks said pleasantly, 'I'll be talking to you.'

There was a pause, a few seconds, long enough for me to realize that Marks was no longer on the air. Long enough for Liam to urgently bang the roof of the wheelhouse. Long enough for the *Quo Vadis* to dig her stern into the waves and swing her bow towards the plodding *Castledawn*. They were coming at us again. They were faster, bigger and better armed. As I watched her start to cover the distance between us, I saw men take up firing positions on her deck; at least three in the all-weather jackets and one man in a khaki jacket, whom I took to be Canning. I couldn't see into the wheelhouse, but I reckoned that Marks and the American team leader were there. Deirdre looked at me for help.

'What do I do?' she asked.

'Hold your course until they are closer, then swing her

round towards them,' I said. Meeting bow to bow meant they had a smaller target to aim at, and hopefully would mean we were engaged for less time. It wasn't enough. I saw guns begin to spit fire from the deck of the *Quo Vadis*. The guns they had were meant for close-quarter action and they weren't hitting us yet, but it was only a matter of time. I forced myself to think as I raised the FN to my shoulder. Through the big scope, I sighted on their wheelhouse. It suddenly occured to me that their skipper was vulnerable. They couldn't have organized their own boat in such a short time, so they had to either hire one, or hold a gun to the skipper's head. Either way, he couldn't be happy. I put the big scope on their wheelhouse windows but I couldn't see through the anti-glare glass. I stepped out on to the wing of the bridge and tried to level the rifle, but it wasn't going to be easy. The boat pitched and corkscrewed as Deirdre brought her around, and the wind tore at the barrel, making it almost impossible to fine-tune the lateral movement of the rifle. I squeezed off two shots. I might have frightened the odd seagull, but I had no discernible effect on the bridge of the *Quo Vadis*.

I looked up and saw that Liam was hunkered down under the stubby communications mast. He looked calm and clear-eyed.

'The bridge,' I shouted up, the wind carrying my words away. 'Shoot at the skipper.' He nodded briefly without looking down. He had thought of that one.

The *Quo Vadis* was covering the water now with terrifying speed. As I looked down, a line of bullets stitched the water and thudded into the gunwhale. I ducked back into the wheelhouse where Deirdre, white-faced, was trying to wrestle the wheel around. As I did so, I heard Liam open fire. Splinters of wood and sparks flew from the window surrounds of the *Quo Vadis* bridge, but astonishingly the bullets seemed to miss the glass. I stepped out on the wing again and blazed away from the hip. I saw the glass shatter in one of the portside windows but she kept coming on, and the men on deck were making their shots count now. I saw the wood of the wheelhouse door ripple and bullets thudded into the chart drawer behind me. Liam had changed magazine and I heard the rattle of semi-automatic fire above my head and saw the men on the deck of the *Quo Vadis* get their heads out of the way as bullets scythed the air above them. The respite was brief. As Liam switched magazines again they all opened fire as one. A hail of bullets hit the portside of the *Castledawn*. I flattened myself to the wall as splinters of glass and wood filled the air, instruments smashed and angry sparks flew from the fusebox mounted behind my head. I felt something hit my forehead and a wave of panic came over me as blood poured down my face and momentarily blinded me. I cleared the blood with my sleeve and started firing at random, the big 303 bullets thudding through the wheelhouse door and hopefully finding a mark.

The wheelhouse door swung open, the lock shattered. The *Quo Vadis* was almost on us, the men on the deck momentarily unsighted by our forecastle. As I watched, she swung out, seemingly intent on pulling back in and dealing the side of the *Castledawn* a hammerblow. I don't know if it was by instinct or intent, but just at that moment Deirdre swung our own bow into that of the attacking boat. I could hear her timbers groaning under the pressure but the weight of our hull meant that the tug couldn't slam into us, pushing us back until we were side by side in the raging sea, gunwhale against gunwhale, metal and wood splintering and shrieking, neither ship with an advantage over the other. I slammed the bolt of the rifle back and felt it click on an empty chamber. Above my head Liam's gun was silent, either jammed or empty. I found myself looking directly at the four men on the deck of the *Quo Vadis*. I was staring into the eyes of one man in particular and it was the face of a type I recognized. Pleasant, even features. An arts degree in some obscure Midwest college. Then Langley Virginia for several years' training. Africa next perhaps, or a minor intelligence posting in the Middle East. The face of a Central Intelligence Agency careerist. Well-educated but ultimately vacuous. Well-travelled but ultimately contemptuous of other races. I saw the machine pistol in his hand and I saw him raise it and I knew he would kill me in textbook fashion, kill all of us without compunction or regret because he believed he served a higher cause which had abrogated all morality to itself. I looked into his pale eyes for what felt like a long time and I seemed to be looking into the pit of hell. I sensed rather than saw his colleagues train their guns on the wheelhouse where Deirdre stood alone and I knew that she could not escape and that this man regarded my soul as his own. And it was at that very moment, as we stood on the brink, that Regan burst through the door of the sleeping quarters like a vengeful imp that had itself escaped from the abyss.

He had his Steg in one hand and my Glock in the other. A bloody flap of skin fell over his forehead and I realized that he had indeed been thrown into the engine bay by the earlier impact and had been knocked cold. But he was awake now and by the look of him was as mad as hell. I had heard about the Regan temper but this was the first time I had seen it. Hooking one arm around the trawl gantry on the side of the *Castledawn*, he leaped on to the rail, heedless of the bucking sea, or of the deadly crushing gap that opened and closed between the two boats. Firing both guns at once, he felled the man who, seconds before, had had me in his sights, and sent the others scattering. Keeping the Steg trained on the deck and firing in short bursts, he tilted the Glock so that it was pointing at the base of the wheelhouse and emptied the magazine into the wooden underside of it. The tug skipper had been brave until then, but the bullets coming through the floor must have done for him. The *Quo Vadis* swung violently to starboard, moving so abruptly that she almost broached to in the heavy seas, and sent her deck complement tumbling for cover. Regan spotted Canning.

'Canning, you half-bred fucker!' Regan yelled, firing off what was left of the magazine at him, then pulling a pistol from his trouser waistband and firing wildly. I remembered what had happened to the famine dock and thought for one moment that the man was sizing up the growing gap between the boats in order to leap it and conclude his business with Canning. Liam tumbled, whooping, from the roof beside me and ran to get a fresh magazine for his pistol. I saw the stern of the *Quo Vadis* lifting from the water and had an idea. Cursing myself for not remembering, I grabbed the shotgun from the shelf underneath the navigation bench in the wheelhouse. There was a growing distance between the two boats but I bided my time until the stern of the *Quo Vadis* was clear of the water and her rudder half-visible before I squeezed off both barrels. I saw flakes of paint scatter from the stern of the tug as one barrel slammed harmlessly against the metal plating. But with the second barrel I thought I saw the blade of the rudder flinch violently before it buried itself in the foam, and before another wall of sleet swept towards us, obliterating the other ship as if it had never been there.

Regan pushed into the wheelhouse, bristling with adrenalin charge. He was covered with oil and blood. Liam swung himself down from the ceiling. He was blue with cold but he grabbed Regan and shook him by the shoulders.

'Christ, Regan, but you're a warrior, a bloody warrior.' Liam was elated. He had been chased for a long time but this time the prey had turned and bitten back.

'I fell into the engine, else I would've been out before,' Regan said. 'We would have had the lot of them.' Both men were full of the elation of battle, and I felt it myself. We weren't feeling the salt spray or the cutting wind coming through the broken door and wheelhouse windows. There was a smell of cordite in the wheelhouse and I could see Liam's and Regan's blackened faces and knew that my own looked the same. Liam slapped me on the back and shook his fist in the direction of the departing tug. When you have the light of battle in your eyes, it blinds you to other things. Liam and I didn't hear it. It was Regan who turned at the whispered word 'Liam', and turned in time to see Deirdre slump sideways from the wheel and against the wheelhouse wall, her face pale and a rose of blood growing on the material of her blouse just below her left breast. 'Please,' she said, and a trickle of blood ran from the side of her mouth.

10

Any doctor in a war zone will tell you that gunshot wounds are complex and strange things. Someone will die of shock from being nicked by a low-velocity slug. Someone will walk for a mile after a high-velocity shell has passed through their legs without realizing that they have been shot. Bullets will fragment inside the body. A lead slug moving at low speed will bounce off the skeletal frame inside the body like a steel ball in a pinball machine, destroying as it goes. Fragments of cloth from clothing will be driven deep into the wounds, causing them to fester. Badly injured patients will be up and about in days, joking with nurses. Men with minor injuries will huddle under the blankets, their eyes full of fear, unable to contemplate the brush of death's cloak.

Regan was the first to hear Deirdre and he was the first to move, kneeling by her side, looking first for other wounds, then lifting the fabric of her blouse away from the small, white-lipped wound just above her bottom rib. Deirdre's breathing was quick and shallow. She fixed her eyes on mine and followed me as I moved but she seemed to be somewhere else, concentrating on something very complicated and very far away.

'There's no exit wound,' Regan said, 'the bullet's still in her. Machine-pistol, I'd say.'

Liam knelt on the other side of her. He brushed her hair gently out of her eyes. He opened his mouth to say something, then shut it again. He looked up at me with a mute hopelessness in his eyes.

'She's well into shock,' Regan said. I had already pulled a blanket from under the map desk, but I knew that we had to get her below. The wheelhouse was too exposed with half the windows shot out. With any bullet wound, shock is an enemy, and she needed to be in a warm, dry place. I was hoping that shock was the source of the dry, shallow breathing. I put my ear to her chest beside the wound. I could hear the characteristic sucking rattle of a lung wound. She must be bleeding internally, and God knows what else the bullet had hit. Apart from anything else, it ruled out morphine and the pain would be hitting her soon. I knew enough about field first-aid to know that morphine suppresses lung function, and she was having enough difficulty breathing without that.

I turned to Liam. He was looking at me and I didn't need to ask what he was thinking. There was a pinkish foam on her lips. Her eyes were still open but I wasn't sure how much she was seeing. I went to the short-wave. I looked at Liam and Regan, all of us knowing without it being said that the next move would probably deprive both of them of their liberty for the next twenty years.

'What are you waiting for?' Regan said, and turned back to Deirdre. I punched the button for the marine emergency channel. I got an immediate response. A calm female voice.

'Emergency response. Please state your name and position.' I gave our name and position.

'Nature of emergency, please?'

'We have a critically ill crew member requiring immediate evacuation.'

'What is the nature of the injury please?'

'Gunshot wound.' There was a brief hesitation, then the calm, professional voice went on.

'Please confirm that, *Castledawn*.'

'Our crew member has been shot in the chest with a low-calibre firearm. There is internal injury.'

'Roger, *Castledawn*. We'll be scrambling a helicopter from Lisburn, should be with you within twenty minutes.' I liked this calm voice. The professionalism that figured it was none of her business how my crew member had acquired her wound. The professionalism which would require her to contact the security services the minute I was off the air.

There wasn't time to dwell on it. I realized that there was no one at the helm of the *Castledawn* when a wave caught us beam-on, swamping the deck and sending a flood of icy water half-way across the floor of the wheelhouse. I grabbed the wheel and straightened her up, then pulled Liam towards me and thrust the wheel into his hands. He was about to protest, but I silenced him. We couldn't afford to leave the wheel unattended. And the *Quo Vadis* was still out there somewhere.

Using a blanket as a stretcher, we got Deirdre down into the stateroom. At least it was warm there. She was lapsing in and out of consciousness, and her breathing seemed shallower again. Regan laid her on the bed with a gentleness I hadn't expected. He sat on the bed and began to talk to her – soft nonsense talk, it sounded to me, with Irish and dialect words mixed in, but she responded to him, opening her eyes and raising her face to his like a child listening to a bedtime story. After a little while, her eyes closed but her breathing seemed more regular and a little colour seemed to have returned to her cheeks. I didn't have time to wonder at what he had done. I ran topside and gathered all the weapons. The shotgun and the sniper rifle went over the side. The Steg and the two Glocks went under the engine block. If they were found, I could claim they were mine and take my chances. I thought about making up a cover story but I realized there was no point. Once they identified Regan and Liam, they would draw their own conclusions.

After that, there was nothing to do but sit and wait for the helicopter. That was when the enormity of what had happened began to set in. I had seen too many men shot in the way that Deirdre had been shot. I knew that her chances were even, at best, and with every minute that ticked away, they became less. I couldn't shut my eyes without seeing her face. I couldn't let a thought into my mind because with that thought came the knowledge that she had been led into this by Liam and I, the two men who professed to love her best. When Liam turned to look at me, I saw the same bleak realization in his eyes. Sooner or later, life strips away the last residual romance from those of us who started out dreamy and idealistic. We sank into silence and despair, and there was no other sound in the wheelhouse as the *Castledawn* furrowed the restless waters like a hopeless barque bearing the glittering, cold body of a warrior princess to her final rest.

It seemed longer, but the chopper was with us within twenty-five minutes of Deirdre being shot. A yellow Sea King with RAF roundels on its sides, emerging, almost at mast level, from the spume and sleet. For a moment, I thought that they had sent a conventional air–sea rescue team. Then I saw the barrel of a sub-machine-gun protruding from the winchman's hatch and a metallic amplified voice ordering us to down all weapons and prepare to receive a boarding party. I went into the bridge and raised them on the marine channel.

'You're welcome on board,' I said, 'you won't meet any resistance.' There was a silence which implied that they'd see about that, then the side door of the Sea King slid all the way back and three ropes dropped to the heaving deck of the *Castledawn*, closely followed by three heavily armed men wearing survival suits. They abseiled swiftly to the deck. Impressive, I thought, although a bit foolhardy. I noticed one of them collide with the old winch casing and land heavily on the deck. When he got up, he had trouble putting his weight on his right ankle although he was trying to hide it. I filed it away. Otherwise, they did everything right and within a few minutes Liam and I were sitting with our backs to the wheelhouse wall with plastic ties on our wrists. Regan emerged from the stateroom with his hands up and got the same treatment. Only then did they allow the winchman to lower a stretcher to the deck. They brought the stretcher below and emerged with Deirdre strapped to it. She looked very pale.

The stretcher was clipped to the winch cable and at a signal from one of the men, it began to rise. Even before the stretcher had reached the helicopter, the pilot had started to bank away. Within seconds, the helicopter had disappeared into the low cloud. As I watched, I forgot about Sirius. I felt bleak and empty, and underneath the emptiness, the beginnings of a burning anger towards the men who had shot at us. It must have showed in my face. I looked up and saw one of the boarding party watching me. He had the eyes of an older man and the eyes narrowed as he looked at me. I would have to watch myself with him.

One of the others seemed to be an experienced seaman. He took the wheel while the older man dictated a new course to him. As far as I could work out, it would take us close to Belfast. We were virtually ignored after that. The older man, speaking in a soft English, West Country accent, directed the others to board up the shattered panes of glass on the port side of the bridge. They found my stock of plywood in the forecastle and began to work. They had finished within the hour. One of them examined Regan's scalp, then took a field dressing from a pouch at his belt and expertly covered the wound. Otherwise, they were wary and self-contained. We were sitting in an inch of sea water, but none of us complained. Liam seemed lost in thought and Regan seemed asleep, or, to be more accurate, in a state of suspended animation, unaware of his surroundings. I calculated it would take us close to four hours to get to Belfast.

The older man watched us disinterestedly. He had obviously been told to deliver us and nothing more. That meant there would be a reception committee. I wasn't looking forward to it. It might be the police and we might be brought to an RUC station and put into a nice, warm cell, but I doubted it. More likely, there would be hard-faced men waiting for us and we would be brought to a place which was neither nice nor warm.

11

I was right. It took four hours to get to Belfast and it was dark as we entered the mouth of the lough. You could see the lights of houses glittering on the slopes of Cave Hill. I felt a kind of nostalgia for what I imagined going on in those houses. The smell of cooking, children's schoolbags thrown in corners, favourite programmes on the television, the warm glow of life the way it was meant to be lived, without danger and without terrible regret. From my position on the floor of the wheelhouse, I could just see the tower blocks of the nurses' homes beside the Royal Victoria hospital. They would have taken Deirdre to the Royal, a hospital with more experience than most in dealing with gunshot wounds. I thought about the gleaming high-tech operating theatres they had built to deal with trauma wounds. But I couldn't stop the picture of the gloomy Victorian morgue coming into my head.

As far as I could see, we were heading towards Queens Island, the reclaimed land where the shipyard was located. The storm seemed to have abated a little, but there was an ominous, oily swell which suggested that this was only a temporary respite.

The channel became narrower, and through the starboard windows I was able to see rusted cranes, abandoned machinery, a mournful landscape of empty shipyards and abandoned dry docks. The shipbuilding industry here was reaching the end of almost a hundred years of decline, a decline that was already under way when the *Titanic* and the *Lusitania* rolled down the Harland & Wolff slipway. The men seemed to know where they were going. After twenty minutes of this, a radio crackled to life at the older man's belt, but he stepped out on to the wing before he replied. While he was gone, I tried to push myself up against the wall of the wheelhouse to get a better view of our position, but all I could see was the heavy wooden piles of a Victorian dockside. The older man came back in and saw me. Almost casually, he backhanded me with the heavy 9mm pistol he carried in his right hand and I felt pain across the side of my face and then blood. The man turned away from me and peered through the wheelhouse windows. There was nothing personal about the blow. It was simply a way of telling me that no liberties were to be taken. One part of me admired his professionalism, almost sympathized with his point of view. The other part wanted to hold him face-down in the bilges until his eyes popped out. I tried to keep the angry part to the fore. I might need it in the following hours.

Eventually the *Castledawn*'s single engine slowed. One of the soldiers went out on deck and I felt the boat bumping against what sounded like a wooden dock. The hull recoiled as ropes took the strain. We were back on land.

They wasted no time. We were hoisted to our feet and pushed out of the wheelhouse door. We had been sitting in the cold for hours and were cold and unsteady on our feet. I saw Regan stumble and fall against the wheelhouse. The younger soldier pulled him roughly to his feet and when Regan stumbled again, slammed him against the side of the wheelhouse. I could feel the anger again, and I could feel Liam tense beside me. I remembered Regan's gentleness with Deirdre and I eyed the young soldier darkly. His card was marked, and if I got the chance, which I doubted, he would know about it.

I wasn't really in a position to be thinking such thoughts. I felt myself hoisted up on the gunwhale. There was a two-foot gap between the dock and the boat. They pushed me in the back and I sprawled on to the rough wooden planks. My hands were still tied behind me and I skidded across the dock on my face. I decided that the men had another black mark against them. I might as well keep score.

We were at a small dock, carefully chosen so that you couldn't see beyond the small, low-roofed sheds that surrounded it, and no one else could see in. The wrought iron and metal of the gates was old and rusted but I saw new chains and locks on them. I wondered how many men had walked the same path as the one we were now following. I wondered how many bodies, discreetly coffinned, had been carried across the dock and loaded into the hold of some small merchant navy tender. During the late eighties and early nineties, it had become policy to deny military fatalities, particularly during covert operations. But men were killed and then a week or so later a small paragraph would appear in one of the London papers to say that three soldiers had been killed during a training accident in some obscure military camp. The policy was to preserve military morale, denying propaganda to the IRA. I was never sure if it achieved either objective. I thought it only added another layer of deceit to the Irish war, another whiff of cloak and dagger.

We were half-walked, half-carried towards a big corrugated shed, the size of a small hangar. I noticed several cars parked to the side of the shed. The kind of nondescript vehicles used by undercover forces. Q cars, they called them. The flash of anger had cleared my head and my mind felt oddly lucid. I realized that this was no conventional police or army operation. If it had been, there would have been massive back-up, helicopters, the area swamped with soldiers, not just a few cars parked discreetly behind a shed. It wasn't good news. With all the paraphernalia of a joint police/army operation, you had a certain degree of protection. The quiet bullet behind the ear wasn't an option. But in this case it almost certainly was. In fact, the whole thing might have been set up towards that end.

The big doors of the shed slid open and we were pushed

inside. It took my eyes a moment to adjust to the darkness, sparsely lit by unshaded bulbs high in the ceiling. Metal junk was piled in the corners of the shed, the detritus of the Industrial Revolution. There were two more soldiers standing in the shadows, both carrying Heckler and Koch automatic rifles. There were smells of diesel oil and seawater, and the shed was bone cold. At the end of the shed, I could see two more men. One was sitting on an oil barrel. The other was standing. Squinting through the gloom, I tried to make out their faces, but I couldn't. The place gave me a bad feeling. It was cold and echoing and felt more like a place of dark judgement than a derelict shed in a derelict corner of an ailing shipyard. There was a sense of sickly evil about the place, that I had come across a few times in my career.

A few years ago, I had a call from an old friend, a press photographer, who wanted to go to Turkey and do a feature on the Turkish war against the Kurds. I wasn't doing anything at the time and I went with him, mainly because the photographer was the type of man who always seemed to irritate authority figures beyond measure with the sense of imminent anarchy that seemed to accompany him. It was a part of the world I was interested in, and a little knowledge of conditions on the ground could be useful. It was a long and difficult journey but eventually we found ourselves in a small village on the border with Iraq. This village continually changed hands and had been shelled almost to oblivion. The Kurds were in control at the moment and the local commander took us to see a bunker he had apparently stumbled upon.

We went down into the bunker from the heat of the desert noon. It was cool and dry and our boots made a shuffling sound on the sand-covered steps. There was a strange smell in the air. We turned the corner into the bunker. There wasn't much in it. A desk and chair, a battered filing cabinet and a strange contraption in the corner.

The commander said it was a torture centre which had been used by the Turks against Kurdish prisoners. In truth, it could have been used by the Iraqis against the Kurds, or by the Kurds against the Kurds or any other combination you could think of. It suited the purposes of this man to blame it on the Turks. He stood at the entrance to the room with a benign smile on his face while I stepped forward to examine the device, which took up one corner of the room. Essentially it was a metal bedstead suspended from the ceiling by means of a pulley. There were leather straps at each corner of the bedstead. Underneath it, there was a filthy gas cooker attached to a yellow gas cylinder. There was a horrible ingenuity to it. A man, or a woman, would be strapped to the metal bedstead, then lowered on to the lit burners of the cooker. I tried not to look at the top of the cooker and the matter that was caked on it, but I knew that the smell I had got coming down the stairs was the smell of burned flesh.

The Kurdish commander gave the device a name. By the time we had got back to London, I had forgotten it. It didn't matter anyway. No one wanted the photographs, or the accompanying piece I had written. You find that these devices are always given lurid names. The Crab. The Tiger. It increases their terrible allure, makes them more frightening to a civilian population, cloaks the torturer in what he believes to be a dark glamour.

I couldn't swear that similar things had happened in this building. But it gave me the same feeling. There was a strange psychic tide in the place, as if haunted by the screams of the maimed and tormented. I knew that Liam had got the same feeling. When I looked at him, I could see the whites of his eyes in the darkness, the sheen of sweat on his skin. I wondered if the soldiers were aware of it. There was a certain sense of decorum now in the way we were guided rather than pushed towards the two figures at the far end. I recognized the standing man first. The detective Whitcroft, older than he looked in his photographs, staring at us with a dark, unreadable look. I hadn't expected the other man. It was Curley, Somerville's right-hand man. I knew that Curley rarely travelled beyond the Park. Only an exceptional need could have driven him here, and that worried me.

The three of us came to a halt in front of the desk and there was a long pause. Curley was looking at me with a half-smile on his big, open countryman's face. Whitcroft was staring at Liam and he wasn't smiling at all. It was Whitcroft who made the first move. He came around the front of the battered desk and, without breaking stride threw a punch at Liam. Liam must have known it was coming and he rolled with it. Otherwise, it would have broken his jaw. But it was still a hard punch and he went down, a dazed look in his eyes. He put the side of his head on the ground and spat out a tooth and didn't bother trying to get up again. Whitcroft examined his knuckles, then stepped quietly back behind the desk.

'What about my sister?' Liam said shakily. 'How is she?' No one answered him.

'I'm very disappointed in you, Jack,' Curley said to me. You could tell he wasn't used to fieldwork. The sentence sounded like something you would hear from a Bond villain, and I almost laughed in his face. Almost, because I knew both by reputation and experience that Curley was capable of almost anything.

'You were sent to retrieve something,' he said, 'and you didn't do it. We're taking a dim view of it.'

'I was bringing it back,' I said. 'I was just taking the scenic route.' Two could play at bad movie dialogue, I thought. Curley wasn't a man for flippancy. He came round the edge of the desk and kicked me hard in the stomach. I tried to go down. I wanted to go down, but one of the soldiers held me semi-upright. The extra stone around my waist might have cushioned the blow, but the pain was searing, and I felt as if Curley's heavy brogue had torn muscle.

'I'd prefer it if you'd listen to me and not talk. You were supposed to find something for us and return with it immediately instead of indulging yourself in a reunion with a little bastard of an IRA man and his slut sister.'

Everybody had forgotten about Regan. Apart from everything else, he must have had the suppleness of a snake. He had sat on the ground beside Liam and somehow worked his hands, which were tied behind him, over his feet so that they were now tied in front of him. He launched himself from a sitting position and was on Curley before anyone had time to react, clubbing him to the ground with his tied hands. He slipped his bound hands over Curley's head and around his throat and began to throttle him. Two of the soldiers were on him in an instant, beating him with the butts of their weapons, but Curley's face was purple and his tongue was starting to protrude before Regan was finally prised off him.

Curley gradually worked his way into a sitting position, then to his feet, shrugging off any help. He stood with his back to us for a long time, feeling his throat. I wasn't able to see the expression on his face. I was glad. The reference to Deirdre had been meant to sting, but now that we no longer knew whether she was alive or dead, somehow Curley's malice had been deprived of its power. I could see that Liam had allowed it to pass over his head as well. Regan was a different matter. He had risen to the defence of the girl and we all knew that he would pay a price.

After what seemed like an age, Curley turned back to us, his face composed. The soldiers had bound Regan's hands and legs and had added an extra tie between his elbows to stop him slipping his hands out again. Curley walked over to him. Regan was lying on his side and Curley stopped so that his brogue was just beside Regan's face. Regan glared at him without speaking.

'I don't think you men realize the situation you're in,' he said eventually. 'You know, I've heard it said about old people who are ill that in fact they would be better off dead. That's the place the three of you are in. You would be better off dead.'

His foot smashed into Regan's face. He did it again and again. I felt a spray of blood spatter across my own face. When Curley had finished with Regan's face, he worked on the rest of his body. He worked methodically. He was a professional and this was a beating which was intended to inflict pain and eventually to kill. This was what I had sensed when I came into the shed, with its darkness that seemed to cloud your being. I felt myself pulling and twisting at the plastic ties around my wrists until the skin was torn but I couldn't shift them and then a soldier was standing over me and another over Liam so that we would know the futility of attempting to get free. And the beating went on, Curley grunting now with the effort. Yet through the whole thing I could see Regan's eyes in the blooded mask that had been his face. He seemed calm, to have retreated into that interior place I had seen before. And all the while his gaze never left Curley's face, as if he intended to implant the man's features into his own DNA, the very matter that made him, so that this hour could never be forgotten. I could feel the soldiers shift uneasily and I saw one of them look towards Whitcroft who had remained in the shadows and who seemed to represent the only other authority in the shed. His features remained inscrutable, the face of a hard border cop who had seen much. And perhaps it was that diamond hardness that gave authority to his voice when he spoke.

'Curley.' He spoke the word, but it seemed emphatic for all that, and Curley stopped. It may have been out of respect for Whitcroft but I suspected that it was because Curley was a long way from home and he needed Whitcroft's local knowledge. It seemed fairly clear that they had joined forces because Whitcroft wanted Liam and Curley wanted me. Curley stared down at Regan, almost as if he couldn't see him. Then he took a small revolver from his jacket pocket. Regan didn't flinch and his expression didn't change.

'That's enough,' Whitcroft said. 'You've had your crack. It's time to do what we came here to do.'

Curley turned to look at me, raising his eyebrows. I nodded wearily. For the moment I couldn't see any point in defying him. Besides, he was smiling now, the gun dangling by his side, Regan seemingly forgotten. I wondered if Curley was sane.

'Where are the things?' he said. It occured to me that Curley didn't know precisely what I had found on the mountain. It was a typical Somerville ploy, and conventional enough – keeping people in the field ignorant of everything except the information they needed in order to function. But I had always thought that Somerville and Curley operated as one.

I stored the insight away. I seemed to be doing a lot of that recently in lieu of acquiring insights that I could actually use to get us out of trouble.

'They're in the boat,' I said.

'Take him to the boat and let him show you where they are,' Curley said to the soldier who had remained standing over me. 'Don't let him touch anything, even a handrail. If you have to turn your back on him, shoot him in the leg first.'

As the soldier led me away, I risked a look at Regan. His eyes were closed and I couldn't tell if he was breathing or not. I knew that Regan had entrusted me with his life as surely as Deirdre had entrusted me with hers. I was the professional. If I had followed orders, they would both be all right. It was a bitter thought.

On my way out of the warehouse, I had checked the forces ranged against us. As far as I could see, there were only five soldiers, making seven altogether, including Curley and Whitcroft. Something else backed this up: there were only two cars. When you are in trouble, always look for the mundane detail. Two cars would take seven or eight men. This information had another implication. There was no room for the three of us who had arrived on the boat. If I'd worked it out properly, there was room for one man. That meant two of us weren't leaving the dock. Perhaps Somerville and Curley judged me valuble enough to take me out. Perhaps not. Perhaps Whitcroft wanted to return to the border in triumph with Liam in chains. Either way the outlook was bleak for Regan if he was still alive.

The wind had got up again when we got outside and I staggered as it buffeted me. I received a clip around the ear with a gun butt for that. I almost welcomed the pain for the anger it brought, the clarity. As I scrambled on to the *Castledawn*'s deck and plunged down the companionway to the engine room with the soldier hard on my heels, I knew that only one of us was coming out alive.

I had vague notions of getting a gun or one of the grenades out from under the engine block. Once we were in the cramped engine room, I realized that I had been deluding myself. There was no way a man with his hands tied behind him could get in under that engine.

'Where is it?' the soldier said. His voice was flat, almost mechanical. This was a man who would obey his orders to the letter. I thought desperately; he didn't know what he was supposed to be looking for. Curley couldn't tell him because he didn't know either, but he wasn't going to admit that. It was a weak point. The photographs and other evidence were in fact in my stateroom. I kept thinking. There was a small shelf above the oil pressure gauge where I kept a workshop manual for the engines. There was also a set of drawings of the steering gear and hydraulics. If you didn't look at them too closely, they could be anything. I nodded at them.

'The drawings,' I said, 'beside you.' I cast my eyes frantically around the engine room. Any of the tools Regan had neatly laid out on a cloth would have served as a weapon, but the soldier knew that as well as I did, and made sure I couldn't get near them.

In the end, he did for himself. He wasn't going to reach for the drawings while I was standing beside him. He turned me round so that I was facing away from him and pushed me to the other side of the engine room, where the hose for the compressor was resting on a shelf with one of the diesel jets still attached to it. He'd pushed me with such force that I hit my head off a protruding pipe and half-fell, getting up with the hose and jet wedged under my arm. I tried to remember if I had turned the compressor off and decided that I hadn't. I tried to remember if I had put enough fuel in it to keep it running for hours on end. I couldn't recall the answer to that one either.

It wouldn't have worked if Regan hadn't been knocked cold before he could finish clearing the jets. It wouldn't have worked if I had been facing him, because I wouldn't have been able to bend my fingers back up to get them on to the trigger-type control on the hose. It wouldn't have worked if the jets hadn't been full of oily sludge, or if, in spite of what he had been told, the soldier hadn't taken his eyes off me momentarily as he reached for the maps, which gave me time to take a rudimentary aim, waiting for the moment when he looked back at me. I hit the trigger and a toxic blast of compressed air and filthy oil hit him right in the eyes.

I would have died then anyway if I hadn't dived for the bilges. The soldier was well trained and, painfully blinded as he was, he swept his weapon up to waist level and started firing at the place where I had been standing. Somehow the trigger mechanism of the air hose had jammed open and the hose writhed like a snake in the narrow space. It struck the soldier on the shoulder and he staggered back, firing another burst at an invisible enemy. I almost felt sorry for him. He was effectively blind and no match for me even with my hands tied behind my back. The next burst warned me against complacency, however, as spent bullets ricocheted around the confined space. I got the engine block between us. He was inching backwards, feeling desperately behind him for the companionway opening, but he was three feet to the right of it. The air hose hit him again and he squirmed away from it, firing again until the hammer clicked on an empty cylinder. He pulled a Luger from his belt. I gave him one chance. I already had a pair of pliers in one hand, and had the jaws around the plastic ties.

'Drop the gun,' I said. 'You can't . . .' It just goes to show you that it doesn't pay to do too much talking in these situations. The second sentence gave him time to get a fix on me, and with lightning reflexes and almost perfect aim he got a shot off in my direction. I didn't have time to duck and I heard the bullet whistle past my ear. That was enough. I felt the pliers bite through the plastic ties. I reached under the engine and took out the first gun I found which was Regan's Steg. I switched it to single shot and I put a bullet into the man's chest.

In television or film, a bullet is a dramatic convention. You throw up your arms and die if the plot requires it. You are wounded but struggle on bravely if that's what is required. But real shooting is different and there is real horror in it. I came around the engine and saw the man on the metal decking. He was in a terrifying spasm, his weight resting on his heels and shoulders, his back arched, his body racked with huge nerve damage. His eyes had rolled back in his head and he was making an eerie, high-pitched, bubbling sound.

In these situations, you do what you have to do. I shot him in the forehead. One dead this night, possibly two, depending what damage had been done to Regan. And certainly more to come. I stared down bleakly at his dead eyes. Somebody's son, somebody's brother. Except you can't afford to think like that. You have to say to yourself that he tried to kill you, coldly and without compunction. That was the way to justify the killing. Except that the words didn't seem to fill the moral vacuum the way they used to.

I pulled myself together. I had very little time. Any minute, someone would come looking for me.

Two minutes later, I climbed over the gunwhale on to the dock. I was carrying every weapon I could find on the boat, including the pistol from the wheelhouse and the dead soldier's 9mm. The three stun grenades made an uncomfortable lump in my trouser pocket. There were four soldiers left. They wouldn't call for back-up. I knew the mentality. They were the élite. It would be unthinkable for them to ask the ordinary squaddies for help. Not only would it be humiliating, it would go against every tenet of their basic training, which was to be self-sufficient, to handle crises themselves.

I studied the big hangar, aware that time was short. They had made one big mistake. It was a mistake encouraged by the system. The training received by Special Forces had become so specialized, often to the point of being esoteric, that basics were neglected. And a basic of the situation here would have been to have someone outside, guarding the shed. It wasn't overconfidence. They simply hadn't thought of it.

It didn't make my task that much easier. It just meant that I wouldn't be shot down before I reached the door. I saw a ladder leading up the side and there were skylight-type windows at the very top which would provide a tempting firing point. Or at least they might have done twenty years ago. But there was a sharp pain in my stomach from Curley's brogue every time I moved. There was also an extra inch covering the seat of that pain and a weariness in my limbs that resented the very idea of that ladder, and a sudden aversion to the thought of the icy wind sweeping in off the lough. I cast about, looking for a back door, a hidden entrance. And then the anger returned. Anger, not only for Deirdre and the brutalized Regan, but, if I was honest, anger that I was no longer able to swarm up ladders, burning with self-belief and a sense of the rightness of my cause. But some part of me did stay clear and cold enough to check that the weapons were cocked and ready, then I simply slid back the big door, walked into the shed and started firing.

As a strategy, if it could be called a strategy, it was partially successful. I hit the soldier nearest to the door and saw him go down. A second one came at me and I recognized him as one of the men who had abseiled on to the deck, the one who had fallen against the winch. I took a chance that it was him and feinted to his right. The ankle he'd hurt gave way long enough for me to get a shot at him. The round went straight into his body armour, but he stayed down. I ducked down and slid the Glock across the floor towards Liam and saw him catch it and roll out of sight.

That was as good as it got. A hail of fire from at least two weapons struck the spot where I had been standing. I dived for a pile of metal debris at the corner of the shed. I had only a glimpse of the scene in front of me before I hit the ground. I tried to hold the picture in my mind, to create a moment of stillness in the chaos. I shut my eyes. I saw the scene around the desk where Regan was still lying on the floor. He was alone. There was no sign of Whitcroft or Curley. Suddenly and inexplicably, I felt tired, utterly fatigued. I leaned my forehead against a piece of angle iron in front of me. I heard six or seven shots being loosed off, an odd, irrelevant sound, which only made sense to me when I realized that the gloom in the hangar had deepened. The shots were answered by a rattle of machine-gun fire. I tried to make my exhausted mind put it together: Liam shooting out the lights, and one of the soldiers aiming shots at the muzzle flash. I wasn't functioning and I knew it. I palmed a benzedrine tab from the pouch in my back pocket and swallowed it. Better to die of an amphetamine-induced heart attack than a bullet, I thought. The speed hit me quickly. It had to. There were two echoing bursts of gunfire in the darkened shed. Covering fire laid down. They knew where Liam was and they were moving in on him. I knew he was aware of my position and would be leaving that flank open. At the very least, I could cover him. I put the barrel of the Glock over the angle iron and squeezed off a burst, as much to let him know that I was still there as anything else.

I had no illusions about our situation. The two men we faced, assuming that Curley and Whitcroft had pulled out, might have been overtrained, but this was the kind of circumstance their training was based on. I had some idea of what technique they might employ, but Liam had no formal training. Still, as far as I could see, the two men reckoned Liam to be the real danger and were moving to take him out first. I can't say I was particularly flattered. To remind them that I was still there, I pulled out the pin of one of the stun grenades and lobbed it into the middle of the floor. I didn't put any particular thought into it. The intention was to create a little space for Liam.

The noise was deafening. The very fabric of the shed boomed and shook and reverberated. My ears rang. I had underestimated the amplifying effect of the metal shed. I risked a swift look over the top. I could see nothing. I couldn't see Liam. I couldn't see the two soldiers. And I couldn't see Regan. The space in front of the table where the body had lain was empty. Regan had gone.

The disappearance of Regan gave me an eerie, unsettled feeling, as though he had somehow been spirited away by the shades which inhabited this black place. I had always had a feeling my life might end in a place such as this. Somewhere strange and dark and unredeemed. I shook my head to rid it of such fancies and I felt another rush from the amphetamine. We'd got this far. In the darkness, I heard a single shot and then a man's cry, a piteous sound that went on and on and pierced you right to the very soul. Something that has been happening to men on battlefields since war began. The desire to be beside that crying man and to snuff out that terrible cry with knife or gun, to snuff out the knowledge that it might be your own voice.

The cry went on. I knew that it could be Liam. He was a brave man, one of the bravest, but that didn't mean that he wouldn't cry out in pain, in a lament for his own mortality. The sounds men make in the heat of battle or in mortal pain sometimes do not appear to come from a human throat. You would often hear eyewitnesses to a mortar or rocket attack in South Armagh referring to the surviving soldiers as having squealed with terror. I thought it was a figure of speech until I was close to a bomb attack and saw soldiers run away from the seat of the blast, throwing away their weapons as they ran, and squealing, a high-pitched girlish sound, the sound of men beyond fear.

The noise went on until I thought it would never cease, then suddenly, over it, I heard a rattle of gunfire. The man's screams continued after the shots, then I heard Liam's voice.

'Come on out, Jack, I got the two boys, and Curley and Whitcroft ran like hares when the shooting started.'

I came out cautiously and followed the scream to its source. Liam was behind a pyramid of packing cases. The noise was coming from one of the soldiers. He was lying on the ground and rocking himself from side to side. There was a hole in his leg and another in the side of his face. You could see broken teeth through the wound. A few yards away, the last soldier lay face-up on the ground. It seemed to me that the screaming man had been used by Liam as bait in a trap for the other, older man, who, despite his experience, had felt compelled to come to the aid of his young colleague.

'What'll we do with this crying bastard?' Liam said, poking him with his boot. I wasn't used to such brutality of word or gesture from Liam. The barrel of Liam's weapon was pointing at the man's head. Before he could fire, I moved swiftly. I knelt beside the man and ripped open the pouches on his belt until I found what I was looking for. His first-aid kit would contain syringes of morphine. I found a belt of four of them and ripped open the packaging. I dug the syringe into his thigh through the battledress and depressed the plunger. I gave it a minute. When the screaming had abated but not stopped, I gave him another one. The sound dropped away to a low moaning almost immediately, and it became possible to feel for the young man as a human being again.

'You'd be better off looking for Regan,' I said, 'instead of standing there like some butcher's assistant with a boltgun.' The words were harsher than I had intended. I knew what was going on in Liam's head. His brutality was a response to the fact that his sister was in hospital, perhaps dead. But I suppose that was what worried me. It came to a point where brutality was the only answer. I looked up at him and was relieved to see that he looked shame-faced. He moved off, looking for Regan. I joined him. There was a trail of blood leading away from the place where his body had lain.

When we found him, he was still moving, lifting himself up on his hands painfully and dragging the weight of his body behind him. His hair was matted with sweat and blood. His eyes were fixed on some invisible goal and we had to talk to him softly, whispering in his ear, for several minutes before he stopped forcing his broken body towards shelter.

When we had carried him back to the *Castledawn*, Liam wanted to put him in the stateroom, but I brought up a campbed and lashed it to the map table. I didn't tell Liam, but I knew that we had no choice but to head out into that storm, and there was a fair chance the *Castledawn* wouldn't make it. In that case, I wanted Regan somewhere I could get him into a liferaft. I broke open another of the morphine syringes and gave him half of it.

Our survival chances on one engine in a storm were practically nil in any case. I needed time to put the dismantled fuel-injection system back together, but we couldn't stay where we were. Liam cast off and we slipped away from the dock. We ran without lights through the piers and jetties of the docklands, a furtive shadow on the dark, oily waters. There was no other traffic in the channel beyond. The big bulk carriers would ride out the storm at sea. Small craft like ours were well tied up in snug little ports. I felt a pang of longing and self-pity at the thought of seamen, their vessels safely aport, sitting with their families and listening to the wind tear around their roofs. Except that it wasn't just sentiment. It was the speed wearing off and the beginnings of the dull, anxious amphetamine comedown. I thought about another tab, but I only had a few left and we would need them during the night.

After twenty minutes, I found what I was looking for, a hulk half-submerged twenty metres from the main channel. I made fast to her, told Liam to take a watch and to do what he could for Regan, while I went below to work on the engine.

It took a little short of two hours to put it all back together. This time, the engine started immediately. I promised myself a swig of the Redbreast bottle as a reward for my mechanical prowess and made my way topsides. There was another positive awaiting me there. Liam was drinking tea, but the whiskey bottle was sitting on the map table. And half-propped against it and holding his own mug of tea was Regan. He looked terrible. His eyes were red-rimmed slits in the middle of swollen, blackened skin. His nose had been badly broken and pushed sideways. I noticed, on the hand that held the mug, that one or more of the fingers sat at an unnatural angle. He didn't seem able to use the other arm at all. He lowered the mug from his mouth to say something to me, but his lips were too broken and swollen to speak properly. I thought about warning him about the dangers of alcohol and morphine together, then thought better of it. If the beating didn't kill him, he could take his chances with the drink and morphine.

'He says, who was that bastard?' Liam said, handing me a mug of tea and pouring a shot into it.

So I told them about Curley. Regan grunted and said something. I couldn't make it out, but I thought it was something along the lines of 'Some friends you got.' I had to agree with him.

It was half past one and I was anxious to get going. Before Regan had a chance to protest, I gave him the last syringe of morphine. While I was waiting for it to take effect, I got the marine forecast. I didn't need to be told how bad it was with the wind shrieking through the mast, and the communication mast rattling like a thousand devils. Severe storm warning. Winds gusting to force twelve. Heavy, broken swell. I turned it off. When I looked round, Regan was asleep. I knelt over him and straightened his nose as best I could. I broke a piece off an old wooden scale to serve as a splint and straightened his finger. He cried out in his sleep as I did so. I taped the finger to the splint.

When I looked up, Liam was watching me. I saw that he had Regan's mobile phone in his hand.

'I rang the hospital,' he said. 'She's critical, that's all they would tell me.'

'She's alive then,' I said. 'She's alive, Liam, and you know what she's made from.'

Liam looked at me. He wanted to believe in her strength, but he had seen too many gunshot wounds. So had I.

I looked at the phone. A mobile phone when it is switched on, is as efficient a tracking mechanism as was ever invented. Any half-efficient organization with an interest would know our position down to a few yards by now.

'I thought of that,' Liam said, reading my thoughts, 'but do you not think they know where we are anyway?'

He was probably right. I went outside to cast off the ropes. Another half an hour would take us out of the lough. I went back up to the wheelhouse and checked the wooden boards that now covered half the windows. Liam took the wheel as I got a power socket and some self-expanding bolts and made the sheeting as secure as I could. In a storm, a flooded wheelhouse meant disaster. After that, I went down to check the bilge. There was a little more water in it than there should be. The water itself wasn't a concern, but the thought of a sprung plank was worrying. I inspected the place where the tug had struck the *Castledawn*. The damage appeared superficial but there might have been some harm done below the waterline.

As I emerged on deck, it was awash and the boat was pitching violently. I got myself back to the wheelhouse. There was one more job I had to do before we got out of the lough and into the maelstrom beyond. I took over from Liam at the wheel and poured us both a Redbreast. I had been waiting to speak to him from the moment we had first been hit by the tug, and I knew I had better speak now. Neither of us could tell what the next twenty-four hours might bring, and there was one burden that I could lift. Liam sat down at the map table and took a drink from his glass. He stared blankly into space. There were dark shadows under his eyes and his face was lined. I didn't want to broach the subject on my mind, but I knew that I must. I knew that I would be relieving him of one burden but replacing it with another, perhaps more onerous, burden.

'Liam,' I said softly, 'we have to talk about Berlin.'

12

The look he turned on me was ashen, haunted. For a moment, his eyes were two black pits and I was glad I had to turn away from him to correct the course of the *Castledawn*.

'What about it?' he said, with a deceptive gentleness in his tone. 'What about Berlin?'

'It's about Eva,' I said.

'How did you know her name?' he said. He was intent now, totally focused.

'About how she was killed and why,' I said. A particularly large wave hit the bow and drove the *Castledawn* sideways. I knew that there wouldn't be much time before I would have to give all my attention to the helm.

When I turned back, Liam was on his feet. I could feel the tension emanating from him. A pulsating, animal energy.

'I can't give you details of sources, Liam, except that I would stake my life on the integrity of the man I spoke to.'

'Tell me.' He spoke flatly, but his voice was full of menace.

'The first thing is that Eva did not give them the information about the Slieve Bloom operation. They already knew about it. They were looking for detail and she wouldn't give it to them.'

I watched as Liam absorbed the implications of this. I wondered how long it would take to hit him. I had tried to think my way into her mind, and in a way I thought I had; the painting she had done had given me some clue to her character. She had been complex, unreliable to the point of betrayal, and totally involved with life in a way that I could never be. She had started off by selling out Liam, by getting involved in a double life, but if I was right about the painting then she was operating to a different and deeper level of integrity than most of us were capable of. At some point, she had recognized the place where the game she was playing led, and she had decided she wasn't a player any longer. She had stopped and had determined in some iron part of her that she would not go on. They had tortured her and degraded her, but I think she turned away from them into an interior place. It wasn't just the heroin that had taken her on to a different moral plane. It was a recognition of her own worth and place in the universe. I envied her.

'There isn't any doubt about this, Jack, is there? I couldn't stand to find out that this wasn't true.'

'It's as certain as it can be,' I said. 'The man who gave me the information is a man of integrity and he asked me no price for it.'

There was anguish in Liam's eyes. I saw the realization dawn on him. That night, in the Berlin apartment, he had accused her of betraying him. She had denied nothing and had walked out into the night and towards the death that was beckoning her. He had done nothing to stop it, had impelled her towards it.

I turned my attention to the sea. All I could see in front of me was darkness, broken by a few lights. Not many lights. A long time seemed to pass and I didn't turn around. I didn't want to. Yeats said that too much suffering makes a stone of the heart. I was never sure if he was right or not. It was an aesthete's view of suffering. I thought that too much suffering simply breaks a man. I think Oscar Wilde knew that, and knew that he was broken when he left prison. I was afraid that I would see Liam broken if I turned to look at him. But I had underestimated him. He had absorbed the other implication of my information.

'Where did it come from then, Jack?' he asked. 'If she didn't tell them, who did?'

A theory had started to form itself in my head, but it was the wrong time to share it with Liam.

'I don't know, Liam.' I turned to look at him. He was

watching me closely. I had the uncomfortable feeling that he knew exactly what I was thinking. A small, steely smile tugged at the corners of his lips.

'All right, Jack,' he said, 'all right. But when the time is right, I want you to tell me what you suspect.'

I nodded. Another wave drove into the bow of the *Castledawn*, burying it in foam. Liam was still watching me.

'Something else on your mind?' he asked.

'I hate to say this,' I said, 'but in ten minutes' time, we're going to be in the worst storm I've ever seen . . .'

'Yes . . .'

'And I'm bloody starving.'

Liam shook his head.

'I should have known that was coming,' he said. 'I'll take the helm.'

'Keep her head on to the waves,' I said. 'I've got some ciabatta in the freezer I can do something with.'

Liam shook his head again, a wry grin on his face. I heard him muttering 'ciabatta' to himself, as I went down the gangway towards the galley.

The galley was in darkness. Two minutes in the microwave would defrost the ciabatta. There was a jar of pesto in the larder, and a hunk of Parmesan. That, and a flask of coffee, would stave off hunger. Liam was laughing, but hunger and fatigue are enemies at sea. I could almost smell the Parmesan as I stretched for the light switch. My hand never reached it. I felt the hard barrel of a gun pressed into my ribs before I heard the voice, the voice of a professional, a hard, cold voice.

'Don't fucking move, Valentine. Don't move a muscle, or I'll blow you apart.'

13

I thought about a reflex attack on the man. But the thought faded as soon as it appeared. There was no room in the galley for such a manœuvre. I knew I should have checked the boat before we set sail. Now it was too late. I leaned back against the wall, suddenly feeling very weary.

'You don't give up, do you, Whitcroft?'

He gave a grim laugh.

'Around the border they call me "The Mountie", Valentine. I always get my man. Good thing you got Regan on board as well.'

'Kind of a bonus, is it?'

'Under other circumstances it would be, but this time that's not what I'm after. How's the girl?' I wondered at the sudden change in tone.

'Critical,' I said. 'Critical but still alive.'

'That's the thing with people like your friend Liam, going in with all guns blazing like some sort of fucking cowboy. The innocent get hurt.'

'That's war,' I said, wondering why I seemed to be debating the morality of armed conflict in my own galley with a man who had a gun stuck in my ribs.

'It's always an easy answer,' he said. 'People say it's a war and then that lets them off the hook.'

'What do you want, Whitcroft?'

'Go and stand at the far side of the galley.' I did as he said, feeling my way in the dark. When I had done so, he turned on the light.

Whatever this chase had done to the rest of us, it didn't seem to have done Whitcroft any good either. There was stubble on his cheeks and mud on his shoes and raincoat, and his eyes were sleepless. He said nothing, staring at me for a long time before he placed his revolver on the bench beside him. I watched him warily.

'When it comes to war,' he said, seeming to be talking to himself, 'there's more than one way of skinning a cat. More than one way.' He sighed. 'I was sorry to hear about the girl.'

I felt a faint glimmer of comprehension. I remembered Eamon in his bar in Dundalk, talking about a source in the senior ranks of the security establishment. Could it be Whitcroft? If it was, then security policy along the border had been compromised perhaps for decades. I looked into those red-rimmed, slightly watery eyes and wondered about the knowledge concealed behind them. I sensed a man not unlike Eamon, a strategic thinker, ruthless, a player of the long game.

'What do you want with Liam, then, Whitcroft? Why is he important to you?'

'I need to talk to him.'

'About what?'

'You know that he's been singled out as a target?'

I nodded warily.

'I also know that he isn't the target, that the wrong man has been singled out,' I said.

Whitcroft looked at me and I sensed a new respect in his look.

'Well, then,' he said, 'we both know the same things. I suppose you also know that Liam is a key figure in the movement. Perhaps the key figure, the man the rank and file look up to. A legend, in fact.' There was a weary contempt in his voice as he spoke about Liam as a legend.

'I know what Liam is,' I said, 'and he's no random killer.'

'My brother is not a criminal,' Whitcroft said, quoting the famous border memorial to the hunger strikers. 'Whatever. The point is that the rank and file are badly divided over this issue, to the point that the movement is in danger of a split. They'll go back to war before they'll allow a split to develop, and I won't allow that to happen. There's been enough killing.' There was a kind of passion in his voice now, the weary passion of a man who has seen too much death.

'My job is to find who ever informed on the Slieve Bloom operation and bring Mellows back in from the cold,' he said. 'I'm after him to talk to him, not to kill him.'

'I'm glad to hear it,' a soft voice said from behind Whitcroft, 'I'm fierce glad to hear it, for I nearly put a bullet in you where you stood, Whitcroft, and maybe I still should.'

'I don't think so, Liam,' I said. 'There's more here than meets the eye.' Liam stepped into the galley and I saw him noting the gun on the table.

'It would appear so,' he said. Suddenly I felt the boat shudder and heel.

'Who's got the helm?' I said, starting from my position.

'Regan,' Liam said. 'I had to come down to see what happened to you.'

'He's not fit to handle her in this weather,' I said urgently, as the trawler bucked again. 'Put the gun down, Liam. You can settle your differences later, but for now you're the crew of my boat.' Liam looked Whitcroft in the eyes, that strange, appraising look he shared with his sister. He nodded very slowly to himself, then lowered the barrel of the gun.

'For now, Whitcroft,' he said, 'for now.' I pushed past both of them and ran for the wheelhouse.

Regan was just barely holding on, trying to work the wheel with one hand while keeping his battered frame upright. I grabbed the wheel and turned to Whitcroft, who was right behind me.

'Help him, for Christ's sake,' I said. Whitcroft caught Regan as he fell sideways, and half-lifted, half-dragged him towards the camp bed. There was a funny look on Whitcroft's face and I thought he would drop him when Regan turned his face to Whitcroft's and showed what was left of his teeth in a parody of a grin and said something which sounded suspiciously like a request for a kiss.

Although the request was facetious, Regan knew that Whitcroft had saved his life in the shed, beyond a shadow of a doubt, when he had stopped Curley's brutality.

For the first time since the shooting, I turned my attention to the sea. I had never seen anything like it. Beyond the shelter of the lough, the sea boiled white, a maelstrom of white foam, the waves confused beyond measure, coming from all directions, the worst kind of sea. I didn't need a weather forecast to tell me what lay ahead of us.

'I'm sorry,' I said quietly, 'I can't take you into that. I'm going to turn back.'

'I don't think turning back is an option,' Liam said quietly. 'Look.'

I turned to the side window of the wheelhouse. About five hundred yards from our port quarter, running slightly behind us and cutting us off from safety, was the slender, sinister bow of the *Quo Vadis*.

She must have been waiting for us in the lough. Whoever was aboard her had access to some sophisticated technology. We had been on a screen somewhere the whole time we had been in the harbour area. My heart sank. The *Castledawn* was a seaworthy vessel, but she hadn't been built with these vast seas in mind. The *Quo Vadis*, on the other hand, was designed to put to sea in the worst of weather. Though even she wouldn't find this storm easy going.

'First things first,' I said. 'If we're going to get out of this alive, I need total cooperation from the crew. That means you and Whitcroft, Liam. Whatever you need to work out, do it when this is over. You haven't the luxury of watching your backs. All right?' Both men nodded warily.

'Right, Liam, I want you to check the bilge and make sure the pump is all right. Whitcroft, make sure Regan is strapped in, then get us some food from the galley. Get moving. We only have a few minutes.'

I looked at the *Quo Vadis* again. She wasn't making any attempt to get closer. I studied her movement in the water. She seemed to be moving oddly as she came down the face of a wave. I started to wonder about the speculative shotgun blast I had aimed at her rudder. Had I done any damage? There was certainly something strange about her motion. I took a little heart from that. If she was putting to sea in this storm with rudder damage, then her captain was a fool. But then, considering the men he had on board, he probably hadn't been given a choice in the matter. In any case, her close-quarter manœuvrability would be compromised. It wasn't much, but it was something. I thought about this for a moment and then the sea hit us.

The keel of the *Castledawn* had been laid in Bill Quinn's boat-yard in Kilkeel in 1953. During the war, a German U-boat had surfaced among the Kilkeel fleet as it fished off the Isle of Man. He had ordered all the crews on to the smallest boat, then he had sunk the rest by gunfire. It took a few years for the fleet to be built up again, but the *Castledawn* was the pride of the fishing village. Clinker-built to a Cornish design, she had taken everything that came with a hard working life. But she was an old boat now, entitled to gentle treatment. Instead, she was facing into the worst storm she had ever encountered. As the first wave tore at her, I thought momentarily of the skilled hands that had put her together in the calm of a post-war boatyard, the hands of men long dead, in most cases. I hoped that their shades were looking kindly on her now. I didn't look back for the *Quo Vadis*. I didn't have time. I braced my legs against the wheelhouse floor and tried to feel the motion of the boat, the flex of every plank on her, the impact of every wave. It was the one advantage I had over the *Quo Vadis*. The wooden hull of the old trawler flexed and was responsive to the sea. You could almost say that the wood remembered past storms, knew how to react to them. The deck in front of me foamed with white water, the seas breaking over the forecastle at will. I risked a quick glance backwards. Such were the seas that the afterdeck rarely appeared above the water. The only thing that protruded above the angry sea was the wheelhouse, and within minutes it was taking such a battering that I wondered if it would be carried clear of its mountings. I glanced the other way, towards Regan. He was awake and looking at me. I could see the whites of his eyes. Liam braced himself against the corner of the cabin where he could look for our pursuer, not that anything was visible through the spume and foam that surrounded us. I realized that the broken waves, the tearing, corkscrew effect, was probably a result of the tidal surge in the lough. I gave up any thought I had of staying close to the shore and pointed her bow towards the open sea. At least with the waves coming from one direction, we might have a chance.

Such was the power of the waves striking us that we appeared to be making little progress, the boat seeming to be pushed back towards the shore, but gradually I noticed the lights of the shore receding, the corkscrew effect becoming less pronounced. As if to make up for it, the swell seemed to double in size. From the decks of an ocean-going liner, they might have appeared majestic. From the wheelhouse of a small trawler, they were terrifying. Whitcroft appeared from the galley. He had no food and no coffee with him. I couldn't say I blamed him. He tried to say something, but I couldn't hear him above the sound of the wind and the waves. I turned back to the sea. As the bow rose out of yet another monstrous wave, I noticed something different. The metal guard rail that ran along the top of the forecastle was gone. Some superhuman force had wrenched the flanges of the railing from the metal seats. I tried not to think about it. I motioned Liam to me and shouted in his ear that he was to check the water in the bilges. I didn't want to start the pumps unless there was something for them to work on. The mast top spot blinked and then went out. I think I was glad that I could see less of the murderous sea. I didn't know then how costly the lack of that light would be.

Liam came back and indicated with his hands the depth of the water in the bilge. Just over a foot, I reckoned. Not too bad if you were within sight of port. Not too good if you were heading straight into the heart of the kind of storm that only comes along once every century.

I shouted in Liam's ear again. He picked up the words '*Quo Vadis*'. He shrugged. I'm not sure if the shrug meant that he didn't know where the tug was, or if it meant that the storm was probably going to drown us all so it wouldn't matter anyway. I knew that I had one small advantage over the tug. The metal hull had to cut through the massive waves, making it extremely difficult for her to hold a heading with a damaged rudder. By contrast, the wooden trawler rode on top of the waves. That was the theory, anyway, although it was hard to believe she was riding on top of anything.

An hour passed. I looked down and saw that my knuckles were white where I gripped the wheel. I tried to make them relax, but they wouldn't. I looked quickly around the wheelhouse. The other men's faces were pale and strained and their eyes were starting to glaze over, the way the eyes of disaster victims glaze over. They were all brave men in their own way, but the screech of the wind tore at their frayed nerves, and their idle imaginations started at every creak and groan. And then no one was idle any more. The *Castledawn* took a rogue wave on her beam. It drove us over to port, heeling over further than I thought she could go, and I thought I could feel the start of the vertiginous roll that would come as she reached her point of no return and went beyond it, gathering speed in her capsize. Then, under the terrible strain of tons of water, the lock on the wheelhouse door burst and suddenly we were waist-deep in cold, turbulent water. More than waist-deep, for the recumbent Regan, helplessly strapped into the camp bed, had disappeared under the water. I felt myself being driven across the wheelhouse, my feet pushed out from under me, one hand still wrapped desperately around the spokes of the wheel, my head being forced underwater, then bursting free. I saw Liam powering through the water towards Regan. I saw Whitcroft, feet braced against the door, his back against the wheelhouse wall, trying to force the door closed. And then, slowly, in a motion which seemed to span all of eternity, the *Castledawn* started to right herself, fighting the weight of water on her deck. The night was full of weird sounds, the creaking of timber strained beyond measure, the rush of tons of water, the wind howling through the open door. With one final shake, she was free of the water and riding head-on into the storm again. Whitcroft managed to push the door shut, although the wheelhouse was still knee-deep in water. Liam pulled Regan from the water, spluttering and choking. There was a moment of quiet as the wind seemed to die away. We met each other's eyes, pale-faced, exhausted. I wondered how much more the *Castledawn* could take. But she had righted herself. Against all the odds, she had come back from an impossible angle. I reminded myself of that. Then the storm hit us again.

14

It is a short crossing between the north-east coast of Ireland and the south-west coast of Scotland, one that isn't known as being particularly tough. Normally the narrow opening, almost a strait into the Atlantic, prevents the swell from building. It is extremely rare that a wind will build at the particular angle of a few degrees off north-west which will channel it precisely into the narrow strait between the land masses. It is even more rare that the same wind will build to such an intensity that it drives the water in front of it, building wave upon wave, piling them on top of each other as the mass of water rushes into the channel faster than it can escape. And it is almost unknown that, with all these factors in place, a low will slow to a halt in the Atlantic and allow the wind to build for hour after hour, constructing towering breakers of almost unbelievable power.

That was the storm we had faced. Twice more, a massive breaker drove the *Castledawn* sideways, and each time she righted herself. Both pumps were going full-time now. Tiny gaps opened in the trawler's hull as her timbers worked apart. The pumps were holding their own, but only just. We were in the middle of the channel now, and, I believed, beyond all help. Even the most experienced chopper crew would not have been able to pluck men off the wildly pitching deck of the *Castledawn*. Water still sloshed around the wheelhouse and my legs had gone numb from the cold. I'd taken the last amphetamine tablet an hour ago. I hadn't offered any to the others, even though they looked dangerously fatigued. Regan in particular seemed to have only a feeble grasp on consciousness. But the way I looked at it, I had to keep the helm, and I needed all the help I could get. If

I lost control, then it wouldn't matter what state the others were in because the boat wouldn't survive.

As if to underline our isolation, I heard a loud bang on the roof of the wheelhouse and seconds later saw a flash of orange fly past the window and into the night. Our liferaft had been carried away, automatically inflating itself as it was torn away. Liam saw it too. He looked at me and shrugged. He was right. If the boat started to founder, the chances of getting to the liferaft were slim anyway. He shouted to me that he was going back to check the pumps. He seemed to have given up on the *Quo Vadis*. It made sense. Even with full steerage, the tug skipper would have had enough on his hands without worrying about trying to board us.

Five minutes later, Liam was back. He looked worried.

'There's a foot and a half in the bilge,' he shouted, 'rising fast.'

'Check the hull, as far as you can,' I shouted back. 'There's got to be a leak somewhere.'

I didn't know if it was my imagination or if the steering was starting to feel sluggish in my hands. The sluggishness caused by too much water in the bilge could be disastrous in stopping the boat recovering between waves.

'You'd better give him a hand,' I told Whitcroft, privately hoping that the two men could refrain from the temptation to put a bullet in one another when they were below decks.

'You take the portside,' I told Whitcroft, 'Liam on the starboard. Get moving.'

My hope was that it was a sprung plank, something that could be fixed temporarily. But I couldn't stop other dark thoughts from entering my head. A leaking propeller shaft. A tear in the hull from some floating object. Things that couldn't be fixed outside a boatyard. If the masthead light had been there, I might have seen what was wrong. As it was, Liam and Whitcroft were back within ten minutes to say they had seen nothing and the water was still rising. I had to think quickly, but my mind refused to work. A combination of weariness and the amphetamine seemed to send me into a strange fugue. For some reason, my mind drifted back to the souterrain on the mountains and the skeletal remains of a man. The bleak peace of the place. The empty sockets of the skull, inviting your gaze, tempting you to share the strange thoughts of the dead.

The *Castledawn* pitched, sending cold seawater over my legs. At the same time, I was aware of Whitcroft beside me.

'Come on,' he said roughly, 'get thinking.'

'Could be anything,' I heard myself mumble through lips numbed by the icy cold in the wheelhouse.

'Start eliminating things,' he said. Elimination was the oldest investigative technique.

'I think it's something underneath the boat,' I said, 'something that can't be fixed.'

'Are you sure about that?' he demanded. 'Are you absolutely certain?' I shook my head.

'Then eliminate that,' he said. 'Eliminate the things you can't do anything about and go through the possibilities. Come on, Valentine.'

Liam came into the wheelhouse.

'Another six inches in the bilge,' he said quietly. This time I could definitely feel the weight of water. The boat was slower to climb a wave, slower to recover when she rolled, I thought. I started at the stern and worked my way through the boat. I couldn't think of a single repairable fault.

'Keep thinking, Valentine.' I could feel Whitcroft's eyes on my face. I wondered what it was like in one of his interrogation rooms. He was said to have a high rate of extracting confessions from suspects. Some interrogators use violence. The best can use the burning power of their consciousness, and I felt that now from Whitcroft. I tried another method. I realized that I had seen the boat stripped down only once, the summer I had spent refitting her. I allowed my mind to drift back to that time. It had been a good summer and I had taken her out of the water at a small boatyard down the coast from the house at Kintyre. I remembered the heat of the sun on my face, the smell of tar and woodshavings. I remembered the feel of the chisel in my hand slipping into the old wood of the trawler and finding at the heart of it the green sap, fresh as the day the tree was cut, and the turpentine scent of pine sap rising in the warmed air. Quiet days, except for the gentle noise of wood being worked, the waves on the harbour wall and the distant squabbling of gulls. Mentally, I walked around the trawler as she had sat on blocks, stripped to the bare wood, much of her decking removed to facilitate the fitting of a new engine. I continued my tour and in my mind's eye I went on to the wheelhouse, again a stripped space with a pleasing utilitarian line to her. I walked to the front of the wheelhouse and looked down on the deck and then I had it, knew with sudden certainty what had happened. I came back to the present and looked down at the storm-lashed deck, the water boiling across it. I knew that we would have to go out on to it, no matter how impossible it might appear. And I knew that if we didn't and the boat sank, then it would be my own fault.

It was when we were putting the *Castledawn* back together. The owner of the boatyard had retired and his son had taken over. Tom Hornett was in his mid-thirties, a skilled shipwright and a man determined to preserve the skills and traditions of trawler building that had been handed down to him even though he knew it was already an archaic craft, its days numbered. I remember him sitting on deck smoking and watching me put the foredeck together. In the middle of the deck there was a hatch down into the hold where my stateroom was. I had intended to leave the hatch where it was, but make it permanent, putting it down with a line of self-tapping brass screws after I had creosoted it to make it waterproof.

'If I were you, I'd get rid of that old hatch,' Tom said in his soft coastal Scots drawl. 'Get rid of it and extend the decking over the hole.'

'She's held for a few years,' I said, 'she'll hold for a few more.' I was eager to get the boat finished and in the water.

'Why leave a weak point?' Tom said. 'The reason that hatch is there is for putting fish into the hold. It's a weak spot and you'll not be putting any fish into it, so get rid of it.' I should have taken his advice.

I gave the wheel to Liam and went down to the stateroom. The hatch was over the shower which I had added at the back. Every time the *Castledawn* dipped her bow, water gushed down the rear bulkhead, running through the planks and into the bilge, accompanied by a nasty creaking noise which sounded like screws being pulled out of wood. I considered the hatch from underneath, but there was no real way to get at it. Even if I ripped out all the plumbing, which might take an hour, it was still inaccessible, and besides, judging by the volume of water coming through, we didn't have an hour. It had to be the deck.

When I came back to the wheelhouse, I was carring forty metres of nylon rope, a sheet of aluminium and a powerful Black and Decker cordless which I'd waterproofed as best I could in heavy-duty plastic. I brought hammer and nails and four wooden battens as well. I reckoned the hatch had lifted on the starboard side and my idea was to bend the sheeting over the offending side and use the battens to hold it in place. Then I had to consider who was to go out. There was only one way to do it: one man to hold the sheeting, one to hold the battens, and one to drill through both and into the wood. I looked across the deck and thought I saw one side of the hatch lifting as water streamed back off the deck. Time was not on our side. I turned to Regan.

'Can you take the wheel?' I asked. He said something and had to repeat it several times before I could make it out.

'Tie me to it,' was what he was saying.

'Lash,' Liam said. I looked at him. 'Lash,' he repeated.

'Seamen are lashed to the wheel in a gale.'

'Jesus, Regan's a poor-looking Flying Dutchman, all the same,' Whitcroft said.

It wasn't all that funny, but for some reason we thought it was, and we were cackling like demons, Regan showing the gaps where his teeth had been, Liam hanging on to the map desk and even Whitcroft indulging in a wintry smile. It only lasted for a minute, but it left us with something which wasn't quite a sense of companionship considering Whitcroft's presence, but was at least a sense of common purpose. I threw oilskins at Whitcroft and Liam and set about rigging up a harness to fix Regan to the wheel. When that was done, I turned to the task in hand.

I knew we wouldn't be able to work without some kind of support on deck. I reckoned that if I could take a rope across the deck, I could run it round the twin pillars that supported the forecastle. This would give two ropes, about three feet apart, that could be held with both hands as we moved across the deck. I got Liam to tie another rope around my waist and told him to feed it out as I moved across the deck. It might just hold me if I was washed towards the rail, although I wondered whether, if I was washed overboard, they would have the strength to haul me back. As I moved towards the door, Liam slapped me on the back and said something, but I had already opened the door and couldn't hear what he had said. I took a deep breath and stepped out.

I had never experienced a wind of such violence. You felt that it could do anything it wanted with you. It was cold and howling and it threw me back against the wood of the wheelhouse and pinned me there with such ferocity that I felt it was almost pointless to try to fight it. But I knew I had to. I put my head down and half-slipped, half-fell down the steps. I landed in a sitting position on the deck. A swirling wave picked me up and threw me under the stairs I had just descended, my head striking the wood with a blow which left me almost stunned. I shook my head and tried to get up.

I wasn't even properly on the deck yet and already I was doing badly. I made sure that the coil of rope was safely tied to my wrist and I felt a reassuring tug from Liam on the other rope. I looked across the deck. It was only eighteen feet to the forecastle. It must be possible to reach it. The deck disappeared under a mass of water and suddenly it didn't look possible any more. I made the end of the rope fast to the trawl gantry and tried to study the movement of the trawler. In the end, I knew that I would have to make a run for it as she rose out of one wave and before she fell into another. I waited until the bow was buried and as the water started to run off, I started across the deck. I had got about half-way before I realized I had underestimated the pitch of the vessel. Suddenly the deck rose above me until it seemed I was trying to run up a vertical slope. I slipped and fell and tried to scramble to my feet. The forecastle reared above me at an almost impossible angle. Then, with a sickening vertiginous sensation of falling from a great height, the trawler crested the wave and started to plunge into the trough. Suddenly the forecastle was below me and I was looking down on it. Once again, I lost my footing, but this time I tumbled headlong down the deck, stopping with a bone-crunching impact as I hit the steel door of the forecastle, just as tons of water covered the deck where I had been standing. Blindly, I reached out and grabbed at the steel rim of the forecastle hatch as the trawler began to climb another wave. I clung there for several more waves before I gained the courage to let go and start winding the rope around the twin supports.

My return journey lacked even the vestiges of control that had accompanied the first leg. I thought I would use the rope to steady myself. Instead, as the trawler reared, I tumbled headlong down the deck, the rope searing the flesh from my palms as I tried to slow myself, coming to yet another sickening halt under the stairs where I had started out. Gritting my teeth, I secured the other end of the rope. We now had a walkway across the deck. I staggered up the steps and felt Liam's hands under my arms. I fell into the wheelhouse and lay there, my teeth chattering and a numbness in my limbs which I welcomed, because I knew how much I was going to hurt when the numbness left me.

When I had recovered slightly, we lashed the tools to our bodies. Liam and Whitcroft looked grim. They had seen how I had fared on deck. It was hard to see how we could work in the middle of this turmoil. I went through what each man was going to do. I told them that we had only minutes to work in, before the cold would start to incapacitate us. I could see Liam looking doubtfully at Whitcroft. He was the oldest of us. He wasn't in particularly bad shape, but his days for running around on pitching decks in the middle of the night seemed long past. Whitcroft saw him looking.

'I don't like it any more than you do,' he said, 'so let's get going.' Before anybody could say anything else, Whitcroft stepped out into the storm as if he was stepping outside the interrogation room for a cigarette. Liam went next. With a glance at Regan, I followed them.

Things hadn't changed on deck. At least I knew what to expect. Liam, who was carrying the sheet of aluminium, was pinned back against the wheelhouse by the wind, while Whitcroft went tumbling under the steps, where he stayed, stunned by the ferocity of the storm. I reached the rope first and began to haul myself across the deck, hand over hand. Water swirled around my knees. It was almost impossible to make progress. When the boat was going up the face of a wave, you were clinging on, trying not to fall backwards. When it was plunging into the trough, you were trying not to be thrown forwards. I glanced behind me and thought I saw Liam and Whitcroft following me through the spume. I realized that I could barely feel my hands. We had to get to the hatch while we still had some feeling left in our fingers in order to work. I took a chance and allowed the next roll to launch me forward towards the hatch, grabbing the ropes at the last minute to stop myself. The pain was dreadful as I lost more skin on my hands to the unforgiving nylon. At least I could still feel something, I thought, before I was almost knocked overboard by the arrival of Whitcroft, and then Liam.

For a moment we formed a huddle around the hatch, sailors on deck during a storm, part of a centuries-old jeopardy. A giant wave hit the *Castledawn* and it seemed as if we were underwater, choking with saltwater, the roar of it filling our ears, the weight of it tearing at our grip on the ropes. Somehow I clung on, my eyes shut, my arms threatening to come out of their sockets. When I opened my eyes, I fully expected to find myself alone on the deck, but Liam and Whitcroft were still there.

'Come on!' I roared. I got down on my knees, level with the hatch. The port side of it was lifted and torn and I knew that we had to fix it there and then. It would only last minutes before the sea tore it away and tons of water rushed into the hold of the trawler, sending her to the ocean floor. At a signal from me, Liam laid the sheeting across the top of the hatch and started shaping it roughly with a four-pound hammer as I struggled to get the drill out from under my coat. The screws were next. As Liam shaped the aluminium into an L-shape, Whitcroft started punching holes in it with a hammer and awl. Three more times a wave crashed over us, but we got the sheeting roughly in place. I took a screw from my pocket and put it between my teeth. But as I reached for it, my frozen fingers fumbled and it was gone into the night. Cursing, I got out another one and it too slipped from my fingers. I managed to get the third into the punched hole and brought the drill to bear on it. It went in. Four more times I did this, one screw in each corner. And each time I lost several screws. I was starting to wonder if I had enough. But the sheet was held in place at least and I could let one man go back.

'One of you go back!' I yelled. They both shook their heads. Another wave washed over us. I started to speak, then shut my mouth. There wasn't time to argue. Another screw went in, and another. A wave knocked me to the deck and the Black and Decker went spinning into the scuppers. I grabbed it and Whitcroft pulled me to my feet. I got another screw from my pocket and pulled the trigger on the Black and Decker. Blue flame arced from the slats at the back of it. I threw it into the sea and reached for the hammer. I put as many nails into the hatch as I could, then I felt another big wave take the hammer from my grasp. It didn't matter. I was too weak to do any more. I could feel the scene in front of me receding. Even the noise of the storm seemed less urgent. I looked towards the wheelhouse. I could just see the dark outline of Regan at the wheel. Even in my tired fugue, I saw that there was something odd about him. There was an intentness there, as if he was watching something very closely. I looked at Liam and Whitcroft. They were looking towards the bow, each with an air of disbelief. I felt the hairs rise on the back of my neck. I was afraid to turn round and had to force my body to move. As I did so, the moon came out, a flickering, sickly moon that cast an unearthly light on the sea, and on the giant wave that towered above us. I felt my knees go weak. I had heard of giant waves but I had never seen one. This one looked like a mountain of water coming towards us, a mountain which seemed to contain its own dark malice. The wind seemed to dip and as I saw phosphorescence dance along the peak of the wave like lightning, I had the illusion that the wave carried its own weather system with it. And then it was on us, the bow of the trawler pointed almost vertically as it tried to climb the huge mass of water. It seemed to take for ever and I thought I heard the engines labouring as they sought to keep the *Castledawn*'s bow pointed upwards. I lost my footing and sprawled across the deck, as did Whitcroft. Only Liam remained on his feet, his eyes calmly fixed on the wave, as if in some part of him he had expected it. On and on the *Castledawn* climbed, and then it seemed we were at the peak, where we were poised for a moment, and Liam turned to look at me with a fierce awe and exultancy in his face. And then the *Castledawn* started to plunge.

I can never quite piece together the sequence of events, although I still wake up at night, soaked in sweat, haunted by the feeling of vertigo that assailed me as the *Castledawn* began her long descent. I heard something break loose and crash down the deck past my head. I found that I'd hooked the fingers of one hand over the edge of the hatch cover and I was hanging from that. I couldn't see Whitcroft or Liam but I could feel the boat struggling to stay in a straight line. Water crashed over me, tearing at my fingers. Then something else, probably a piece of broken gunwhale, hit my arm. I cried out in pain and lost my hold on the edge of the hatch, and started to slide. Looking down in horror, I saw that I was sliding towards the section of gunwhale that had been removed by the bow of the *Quo Vadis*, sliding wildly and inexorably. I tried to dig my fingernails into the very wood of the deck, but it didn't slow me and then, at the last moment, the boat lurched to one side and I reached out with my foot in one last, desperate gambit, feeling the unbroken gunwhale and then one of the short wooden pillars holding it. Desperately I wedged my foot into the gap behind the pillar as the top half of my body slid out over the sea.

And there I hung, unable to move forwards or backwards, staring straight down at the angry sea a few feet below. My ankle was supporting the full weight of my body. The pain was excruciating, and I realized that I had wedged it in such a way that I couldn't free it without someone helping me. I called out and my voice came out not as the controlled voice of a man who has seen much action in his time, but as the desperate wail of someone in mortal danger. 'Help me, please!' No one came. Then the *Castledawn* plunged into the trough behind the giant wave.

*

I remember being covered in water. I remember blind panic and then the kind of peace that people talk about when they recount tales of drowning. It was something that I had always wondered about, where your mind goes on the edge of death. Mine went back to Armagh, to the summer orchards, the smell of appleblossom. It sounds sickly, but it wasn't. It was as vivid as the days I had spent there. And through it all I saw Deirdre's face. Not the young face of those days, but a face that had pain and injury etched on it, stern in its suffering, yet beautiful for all that.

Then I remember nothing more, until I came to, my foot still wedged, the water washing me from side to side. The pressure on my ankle had eased, but the pain was still excruciating. The noises of the storm seemed to be coming from a great distance. I felt hands on my shoulders, pulling me back from the edge, and a rope being put around my waist. Urgent hands worked to free my ankle. The pain blazed up and I fainted again.

When I came to, it took a moment to realize where I was. My eyes landed on a little Keating drawing that hung on the wall. A gentle, elegiac view of the Twelve Bens in Connemara. I considered this for a while. I remembered that I had bought it for a song at an auction. I tried to work out where I had hung it. Not in the croft, I was sure of that. Maybe on the *Castledawn*. That was it. I studied the wall around the drawing. It was streaked with water stains. I wondered where the water had got in. Then I remembered that there had been a storm. But there didn't seem to be any storm now. I realized that the eldritch noise of the wind had gone, and all I could hear was the sturdy thump of diesel engines. I looked down and saw that I was in a bed, then I remembered that I had hung the Keating in the stateroom, and then it came to me about the storm and the hatch and my ankle. I realized my left leg was outside the blankets and was swathed in bandages. The pain was dull and persistent but nothing compared to the screaming agony of the deck.

'What sort of a man keeps tens of thousands of pounds' worth of paintings on a bloody leaky old tub of a trawler?' I heard someone say. I looked up. Whitcroft was sitting at the little desk.

'Safer here than in the croft,' I said. 'I'm not there most of the time. And I never heard of anyone breaking into a trawler to steal paintings.'

'Why not a bank vault?' he asked.

'I want to be able to look at them, so I keep them close by. They're not insured.'

'Uninsurable, some of them, I'd say,' he said. 'I'm not sure how much you're paid, or even who pays you, but it sure as hell wouldn't buy a tenth of what you've got here. I wonder where you got them.'

'I have a shrewd eye,' I said.

'I don't doubt that,' he said with a jaundiced look, 'I don't doubt that at all.'

'Never mind that,' I said. 'How long have I been here, and what's been happening? And where the hell are we?'

Whitcroft told me that we were running a few miles off the coast of the Western Isles. I hadn't told anybody where we were going so they had thought they would hold station until I came round. I had been out for seven hours or so.

'What about the storm . . .?' I began.

'What do you remember?' he asked.

'Not much after we went out on deck.'

'It was hairy,' he said. He told me that when the big wave had hit, he had been flung backwards and jammed in the scupper by water rushing out. When he had pulled himself together, he saw that Liam, amazingly, was still standing in the middle of the deck.

'Like he was in charge of the whole fucking thing,' Whitcroft said, 'the whole bloody storm and everything.' I said nothing. It was the kind of thing that had people referring to Liam as a legend, and I think Whitcroft knew it too.

There was a certain amount of grudging admiration in his voice. He had seen that the legend had substance to it.

'He turned and roared something at me. He told me to get a rope. I couldn't see you anywhere.'

Apparently Liam had seen me and had gone to me while Whitcroft fetched a rope. Together, they had got a rope around me, released my foot and got me back to the wheelhouse. Whitcroft was matter of fact in his telling, but I knew that it must have been a titanic struggle. I had a feeling, however, that there was more to it than that. Whitcroft saw the look on my face.

'Ask your bloody friend Regan,' he said belligerently, 'for he seems to be taking great amusement from the whole thing.'

I changed the subject.

'How did I get here?'

'I carried you with Mellows. I fixed up the ankle as best I could. Far as I can see, it's not broken but it won't carry you too far either.'

'Thanks.' I said. I meant it. 'What about Regan?'

'I'll give him his due,' Whitcroft said, 'he's a seaman. I can't figure it out, but he and his people don't come from anywhere near the sea.' I didn't say anything. It was a tradition in many parts of the border counties to go to sea. Men would walk many miles to Greenore or Warrenpoint. And many a graveyard in South Armagh carried memorials to local men lost on the Atlantic convoys during the war. The sea was in their blood for all that they were a landlocked people.

'He never shifted from that wheel for eight hours, until the storm died down. There were one or two times I thought we were lost, but he brought her back.'

I half-stifled a grin. In five minutes I had heard the detective praise the two men he regarded as his most implacable foes. I mustn't have stifled the grin enough.

'Don't get me wrong, Valentine,' he said in a low voice,

'the place for people like Regan is behind bars. And if somebody had put a bullet in Mellows when the Troubles started we'd all be better off. It doesn't mean they're not brave men. I'm man enough to acknowledge that. But they're both on the wrong side and that makes them the enemy as far as I'm concerned.'

'What about me?' I said.

'I haven't decided about you yet,' he said. He moved slightly in his chair so that I could catch sight of my desk, and the Sirius material which was on it.

A silence fell on the room. I felt weak, my head woolly and my thinking unclear. It didn't take a genius to work out that Whitcroft knew it was there. I pondered my options as best I could. I could refuse to talk about it. Whitcroft was way offside on this expedition and he knew it. Nothing but trouble awaited him if it came out that he had been onboard with Regan and Liam. I could threaten him with the powerful forces who were interested in Sirius. I wasn't sure if that would work. He had appeared in Belfast in Curley's company, if not in fact as part of Curley's team. That afforded him some protection. Or I could bring him into my confidence. If I was right in my assessment of Whitcroft, he was a man that Eamon trusted, as far as trust could exist in the corrosive world they inhabited. I thought feverishly. Probably of any man alive, Whitcroft had the best knowledge of counterinsurgency operations along the border in the early seventies. He could hold the key to all this. I looked at him. He was waiting patiently to see which way I would go. It was this patience which convinced me. If he had known nothing, then he would have probed me about the photographs. But he hadn't. I decided to take the plunge.

'I took those things from a hiding place on the mountain above Ravensdale. They were left there some time in the early seventies . . .' I hesitated. My head swirled for a moment as the memory of the trauma on deck sent waves of weakness rushing through me.

'Wait.' Whitcroft said. He produced a flask of coffee and a round of sandwiches made with the home-cured ham I had hanging in the galley.

'Jesus, Whitcroft,' I said, 'if I'd known you had this, I would have told you anything. I thought interrogation was your big thing.'

He gave me a wolfish grin.

'It is,' he said. 'The point is that you'll feel so grateful now that you'll tell me everything I want to hear.'

I told him everything anyway. The policy of assassination of leading Republicans. The two men who had parachuted in, how one of them had been killed but the other had continued with the killings. My day and night on the mountain. The pursuit by unknown Americans.

'How come this stuff is so important?' he asked, gesturing at the things laid out on the desk.

'I'm not precisely sure,' I said, 'but as far as I can see, one of the men involved in the operation, either in organizing it, or in executing it, has got himself into a position of power and influence, or is about to get himself there. He wants the material back for fear of being exposed. Other people want it in order to use it against him, or to gain influence with him.'

Whitcroft nodded slowly. He had worked in counter-insurgency long enough to recognize the sickening logic of the proposition. He also knew that, although the whole thing sounded far-fetched in the real world, it was bread and butter to people in the covert life.

'I may be able to help you,' he said slowly. 'Let me tell you a story.'

It had been *1972*. Belfast was engulfed in bloody conflagration. The border area was swept by intrigue, and by killing. There was a sense of apocalypse in the air. 'Everybody was scheming about something,' Whitcroft said. Whitcroft had been a young detective, working eighteen-hour days. There was barely time to record one incident before another came along. Politics was everything. You soon started to learn which murders were to be investigated with all resources and which were to be allowed to slide quietly to the back of the filing cabinet. When senior Republicans in the border area started to be assassinated, everyone assumed that one or other of the British Intelligence agencies was involved. Rumours reached them of a one-man operation, a jackal, targetting the men with great skill and a daring which bordered on the reckless. Whitcroft also revealed another detail. The killer had a gruesome trademark. After his victim was dead, he would shoot them in the genitals with a large-calibre handgun.

'Remember,' Whitcroft said, 'these were men of late middle age or older. Wise heads. Men that could have been negotiated with. Killing them was bad enough, but mutilating them was worse. The young ones went into a frenzy.'

Then one night, Whitcroft got a call. A man had been picked up after a high-speed chase on the Newry–Omeath road. His car had hit the wreckage of a burnt-out vehicle left after rioting beside the Albert Basin. The man had been travelling without lights and hadn't seen the wreck until the last moment. He had been stunned, badly gashed and was lapsing in and out of consciousness. The RUC patrol that had followed him had found weapons they had never before encountered in the back of the car. They had taken him to Corry Square barracks. In those days, if you were shot or injured, hospital came after the interrogation, if you were lucky enough to make it to hospital. There was one other thing, the constable said: 'I swear the bastard has a Yank accent.'

Whitcroft drove into the station just before dawn. It was a two-storey barracks, hastily fortified. Exhausted soldiers were dismounting from Saracen APVs in the yard. There was an atmosphere of chaos. But it was very quiet in the place where Whitcroft went. Before the interrogation of prisoners was handed over to the feared Castlereagh and Gough barracks, the cells of Corry Square were the toughest place in the whole island that a man was likely to find himself in.

The Yank, as they were calling him, was tied to a chair in the interrogation room. Whitcroft saw a tall, athletic man, tied up because he was incapable of sitting upright by himself. His head had gone through the windscreen and a flap of skin had been neatly incised along the hairline and now fell almost over his eyes. He was soaked in blood and mumbling to himself. Whitcroft realized it was going to be hard to get anything out of him. But the uniforms had been right. It was hard to make out actual words, but there was a southern United States twang to the man's voice. There was something about the situation that made the other men uneasy and they seemed glad to get out of the room after giving Whitcroft an inventory of the man's weaponry. He noted that it included a large-calibre Smith and Wesson revolver. Not quite a Magnum, but a high-calibre revolver all the same. Whitcroft considered the man. It was an unprecedented situation. There was a smell of politics that he didn't like. As it happened, he was the most senior detective available that night. He had a feeling that this was a situation that wouldn't wait. Decisions had to be made. The trouble was that he didn't know what any of them might be. He circled the man warily. He wasn't sure if he was still conscious or not. The station MO had certified him fit to be questioned, but the doctor was a drunk with a loathing of those he regarded as subversives, so that didn't mean anything. He had said, however, that the man appeared to have broken ribs which hadn't been sustained in the car crash.

As Whitcroft pondered his options, he found himself stooping in an attempt to see into the man's face. He took a pace backwards when the eyes suddenly opened and bored into his. Eyes that were bloodshot, staring from features that were stained with dried gore. Holding Whitcroft's gaze, the man recited a phone number in crisp, authoritative tones. He repeated the number, then his head slumped forward again.

Whitcroft went outside. He told the station sergeant what had happened. The sergeant was an old hand, and Whitcroft valued his advice. The sergeant told him to ring the number, and then to deny that he had rung anyone if there were adverse consequences. 'Curiosity, as much as anything, made me do it,' Whitcroft said. He recognized the London code. The phone was picked up after just one ring and a male voice with an American accent asked him to identify himself and his location. After he had done so, the line went dead. Whitcroft went back to the Yank, who had by now lost consciousness. Whitcroft called an ambulance to take him to Daisy Hill hospital. The man never got there. As the dawn light rose over the station, Whitcroft heard the sound of an incoming helicopter. Within minutes, a Wessex had touched down in the yard. Oddly, it carried no markings. The pilot kept the rotor turning. A second chopper circled impatiently overhead. Two men alighted, both civilians. One was an Englishman. He handed a letter to Whitcroft. It was signed by the chief constable and authorized the handing over of the prisoner to the bearer. When Whitcroft had read the letter, the man took it back. The other man didn't say anything. He was tall, tanned and rangy. 'You could tell by the look of him that he was an American,' Whitcroft said. 'He kept his mouth shut so I wouldn't clock his accent, but I knew he was a Yank.'

Within minutes, the unconscious American had been lifted on to the chopper which took off again.

'And that was that,' Whitcroft said, 'except that a few days later I went to look for the arrest report and the logbook recording his detention. There wasn't anything there. The logbook had gone to HQ for what they called randon monitoring, but the arrest report had gone.'

'Looks like you weren't the only spook working out of Newry,' I said. He ignored that.

'Would you know him again?' I asked.

'I think I already know who he is,' Whitcroft said. 'I've

seen him.' We heard a clatter on the gangway outside the door and Liam burst in.

'Good to see the skipper awake,' he said. 'Request your presence on deck, sir.' He snapped an ironic salute at me.

'As well as that, I need a helmsman,' he went on. 'The ship's boy, aka Mr Regan is near out on his feet.'

'All right, all right,' Whitcroft said, following him out. I'm not sure if he thought it was a dramatic moment to leave or if he was genuinely worried about Regan at the helm. I added it up. Whitcroft didn't give two damns about Regan's weariness. I thought I detected the appetite of the undercover man, no matter how jaded, for the theatrical exit. Whitcroft would tell me what he knew in his own good time. In the meantime, I knew what I had to do. There were two situations that had to be impelled to a conclusion. The first was Liam and his supposed treachery. The second was Sirius. Both matters needed a conclusion forced upon them. In many ways, both were dangerous abstractions; seen by the protagonists the way a sniper sees his subject half a mile away through a high-powered scope. My idea was to bring everybody face to face. Not just the foot soldiers, but the principals. To remind them that the spilling of blood was not something you directed from afar, if they needed that reminder. To have them kill or to be killed if that was what they wanted. To have them make deals if that was what was required. I knew that there would be both killing and deal-making, but it was the nature of the business at this level. If I had learned anything, it was to bring everything to an end at the same time, no matter what the cost. It was, in many ways, a service people like me provided to the powerful, and they were grateful for it. I thought of Liam, and I thought of Sirius. This time, the truly powerful of the world and the relatively powerless would settle their differences in the same place. Both disputes required an arena. And I had chosen it for them.

15

It took me a long time to get on deck. I discovered that I couldn't put my left foot on the ground. I looked around until I found a suitable piece of wood in the ruined head and ripped it from the wall to use as a makeshift crutch. Even then, I was lightheaded and unsteady. The *Castledawn* was still subject to a big swell, although far from the murderous seas of the night before, and it took a long time to get up the gangway to the bridge.

I would hardly have known the *Castledawn*. The wheelhouse looked like the wheelhouse of some derelict vessel moored in a harbour backwater for twenty years. Most of the windows were boarded up. There was still an inch of water on the floor. The panelling was splintered, bullet-scarred in places. The glass of the Decca was broken and starred. The GPA looked intact, but there seemed to be a smear of blood across it. There was a smell of seawater and storm and cordite. I went to one of the intact panes of glass and used my sleeve to wipe it clean so that I could look out on deck. It took a little while to realize what was different. It was obvious that the damage to her side had been caused by the collision with the *Quo Vadis*, that the forecastle rail had been carried away by the storm and that the mast had probably splintered when we hit the big wave. When I looked down, I could see that a piece of the broken mast had been driven into the front of the wheelhouse like some forlorn, misplaced bowsprit. But there was a difference of texture that I couldn't quite place. Liam grinned at me from the wheel.

'We hit some kind of ice storm before dawn,' he said cheerfully, 'I'd never seen anything like it. It was pelting bloody razors.'

I saw that the whole forward deck of the *Castledawn* had been scoured, the paintwork dulled by the abrasion of the ice. In some places it went through to the metal. She was still riding low in the water.

'The pumps are holding their own,' Liam said. 'There's a steady foot in the bilge. We're not shifting it but it's not rising. Long as the pumps hold, we're all right.'

I expected the pumps to hold. I had spent a lot of money on two new marine pumps. But the boat had taken a pounding, and nothing was certain in those circumstances. I shut my eyes for a moment and felt the motion of the trawler. The engines sang proudly and she lifted off the top of the waves, a little heavy to be sure, but with the same lively action as the day she slid off the boatyard slip. She had proven herself and she owed us nothing, but I had one last journey to ask of her.

I looked around the wheelhouse again. I saw Regan on the camp bed under the map table. He appeared to be sleeping, but when my gaze fell on him, he opened one eye. His face was too swollen for me to see whether or not there was a smile on it, but there was a mischievous glint in his eye as he looked back at me, then glanced at Whitcroft and Liam.

'You should have seen them,' he said, 'the patriot and the peeler.' A sound that resembled a laugh came from him and he fell back to sleep. I looked at the others. Whitcroft had a sour look about him and refused to meet my look. Liam stared straight ahead through the windscreen, but a small smile played about his lips. I said nothing. There was a story there, but it would have to wait for another time.

'We did well,' I said, 'all of us. We survived that bloody storm.'

'We weren't the only ones,' Liam said quietly. I didn't have to be told what he meant. I stepped out on to the wing. The wind was bitter but welcome and I filled my lungs with it and looked aft. About a quarter of a mile behind us, holding station with some difficulty, it appeared, was the *Quo Vadis*.

The binoculars had survived with a few more dents added to the one that had been made by the sniper's bullet. I took them out on to the wing and had a look at the *Quo Vadis*. She hadn't fared particularly well in the storm. Her mast and rigging was a twisted and buckled mess, and all her communication equipment seemed to have been carried away. Her wheelhouse was intact but she was down by the head and the skipper seemed to be having trouble keeping her in a straight line. To add to her troubles, I could see that her pumps, like ours, were working full tilt, water gushing from the outlets on her flanks. Still, I didn't like the dogged way she was clinging to our wake. I couldn't see anyone on deck, but I had the uncomfortable sense of cold eyes watching me from her wheelhouse.

I limped back inside.

'So,' Liam said, 'you've got that look in your eye, like you've got something in mind.'

'If that's the way of it, I want to know,' Whitcroft growled.

'We've got business ahead of us,' I said, 'apart from you, Whitcroft.'

'I've got business,' he said, 'making sure the Lone Ranger here doesn't get his fucking head shot off.'

'Fair enough,' I said. Whitcroft was a useful man to have around. And there was still some information I wanted to get from him.

'Come on,' Liam said. 'Where are we going?'

'Shetland,' I said.

'How far is that?' Whitcroft asked.

'Maybe sixteen hours from here.'

Liam whistled.

'You're putting a lot of faith in those pumps,' he said. 'In case you hadn't noticed, we haven't got a liferaft any more.'

'I think I can pull everything together, Liam, get all of us off the hook. And I need a neutral space to do it in.' Liam looked at me for a moment and then shrugged, dismissing the whole thing and turning back to the sea. I hoped his faith wasn't misplaced.

'Listen,' I said, 'I've had some sleep, and Liam hasn't had any. But I need an hour. After that, I'll take the wheel. Can you cope?' Liam nodded. I stepped closer to him.

'Did you get a signal on that cellphone?'

He nodded stiffly.

'They say she's serious, but stable.' As far as you could work out from the evasive hospital jargon, that meant that Deirdre was a full degree better than critical but stable. I felt the weight in my heart lift slightly. But I wondered at Liam's curt response. I thought he was blaming me for bringing her into danger. Then I realized I was wrong. He was blaming both of us.

I went down to the stateroom. I looked into the galley on the way. I shouldn't have. The cooker had torn loose and crashed around the kitchen. The floor was a mess of broken crystal and preserve jars. There was a strong smell of balsamic vinegar and fine olive oil.

In the stateroom, I cranked up the satphone, praying that it hadn't been damaged. It hadn't, and I thanked the instinct that had made me spend the fortune it had cost to make the dish retractable. I cleared my head. I had to make three calls to three extremely clever men, and each call had to be pitched just right. I picked up the receiver, my pulse moving a little fast, my palms a little damp.

Just over an hour later, I went into the kitchen and salvaged what I could. I found some dried pasta and some Parmesan which had only been a little bit soaked in the oil and saltwater that slopped around the floor. To my amazement, I found some eggs that had survived. I knocked together a passable carbonara and brought it up to the wheelhouse. I woke Regan and we ate ravenously. Immediately afterwards, I sent Whitcroft and Liam below. As Liam was passing me, he looked at me and grinned.

'Shetland is it now?' he said. 'Would it be a case of "both sides stalk each other over several years to contend for victory in a single day"?' He threw his head back and guffawed, then went below without waiting for an answer. I stared after him. It was probably the first time an urban guerilla with a taste for quoting Sun-Tzu had formed part of the crew of the *Castledawn*. I looked suspiciously at the battered smuggler in a sleeping bag under the map table and the detective stumbling with weariness as he also headed below, as if they, too, might start dropping obscure quotations from ancient warrior-philosophers, and was relieved when Regan took the bottle of Crested Ten from the map drawer and offered both of us a swig. To be fair to Whitcroft he didn't hesitate. He put the bottle to his lips and took a good hit from it. He handed the bottle back to Regan with a crisp nod. As far as the two men went, it was civility of the highest order.

As we sailed north, I kept an eye on the *Quo Vadis*. As far as I could see, she was struggling to keep pace with us. There was too much dark diesel smoke from her stack for the comfort of her skipper, suggesting she had sustained some engine damage during the pursuit, perhaps from an engine straining to cope with a bent shaft. The twin Perkins on the *Castledawn* sounded sweet, which was the source of some reassurance. There wasn't much else to reassure me. Liam had said that the pumps were holding their own, but I knew by the way the *Castledawn* was settling imperceptibly in the water that they weren't any longer.

On we sailed, past the Western Isles and on towards the icy north. The weather seemed to be holding, the two boats climbing the wide swells with relative ease. As we headed steadily away from land, the sky seemed to darken. I explained to Regan that as we travelled north, the darkness would seem more complete. During mid-summer, the sun never really set. It dipped until it touched the horizon and then rose again. At this time of year, the sun barely struggled above the horizon. I could see that Regan didn't like it. He drifted into an uneasy sleep. I let him go for four hours, then woke him. We were going through the oilfields and the towering shapes of the rigs loomed out of the gloom like huge sullen beasts of iron put there by a vast, alien hand. I never got used to looking at them. Even at a remove of several miles, they towered over all. On television, you invariably see them from the air, but we were seeing them from below. Regan stood beside me at the wheel and watched them in silence for over an hour, turning to gaze at them even as they faded into the dark behind us, as if he owed them some strange, ancient homage that he could not relinquish. It left both of us feeling a little overshadowed and small, subject to other forces.

Regan limped down to the galley and brought up coffee. We laced it with whisky and sat with blankets wrapped around our shoulders against the draughts howling through the damaged wheelhouse. Every so often, I would get up and go out to see if the *Quo Vadis* was still there. As the rigs passed out of sight, I noticed that her progress seemed even more erratic. I dropped the revs a little, to which Regan raised an eyebrow, but I had no intention of losing them. I was going to finish things, one way or another, when we hit the island.

Aside from that, the next six hours were uneventful. We talked quietly and I got to know him. He told me, wryly, how he had courted Deirdre when he was a teenager, and how she had let him down gently. He seemed almost in awe of her. I knew that Regan had a dark side to him. Liam had told me enough of it to make me aware of who I was dealing with. He showed a knowledge of the history of the border areas which was both encyclopaedic and erudite. His other love was racehorses. It was my turn to raise an eyebrow when he gave me the names of horses he owned. I was no racing *aficionado*, but some of the horses were household names and he could have retired on one or two of them alone, but oddly, the value of them never seemed to be important to him. Then there were his children, two little girls. I envied him that.

It was one of those odd, companionable times when strangers are thrown together and admit each other to a degree of intimacy, and some kind of a bond is formed. There is an unspoken agreement not to dwell upon the ugly compromises and missed opportunities that form a large proportion of your experience at our age. An agreement upon simple philosophies, wisdoms that aren't asked to bear too much in the way of scrutiny.

I told Regan how I had first come to the place. Sixteen years old and taking off on an impulse from Glasgow. Not that I wasn't loved. My mother was a well-read Highlander and my father was a docker, a man aware of his own abilities and haunted by the fact that life had never permitted him to display them. He attended to his family duties and drank too much when he regarded himself as being off-duty, and taught me, or at least showed me, that I was not to follow his example. When I took off, I had no great idea where I was going. You don't at sixteen, but a lorry driver who stopped for me told me that there were plenty of jobs in the oil industry in Shetland.

I told Regan how I'd scrounged a lift from a Shetland trawler sailing home from Peterhead. They fed me drink. It was summertime, and I remember lying on the deck in the twilight glow of midnight and looking up at the stars and thinking that I had found life.

The time passed quickly, too quickly, and I was surprised when Liam appeared in the doorway, yawning and refreshed.

'Well, Valentine,' he said, looking at me shrewdly, 'and so to war, is that the way of it?'

It was the way of it. A little way off our starboard bow, I

could see the low shape of Fair Isle, showing grey-blue against the silvery dawn sky. In a few hours' time, we would be in Lerwick.

'Wake Whitcroft,' I said. 'We need to talk.'

When Liam was gone, Regan told me how the two men had been on deck together, when I was hanging off the side of the ship, battered unconscious. It took them twenty minutes to reach me. Twice Whitcroft was knocked over and twice he would have been swept over the side except for Liam. I wondered if it had been tempting for Liam to let his bitter enemy go, even as he must have known that he had been somewhere on the same side all along. I realized, however, that these subtleties wouldn't matter. It would have been a matter of unbending pride to him not to let go of the man's hand.

Liam came back with a crumpled Whitcroft in tow. We were two hours from Lerwick. It was time to outline my plan. I was bringing all the parties together. I could identify underlying themes running from Sirius right through Berlin and into the Slieve Bloom mountains. It was time to put everything into the hat. Either it would be compromise all round, or winner take all. In the latter event, I would be the one to choose the ground.

Liam went along with it straight away. Regan thought about it, then nodded. Whitcroft argued. I wasn't sure if he was a man who disagreed with the concept of possible mayhem, or who only liked the kind of mayhem he engendered himself. In any event, he came round to it, grumbling.

After that, I took him down to the stateroom.

'You said you saw this Yank, the one that was taken into your station,' I said. He nodded slowly. I waited for him to speak. It took a long time. The policeman's habit of confidentiality dies hard.

'I saw him on television a few times,' he said. 'Unnamed. Part of a group around senior US politicians. You know the kind of thing. An unnamed man standing in the background.

You know that he must be important to be in the photograph.'

'If I showed you a selection of photographs, could you pick him out?'

He was amused.

'What do you have, a rogues' gallery of senior American politicians?'

'Something like that. How long ago did you see him?'

'Recently.'

We went through the scanned photographs that Paolo had sent me. As sometimes happens at such times when a sense of fate and things coming home to roost is in the air, he saw him almost immediately. In a group with the President. At a GATT meeting with the Secretary of Trade. His name was Richard Snyder. I studied the face. A face that would have been described as open when he was a young man. Blond hair greying gracefully at the temples. A fit face, a man from some golden southern family taking his rightful place in the service of the nation. He was in his early sixties, but he had kept himself in trim. Though you noticed a slight fleshiness about the jowl, a suggestion of a man of appetite. And you saw the slightly cruel upturn at the corners of the mouth, the secret raptor's look. You could imagine him being impulsive the way a shark is impulsive when it smells blood. And the eyes were empty, with the same ancient void as a shark's eyes. This, then, was Sirius.

'Look,' Whitcroft said. He touched the man's forehead just below the hairline. There was a faint white crescent scar where the man's head had gone through a windscreen on a side road outside Newry many years ago; just as Whitcroft had described.

'Why is he important?' Whitcroft asked, 'I mean, why has this come up now?'

'Not enough information,' I said. 'We'll find out when we get to Shetland.'

He was going to question me further, but Liam came in.

'You'd better have a look at something,' he said.

Liam wanted me to have a look at the bilges. The pumps had given up any pretence of holding their own. The water was rising as we looked.

'How far to Lerwick?' he asked.

'An hour,' I said. He raised his eyebrows in a question. I didn't have an answer. We joined Whitcroft and Regan on the bridge. Liam busied himself collecting the armaments we had left. On the horizon I could see the low outline of the Shetland Islands rising above the waves. I checked the charts. We seemed to be as near as possible to our best approach.

While Liam and Whitcroft sorted out guns, both men working deftly, stripping and cleaning the Steg and the two Glocks, I realized we didn't have nearly enough firepower. I took ten minutes to change Regan's dressing and went down to the engine room to get my stash of grenades. I only just got them out dry. The water was lapping at the bottom of the engine mountings. I urged the *Castledawn* on, then I went back to the wheelhouse. Now I could clearly see the Nab, the huge outcrop of rock that guards the entrance to Lerwick harbour. But the water was almost up to the boat's gunwhales. I asked Liam for his phone. It was picking up a signal from Lerwick. I dialled a number from memory and it answered almost immediately.

'Hello, Kate,' I said, 'I'm coming into Shetland and I'm in trouble.'

When I had run away to Shetland, I had intended to make my fortune in the massive construction site at Sullom Voe, where they were building the terminal for the oil fields. I didn't get any further than the fish factory in the small, dour capital of Lerwick. The workers there lived in wooden huts on site and came from all over Europe. It was a rough, hard-drinking place, and drugs were common, and I took to it completely. Kate Elliot worked there as well, but Kate had bought herself a croft outside the town and was working to do it up. She seemed much older than me, but now I realize that she was in her early twenties. For some reason, she took a liking to me and invited me over to eat one evening. The dinner was macrobiotic, strange, alien-tasting food. Kate's partner Mick was there, a cheerful, shrewd man from Shotts in the industrial heartland of the Clyde. Others drifted in. The talk was, I now realize, fanning the dying embers of post-war political philosophy. But Kate and Mick were ahead of their time, questioning, sometimes offending their companions. Theirs was a cool, philosophical take on things, stripped of jargon and cant. There were few people of their generation who had traversed the previous decades and emerged with their mental vigour intact. They had both travelled in the East. Kate spoke fluent Japanese and had worked as a translator. Mick was the kind of man who could do anything with his hands, fix anything mechanical. He was dark and stocky. She was slim, small, with a freckled face and an upturned nose and an utterly unselfconscious physicality.

I suppose I fell in love with them and they gave me the rudiments of an education, feeding me reading material, books and especially art, which Mick was passionate about. He had me transferred to work with him, which meant going out in a lorry at 4 a.m. and driving around the island, collecting fish from trawlers. It was a good job. Sometimes the sun shone on those rainy islands and you felt as if you were in a world reborn. We'd drive along, smoking roll-ups and arguing about Max Ernst and Otto Dix, although I'd only ever seen their paintings in books.

Then, after I'd been there for a year, we were unloading a trawler, when the cable on a gantry snapped just as a pallet of fishboxes was being swung on to the back of our lorry. Mick was directly underneath.

I knelt with the skipper of the trawler and watched the life drain from his broken body.

We buried him three days later, and a week after that, I

moved in with Kate and gave back some of what she had given me. She suffered some kind of a breakdown and retreated into herself and nothing could shift her. I cooked and cleaned, brushed her hair and talked to her, and sometimes held her in a chaste way.

After three months, she seemed to come round a little. She went back to work and gradually came back to life. She started to laugh again. After six months, we sat one night and drank too much and I leaned across the table and kissed her.

The next morning, she got out of bed and ruffled my hair and went into the kitchen to make breakfast. When I sat down, she told me firmly that it was time to go, not just to leave the croft, but to leave the island. I fought her, but she was right. The following week, the big Aberdeen ferry slipped off into the mist with the customary lone piper on deck playing 'Amazing Grace'.

We'd kept in touch since then, although it was usually by e-mail now. I hadn't seen her for five years. She had accepted the island as her world, and now it seemed I was bringing bloody war into it. She heard the sadness in my voice and told me not to be stupid and to tell her what I wanted. I told her.

We were rounding the Nab now and our little vessel was labouring. The *Quo Vadis* was close behind as the broad expanse of Lerwick harbour opened up to us, the *Castledawn* slowing badly now. The harbour, half a mile across, used to be full of Russian factory ships, rig supply vessels all moored off the main channel. It was empty now. We had a clear run to the pier, but I didn't know if we would make it. Equally worrying, I didn't know if they would risk a ramming or a boarding in the middle of the harbour. Visibility was bad and they might get away with it. I looked at the *Quo Vadis* and saw Canning and Marks standing on deck. If the storm had bothered them, they didn't show it. I was close enough to see the unpleasant grin that Marks had on his face.

'That's it,' I said. 'Give me the wheel.' I gave it ninety degrees to port and hoped my memory was accurate. The other men looked at me as I cranked the engine up into the redline and dodged through a group of small boats. As far as they could tell I was heading straight for the granite harbour wall which supported the two-storey houses there. We weren't moving very fast, but the weight of the trawler meant that we had a murderous momentum. At the last minute, I threw the wheel to one side and she came round with agonizing slowness, grazing the harbour wall before finding the entrance to a tiny beach squeezed between two houses. I threw the wheel over again to get through the dog-leg entrance to the harbour and this time planks splintered against the other wall, but she came round again, with one last effort that wrenched her old sinews. The little beach was in front of us, two small boats drawn up on it that crackled and broke as the trawler's bow smashed them. Then, with a terrible, juddering impact, the *Castledawn* was on the beach, waterlogged, aground, her journey complete at last.

16

We climbed unsteadily over the bow on to the little beach. Liam threw our guns down, wrapped in a sack. I had the Sirius material under my arm. Between us we got Regan over the gunwhale. I looked back at the *Quo Vadis*. She was riding just offshore, but as I looked her engines fired up and she started to head towards the pier. I looked around for Kate. I wanted to be out of there before the locals took an interest in us. Eventually I saw an old Commer van coming round the harbour. It wheezed its way up to us.

'Transport,' I said cheerfully. Liam gave me a disbelieving look. The van clattered to a halt with a sound that suggested something terminal and Kate got out. She had the same fresh face she had had all those years ago, and the same slim figure. And the same taste in expensive clothes that she seemed to indulge without ever spending much money. There may have been other unreconstructed radicals and fish-factory employees driving around Lerwick in a Joseph dress and Prada kitten-heel mules, but I doubted it. She kissed me full on the lips and gave me that look of wistful intimacy she reserved for me, or so it seemed. Liam poked me and nodded towards the pier. The *Quo Vadis* had almost reached it.

'Come on,' I said, 'I'll introduce you in the van.'

We clambered into the back of the Commer and the ancient vehicle coughed into life. I told Kate who everyone was. We were an unlikely crew. The small man who looked as if he had been beaten half to a pulp. The detective in his raincoat, so stained and dirty as to be almost a parody of itself. And the tall weary-looking man with hard eyes. I saw Kate looking at Liam more than once. I wasn't sure if there was sympathy or anxiety in her eyes.

'Listen Kate,' I said, 'we're in a very complicated situation, very complicated and very dangerous and I've put you right in the firing line.'

She didn't say anything. She just turned to me with a strange look, amused but hard to read, as if she had known from the first moment she met me that this was coming.

'Leave her alone Jack,' Liam said from behind me, 'she's with us.' I didn't want to start thinking about where that was coming from. Kate looked at the bemused expression on my face and burst out laughing.

'All right, all right,' I said. 'If you're in, Kate, then drive past the harbour and we'll have a look. Everybody else keep down.'

As I drove off I took one last glance back at the *Castledawn*. She looked utterly forlorn as she lay half-buried in the sand and canted to one side, almost derelict. She had taken us through the storm and now we were abandoning her to a rising tide. I felt a pang. On the one hand in this job there is seldom room for sentiment. On the other hand, sometimes, sentiment is all there is.

I turned my attention to the task at hand. As we passed the harbour Kate slowed. I didn't like the odds. I counted nine men on the dock and I couldn't see Canning and Marks. Some of the men – I was guessing Americans – looked fairly shaken up by the crossing. The one who appeared to be the leader was having a furious row with the harbourmaster. Two deceptively casual-looking customs men watched with interest, ready to board. They were going to have trouble getting their weaponry through. I didn't doubt that they would, but it would take time. Time to make preparations. I let myself slump back against the wall of the van and doze as Kate drove us out of Lerwick.

Ten minutes out of Lerwick, just before we turned off the tarmac road, I asked Kate to stop. There was a little well by the side of the road where Mick would always stop to fill a bottle of water as we went to work. Mick told me there was something special about the well. He said that the ancients gave each place its own sprite and this one had survived. I didn't quite believe him and one day he showed me flat slates inlaid in the ground so that the water from the spring was channelled perfectly into the basin of the well.

'Fuck the sprites,' he said, 'but you have to admire engineering that lasts a few thousand years.'

There was a gap behind one of the slates and I put the Sirius folder in there. Fuck the sprites, but you never know. I commended it to their care and climbed back into the van.

*

It took three quarters of an hour to reach her. Kate's croft. It hadn't changed. There were windchimes outside the door, vegetables growing in a half-acre alongside the cottage, a tabby cat on the windowsill. Inside it was different. Minimalist with an Eastern slant. Cool modern space. A low Japanese table, rice screens, a sleek Scandinavian stereo and a bed made by a young Italian designer Kate had lured back to the croft. Regan and Liam were easy with it. Whitcroft propped himself uncomfortably in a corner and looked around him for all the world as if he wanted to arrest somebody for possession of controlled substances. Kate told Liam to check the chickens she had put in the oven as if she had known him all her life, then she told Regan to sit on the bed. He didn't complain as she gently and efficiently changed his dressings. She looked up as she heard an engine approaching the croft, along the long bumpy lane that led to it. I knew who it was, but I slipped the Glock under my coat just in case.

The car stopped outside and there was a low knock on the door. I nodded to Kate and she opened it. John Stone stood there in the rain. He offered his hand to Kate and smiled apologetically.

'Sorry to disturb you on such an inclement morning, Ms

Elliot, he said in his refined southern lilt, 'but I had to talk to Jack urgently.'

They summed each other up for a long moment before Kate smiled and stood aside to allow the American to enter. He thanked her gravely and stepped into the room. He seemed like an emissary from another world, a formal but perilous underworld. He was stooped and cadaverous, exuding a courtly, world-weary air. He greeted each of the inhabitants of the room by name as if he had known them for a long time. Such thoroughness was second nature to a man like Stone. I could see that Whitcroft was impressed. In fact the two men had much in common, not least in the fact that they both professed the doctrine of the greater good.

Kate offered him a chair, but he waved it away and sat, in the Japanese way, at the low table, grimacing a little as he did so. He apologized for his lack of grace.

'I'm reminded of the great Czech runner, Emil Zatopek,' he said. 'He was asked why he always looked in agony when he was running and he said, in all humility, that he hadn't been given the talent to run fast and smile at the same time.'

'Your timing is good, anyway,' Kate said. 'Will you join us in a meal?'

Stone nodded and seemed genuinely pleased. Kate told us to seat ourselves as best we could. Liam and I could sit at the table. Whitcroft sat awkwardly on a kitchen chair. Regan could do neither and ended up half-sitting, half-lying like a battered Roman emperor. So began one of the strangest meals I have ever had. A strange feast on the eve of battle. It was a little after noon, yet the shadows danced on the roof of the little croft as if it was midnight. Kate put a dish of chicken and brown rice on the table and asked softly if anyone had a grace to say. There was a silence in which it felt natural that any one of us should say grace but it was Stone who spoke first. A simple, formal grace with a southern Baptist dignity and altruism to it. When Kate had served the meal Stone told us about

Sirius, or at least as much as he reckoned was needed, but in doing so he trusted us with a great deal of information, and that trust was a tribute to the people around the table.

'You know who he is?' Stone asked me.

'Snyder,' I said. Stone nodded and smiled. He had expected me to find out.

'How did you uncover him?'

I inclined my head towards Whitcroft.

'Of course,' Stone said. He nodded at Whitcroft in a way which implied professional admiration. It was odd to see the current of respect that passed between the urbane Stone, in a Brooks Brothers suit and overcoat, and the dishevelled, unshaven detective. As it was with the others. A different respect was extended to Regan as a man who was incapable of being owned. And to Liam, who, I think, puzzled Stone. He'd met the political wing of the movement, but he'd never met anybody like Liam. A man who was attentive and shrewd and romantic in a dark and all-encompassing way that Stone's Anglo-Saxon outlook could not quite comprehend.

'What about Snyder?' I said.

'Chairman-in-waiting of the National Security Council,' Stone said. 'A vain and dangerous man, with, I think, ambitions on the presidency.' I said nothing. As far as the rest of the world went, a man like Snyder could do more harm in terms of geopolitics as chair of the NSC than he could ever do in the formalized surroundings of the Oval Office.

'Exactly,' Stone said, reading my thoughts, 'a dangerous man in a dangerous job. Frankly, a bad man.' I said nothing. I wasn't about to indulge in sophistry with Stone. There were many people who would have applied the same description to Stone himself. But I think Stone meant something different. To a man like Stone, bad meant not ordering your life according to certain moral dictates.

'He is desperate to get hold of whatever you have,' he said. 'It's enough to break him.' He smiled, a deceptive, gentle smile. 'And I want him broken. Somerville, on the other hand,' he said, turning to me, 'wants to control him. Correct that. You don't control a man like Snyder. Influence him.'

'Who are the men following Jack?' Liam asked.

'Fundamentally, they are renegades, but they have worked with Snyder for a long time. They share a certain political outlook. Most of them are former security-service personnel. Over the years, Mr Snyder has shown a penchant for stunts, getting his team together and going into trouble spots to represent what he regards as being the American interest. That is how he turned up on your patch, Mr Whitcroft.'

'I don't care how he got there,' Whitcroft said, 'but I do care what he was doing when he was there.'

'He was carrying out a programme of assassination at the behest of certain interests in the British establishment. It was an ideology thing. It is a common misapprehension, you see, that the US government is skewed towards the Irish interest. In fact, particularly then, the opposite has been the case. The State Department in particular is full of anglophiles. The operation went wrong and Snyder lost his partner. But he continued alone and carried out his task with admirable efficiency.'

'If you get the material I took from the mountain, will it stop him?' I asked.

'Yes, it will stop him. And I guarantee that I will cover you with your organization, Jack.'

'There is something I have to do first,' I said. I had a feeling that we were getting an edited version of the Snyder story, that there was something more to it.

'What's that, Jack?'

'I hate to be melodramatic,' I said, 'but I'm going to have a showdown with these boys.'

'If you give me the Sirius file,' Stone said, a little iron creeping into his voice, 'I'll take care of them.'

'No,' I said. 'If I do that, then it will never be over. This way, it's finished for good. Both for me and for Liam. And while

I'm on the subject, this has nothing to do with anyone else.'

'You must be fucking joking,' Regan exploded. 'Look at me, course it has to do with me.'

'You'll have a chance to get your own back,' I said. At that moment, Curley and Somerville would be touching down at the island airport.

'I'll be coming too,' Whitcroft said, 'just to makes sure there's no lawbreaking.' He cracked a wintry smile.

'And afterwards?' Stone asked. 'What about the file?'

'I don't intend giving it to Somerville, if that reassures you,' I said. I'm not sure if he was reassured. 'But first I need a few things.'

'Fire ahead,' he said.

'I want you to contact the Americans and give them this.' I scribbled a set of map coordinates on a piece of paper. 'They shouldn't be hard to find in Lerwick. Its one o'clock now, tell them I'll be there at three.'

'Consider it done,' he said.

'What about the Americans?'

He shrugged. 'It would suit me if none of them came back.'

It wasn't the attitude you usually expected from the Americans where one of their own was concerned, no matter how irritated they were. I said so.

'Listen,' Stone said, 'there are Americans and there are Americans. There is the kind of American who regards it as valid to fire incendiary shells into a compound full of women and children, like they did at Waco. There is the kind of American who regards himself as embodying the values of our society and therefore believes he can do no wrong, who never even questions their own actions, and as the years go on, then the actions become more outrageous. There is that kind of American, and then there is the kind of American I consider myself to be. One who knows the value of a human life. Who knows how to weigh up the moral consequences of an act.'

I knew that Stone would weigh up the consequences, and

then go ahead and add the action to the considerable burden of guilt he carried already.

'Did you bring the weaponry?' I said.

'Outside.'

We went out. A cold mist was starting to blow in from the sea, which suited me. A Daihatsu four-wheel-drive was parked outside the croft. Another man was sitting at the wheel. He was wearing jeans and a fleece, but the haircut and the erect bearing told me he was a marine. He swung out of the driving seat and at a gesture from Stone opened the back of the jeep to reveal a bewildering array of armaments. The marine stood by. Liam and I had the Glocks. Regan had the Steg. Whitcroft picked out a Mk V Uzzi and a lightweight Colt 9mm. An urban drugdealer's arsenal, in fact, which looked strange in the hands of the middle-aged detective. I added a few grenades to the ones I had brought from the *Castledawn*. Liam took a pump-action shotgun. That was it. The marine looked disappointed. But it was a mistake to go into action laden down with firepower. You hesitate, wondering which of your array of weapons to use, giving your opponent the upper hand.

I checked my watch. It would take about forty minutes to get to the place I had in mind. It was almost two.

'I'd better go,' Stone said. 'I have promises to keep.'

I'm not sure if he was quoting Robert Frost, or John F. Kennedy's inaugural address in which he read the Frost poem. In any case, it was finished off from an unexpected quarter.

'And miles to go before I sleep, and miles to go before I sleep.' It was Regan murmuring the lines as if addressing them to some internal audience. For a moment he looked bereft and I wondered afterwards if he had felt something of a premonition.

Stone shook each of our hands. As he was getting into the jeep, he turned and looked at us again. He shook his head and got in. I don't know what he was thinking. We watched him drive off into the gathering mist.

I turned to Kate. She was looking at us with anxiety in her eyes. I had expected her to be angry for bringing this into her home, but it seemed that somehow she had connected with all of the men in the few hours she had known them. Many years before, Kate had believed in auras. I wondered if she saw an aura around us now, because I thought I did, and it was the aura of violent death.

She threw me the keys of the Commer.

'You'll need these,' she said, and then, 'I'll be waiting for you.' Whitcroft and Regan shook hands with her. She looked into Regan's eyes for a long time. Liam kissed her, and I put my arms around her and held her. We climbed into the van. Liam took the wheel. Regan and Whitcroft got into the back and I slid the side door shut, then climbed into the passenger seat.

'Let's go,' I said. The van coughed into life and Liam put it into gear. Kate stood silently in front of the croft, watching us until she could no longer see us, a woman watching men go to war, a timeless, valedictory figure fading into the mist.

17

The atmosphere in the van was quiet, tense, each man alone with his own thoughts, as happens at such times. I explained to them what I had in mind. We would offer them the option of leaving us alone. Then we would fight. There was nothing subtle about the plan. I knew that we would find ourselves opposed by violent and devious men, and that there was no point in trying to second-guess what they might do. They might not be prepared for a straight fight. We had a chance if we struck suddenly and hard.

'Sounds good to me,' Liam said. 'I'm fed up being chased. Time I was doing some chasing.'

Regan looked eager. Whitcroft sighed and looked out of the window as if all the terrible things he had ever dreamed of were about to come true.

I told them about the arena I had chosen. When the oil terminal at Sullom Voe was in the process of being built, thousands of workers were shipped in, and camps had to be built to house them. Hundreds of mobile homes were shipped in and laid out on a grid pattern with narrow tarmac roads running between them. These places had their own shops, bars and cinemas and were in effect prefabricated towns. By the time construction was over, the men had gone. Most of the mobile homes had been sold off, but one camp, the oldest, had simply been abandoned, the old prefabs not being deemed worthy of expensive shipping to the mainland. This was Camp Seven and this was where we would take our stand.

The road ran alongside the island's airstrip. As we passed the wire, I saw a jet looming out of the mist, dominating the small apron. A Boeing 737 with the presidential seal on it. I let out a low whistle. It wasn't Air Force One, or even Air Force Two, but it was part of the presidential fleet, and parked at the end of the steps was the Daihatsu jeep that had carried Stone to the croft. This affair was being taken very seriously indeed if a government jet was being provided to ferry Stone around the place.

As we drove towards Camp Seven, the fog thickened and Liam slowed almost to walking pace. I explained that there was a central block which used to be the canteen and was made of concrete. As well as providing us with cover, it sat on a little promontory which jutted out into the sea, so that it was impossible to flank. I knew that we couldn't beat them by staying in the block, but if things went badly, it was a place to retreat to. Apart from that, I reminded them that all the other buildings were prefabricated and a bullet would go through them as if they were paper.

We reached the rusty wire fence which surrounded the camp. The gates were open and we drove in. Liam went narrow-eyed when he saw the camp. The ghostly shapes of the buildings looming out of the mist, the sense of a once-thriving place now deserted, weeds growing through the tarmac, some of the prefabs toppled by the harsh Atlantic wind. It was a strange, moody, unsettling place and we caught its atmosphere, tendrils of fog floating past the windscreen. I directed Liam to the block. When we reached it, he turned off the engine.

'This is a strange place you've brought us to, Jack,' Liam said. The fog brought a dank, undersea smell with it, a smell that made you think of unclean undersea things, the hands of drowned mariners.

'Never mind the strangeness,' I said sharply. 'Check your weapons and make sure you've plenty of ammunition.'

We pushed open the door of the block. The excitement was building now. I could feel the blood pounding in my ears, the adrenalin surge. It was a long time since I had been in a straight fight, crouched in a building waiting for an enemy. Liam was at a window beside me and he shifted restlessly, sighting along the barrel of the Glock. Whitcroft looked melancholic, but nevertheless held his gun tightly. Regan seemed to have retreated into that still place he had. We waited for them to come, quietly, patiently.

And they came. Walking carefully through the prefabs, spread out in a line, their guns at the ready. Seven, eight of them. The fog obscured my vision. Their faces were intent, for they were hunting and they did not intend to leave without a kill.

'That's far enough,' I shouted, my voice muffled in the fog. They stopped. One of them stepped forward.

'That you, Valentine?' It was the same voice I had heard on the marine band radio. I couldn't see Canning and Marks.

'You want to come out and parley, Valentine? I figure you do, else you would have just shot me. So come on out.'

He bent over carefully and put his gun on the ground then stepped away from it.

'You're not going out there, Valentine, are you?' Whitcroft hissed urgently. In reply I leaned the Glock against the wall.

'For fuck's sake,' Whitcroft said, but I stepped out anyway. The Americans were entitled to this one chance.

The man grinned at me as I crossed the ground towards him.

'You led us a hell of a dance, Valentine.' He was tall, crew-cut. Probably an athlete in his youth. He was a good-looking man but his eyes held the coldness of a small-town boy with simple, small-town convictions turned to evil in a bigger, more corrupt world.

'What's the deal?' he said.

'There is no deal,' I said. 'What we require is that you get out of here and go back home. Otherwise, we shall kill you.'

He threw his head back and slapped his thigh as if this was the biggest joke he had ever heard. But his head snapped back, mean as a weasel, and the hand that had hit his thigh came up with the glint of a bright, lethal blade in it, slashing towards my stomach. He was quick but I was quicker. I caught his wrist with my right hand and deflected the blade away. I palmed the little plastic Russian Derringer into my left hand, placed the barrel against his stomach and blew his spine all over the landscape with a hollow-point mercury-filled shell.

Liam was firing even before I pulled the trigger. The Americans dived for cover. I ducked and rolled towards the block, made a quick decision to dive through the window instead of the door and was glad of it when one of the Americans, anticipating my re-entry to the building, blasted the doorway to pieces. Then everyone was firing, the Americans suddenly starting to realize how uncomfortable their position was. The pump-action was lifting huge chunks out of the prefabs, and the machine pistols stitched their way methodically across the paper-thin walls. We didn't allow a pause in the firing, not for a second, and the Americans were too busy avoiding our fire to direct anything more than hasty shots our way. I saw Liam direct a line of fire across the front of a prefab. The man in the prefab panicked as the bullets moved methodically towards him. He broke and ran. Regan picked him off and turned to Liam with a fierce grin, the light of battle in his eyes.

We could hear the Americans shouting to each other, panic in their voices. I thought the time was right to get in amongst them. I turned to my left to tell Regan and Liam to get ready. As I did so, the words died in my mouth. As Regan turned to say something to Liam, a rifle round hit him in the throat. With terrible violence, he was flung to the back wall of the room. He lay there. With each beat of his heart a massive gout of blood spurted out. Regan was dying, if not dead. I froze. Liam dropped his gun and ran to him. Whitcroft dropped his Uzzi as well. With terrible deliberation, he took a heavy old Webley service revolver from his coat pocket. He pointed it out of the window and took aim. I saw the big old gun kick as he squeezed the trigger and saw the man who had fired the shot tumble from the roof of a prefab.

'Keep firing,' I yelled furiously at Whitcroft. 'The Uzzi, for fuck's sakes.' Their fire was finding its range now. Bullets hammered off the concrete. I moved back, still firing, and looked down at Regan. Normally you see fear in the eyes of a dying man. Sometimes you see terrible agony. But it seemed that Regan had retreated into that solitary interior place and simply did not intend to come back. As I watched him, the breath rattled in the back of his throat and he died.

Liam bowed his head. Whitcroft stopped firing. Then Liam raised his head. There was a dangerous gleam in his eyes.

I cannot explain what happened next. Liam picked up the Steg and his Glock. I had the Russian pistol in one hand, the Glock in the other. Whitcroft also had a revolver and a machine pistol. There were at least eight maybe nine men out there, highly trained men, battle-hardened, resourceful.

They didn't stand a chance.

With a yell, Liam charged through the door, followed by Whitcroft. I followed them. Without deviation, we ran straight for the first prefab, which seemed to crackle and distort as our hail of fire struck it. Two men broke from it and ran and Liam cut them down. I rolled a grenade under a second hut. With a muffled boom and a flash of dull orange light, muted by the fog, it disintegrated. A man appeared at the window of another prefab. Whitcroft deliberately put a revolver bullet into the wall a foot below the window, and the man collapsed.

I believe there is a dark place in war where men go. It doesn't happen to every man, or in every battle, but some men will have been there and will never cease to wonder at themselves thereafter. We were blind to pain, blind to fear, blind to consequence. I saw one of the Americans running away. I chased him and when he turned to fire at me, I shot him, then stood over him with the Glock and fired and fired until his torso was a bloody, sodden mass. I turned then and followed my comrades, throwing grenades into one prefab after another, and they exploded in series with the same muffled orange flare. The air was full of ash and gunsmoke and men's screams. We caught another of the men and all three of us fired at him at once and his body seemed to explode. We saw another running between the buildings and we followed. He ran out on to open ground where the remaining three were throwing themselves into a hired Ford. He ran towards them, waving his arms. The driver spun around in a tight fast circle and didn't see his comrade until it was too late and the car bucked horribly as he went under the wheels. The driver braked, then saw us coming. He missed a gear and stalled. He got it started but the car had gone off the tarmac and the back wheels dug themselves into the mud. He was a grown man but I saw tears running down his cheeks as he wrestled with the steering wheel, tears of frustration and terrible fear.

As we ran up to the car, one of the men in the back discharged a shot. That was all it took. We stood in a line and emptied every weapon we had into the car, the windows and bodywork exploding, the car rocking on its springs with the impact of bullets, limbs writhing in agony inside as we fired and kept firing until even the faintest groan had ceased.

The silence was intense. Liam went down on one knee and covered his face with his hands. Whitcroft cursed and threw the Uzzi on the ground. I felt an emptiness inside, an emptiness that seemed to have been there for ever. As the haze of blood and vengeance passed from us there came a weariness. I wondered how long ago we had left Regan lying in his own blood. Twenty minutes? An hour? It was impossible to tell how long ago this savage and amoral chase had started. I sat down on the ground, overwhelmed with weariness. Then I heard the voice behind us. A soft voice, full of deadly irony.

'That was very nice, boys,' Marks said. 'Very impressive.'

I turned. Canning and Marks were standing behind us, both with rifles in their hands. I was too tired to be surprised.

'Good company you're keeping, Liam,' Marks said, 'Inspector fucking Whitcroft and a Brit secret-service man. I wonder how that would play at home. I wonder what they would think of you then. I wonder, would they think about a particular operation in the Slieve Blooms and who informed on it?'

'I'm no informer,' Liam said wearily.

'You are an informer,' Marks said coldly, 'the worst kind of informer. People looked up to you.'

'At this moment I'm indifferent as to whether you believe me or not, but hear me one more time. I am not an informer.'

'Well, then, it must be the fine company you keep that can't hold their tongues. The fine English women.'

Liam got to his feet. There was a dangerous light in his eyes.

'Do it, Mellows,' Canning said coldly, 'and I'll shoot you down like the dog that you are.'

'You'll shoot me anyway,' Liam said.

'You'll get one in the head,' Canning said, 'but if you move one inch out of line, I'll shoot you in the guts and leave you screaming and watching your friends die.'

Liam shrugged and sat down again.

'How did you hook up with the Yanks?' I said.

'The devious Jack Valentine,' Marks said. 'Does it matter, now that you've killed them all?'

'Humour me.'

'It really doesn't matter,' Marks said. 'We found one of them skulking about and nearly shot him. Then he told us who he was after. We thought we should join forces.'

'Good job you've done on them, though,' Canning said. 'They would annoy you, them Americans.'

'If you're going to do it, then get on with it,' Liam said tiredly. Marks walked over to him, bent over him and spat in his face.

'You're an informer,' he hissed, 'you don't get to choose the time of your execution.'

'Liam Mellows is not an informer.'

Marks looked around wildly, trying to find the source of the voice. He knew the voice and I knew the voice. I had made more than one telephone call.

I raised my head and saw a figure striding through the mist, a man with a long, black coat billowing out behind him, and a battered AK 47 under his arm. The fog seemed to swirl around him, making him seem taller than he was, tall and thin and towering, and I thought I saw Canning bless himself quickly. He carried no stick, and there was the trace of a limp, but this man was not the quiet, unemphatic man whose bar I had visited in Dundalk only a week previously. This man was the personification of generations of rebellion and intrigue; a subtle, intelligent and ruthless man, the measure and more of people like Somerville and Stone.

To my surprise, the first person in the group he acknowledged was Whitcroft. He looked at him and gave him a quiet nod.

'Well, Ronnie,' he said. I realized I had never heard Whitcroft's first name spoken before. Whitcroft nodded back at him.

'Eamon,' he said shortly. I watched Marks's face during this exchange. He looked from one to the other. Eamon possessed an authority that even Marks would find hard to defy. And Marks was utterly confused about the implied intimacy that Eamon had shown with the man who, on the face of it, should have been his mortal enemy. Marks hadn't yet picked up the full implications of the exchange. If Eamon and Whitcroft were willing to reveal their relationship in front of Marks and Canning, it meant that the two men were not to leave this place alive. I felt blank and tired and unable to face further violence, and yet I watched this drama play itself out with a sense of terrible compulsion.

'You know,' Eamon said to Marks, 'this action against Liam Mellows wasn't sanctioned at any level.'

Marks shrugged with elaborate nonchalance.

'It was only a matter of time,' he said.

'Nevertheless,' Eamon said softly.

'Mellows touted on us,' Canning exclaimed.

'Mellows was foolish,' Eamon said, looking at Liam for the first time, 'but he didn't inform.'

'What about the English girl?' Marks said. 'She was running him as an agent.'

Eamon shook his head. 'The English girl told them nothing. In fact, give me a few more men like her and we would have won the war.'

'Somebody informed on the Slieve Bloom job,' Canning said.

'That's true,' Whitcroft said, intervening for the first time. I realized that Whitcroft knew exactly who that informer was, and I watched the scene unfold with a growing sense of horror.

'What was it, Sean?' Eamon said, turning to Marks. 'Was it money?' His voice was quiet and deadly. Marks looked at him, then quickly around him, as though casting about for a means of escape. There was a line of sweat on his upper lip. There was a look of cunning on his face, then his expression seemed to collapse, to be replaced by the kind of look you see on the face of a child – shame at being caught, mixed with relief at the lifting of the burden. It was that quick look of cunning that made me understand. Informers came in many guises, but one of the most common is the man who regards himself as quicker and more intelligent than the men around him, an attitude which ultimately breeds contempt. Special Branch handlers know well how to flatter and manipulate such men. It wasn't money with Marks. It was pride. He looked at Whitcroft.

'You?' Whitcroft nodded at him.

'It's the mistake army intelligence always makes. When they're out on the ground, they're fine. Everything is hostile. But when they get back to barracks, they relax. They think that everybody is on the same side. I was at this Christmas party in Thiepvil barracks and I met your handler. He couldn't help telling me about this great source he had.'

He turned to me.

'That's where you lot go wrong as well, with all your cloak-and-dagger stuff. Get a man drunk and get him talking about his wife and children. He'll tell you anything after that.' Whitcroft didn't look as if he liked himself very much.

Marks sighed and put his weapon on the ground. Canning was looking at him with disbelief. Marks clapped him on the shoulder and shook his head with a smile on his face as though attending to some private joke. He turned to Eamon.

'Can I say a prayer, Eamon?' He was brave, you had to give him that, but his face was ashen and there was a tremor in his voice.

'You can pray,' Eamon said, 'but not here.' He gestured with the gun towards the little hill that rose to the side of the camp. Marks looked at Liam as though he was about to say something and I realized that, for all that Marks would have seen Liam dead to cover for his own treachery, they had still known each other all their lives, had played together as children. In the end, a single word was all he managed.

'Liam,' he said.

'Sean,' Liam replied, as though the speaking of each other's name was an act sufficient to encompass the moment. Marks walked off then, with Eamon following behind. We sat there in perfect silence. I looked up and saw Canning's lips move in silent prayer. Then we heard a single gunshot.

18

After what seemed like a long time, I struggled to my feet. It wasn't over yet. Canning was slumped on the ground, wretched and demoralized. I thought that Eamon would come back and kill him, and I didn't want to be there when he did. I tapped Liam on the arm.

'Come on,' I said. 'This isn't finished yet.' I turned to Whitcroft.

'You're not coming,' I said.

'Why?' Whitcroft said belligerently.

'I'm going to meet a wicked old man,' I said, 'and you don't want him to see you with Liam. If he can't use you, he'll bring you down.' Whitcroft thought about it, then nodded.

'Give me your phone,' I said to Liam. I dialled a number. Stone answered.

'The American team is down. All of them. I need you to come in and clean up.'

'Consider it done.'

'There's another thing. One of our team is down.'

'I am sorry to hear that. Sorry indeed. Which one?'

'Regan,' I said.

'He struck me as a brave, intelligent man. My condolences.'

'Stone, I need you to take care of him, get him home.'

'It will be done.'

'Another thing. Whitcroft is here. He needs to get home as well. Minimum fuss.'

'Also done.' Whitcroft looked as if he was about to protest, then gave in.

'Then I want to meet you,' I told Stone. 'There's a small

pier called Shankly Pier. You'll see it on the Ordnance Survey. Meet me there in half an hour.'

I turned to Whitcroft. There wasn't much to say. We could have felt some sense of triumph, but that was impossible with the loss of Regan. Added to that, the primal ferocity of our response had left us all stunned, almost uncertain, and I did not want to see what was written on a man's face after such an act.

'Come on, Liam,' I said. 'One last thing to attend to.'

The Commer had a few bullet holes in it but was still drivable. By the time we had picked it up and come back towards the gate, Eamon, Whitcroft and Canning were gone. We drove back towards Lerwick. I picked up the Sirius file at the little well. I had picked Shankly Pier not because it was the place where Mick had been killed but because of a memory of driving down to it one radiant morning with Mick and seeing a fully rigged schooner – a Russian-sail training ship in fact – moored off the pier, and for a moment it had seemed a perfect vision of the world the way it should be. But of course it wasn't like that at all. Still, I summoned up the memory and hoped that perhaps the shade of Mick was still around the place somewhere and was looking after what remained of my humanity.

There was one other car at the pier when we got there. We parked and got out. We didn't bother to hide our weapons. I carried the Sirius file under my arm. This would be settled once and for all. As we walked out on to the pier, I saw two figures standing at the end and heard another vehicle pull up behind us, carrying the final protagonist.

Somerville didn't move as we approached him. Curley stood behind him, silent and immovable.

'You've excelled yourself in location this time, Jack,' Somerville said. 'Very melodramatic, I must say. I hope what you have to tell me to explain yourself lives up to it. I assume that is the file under your arm. I'll take it if you don't mind.'

'Wait,' I said quietly.

'The file, Jack,' he insisted.

'Wait,' I said. I hardly recognized my own voice. It seemed that the last few hours had been distilled into it and it seemed harsh and commanding. Somerville seemed to shrink away from it.

We waited. I heard footsteps behind me and saw Somerville's eyes widen. I backed away a little to allow Stone into the circle. He looked old and stooped.

'So,' he said into the silence, 'here we are and here things will be resolved, as is, I think, your intention, Jack.'

'This is nothing to do with you, Stone,' Somerville snarled.

'Sirius is everything to do with me.'

'What the hell is Sirius?' Somerville said.

'Sorry,' Stone said, 'an affectation of mine. A name I put on Mr Snyder. You know, Somerville, something that puzzled me about this affair was how you knew about it. Who Snyder was and what he had been doing in Ireland. I smelt a rat, in other words. And I followed my nose. You'll be interested in this, Jack. It occurred to me to search for the party in British Intelligence who had the bright idea of bringing Snyder in. Guess who I found, in his then guise as a military intelligence officer with a taste for the esoteric, and a liking for the smell of blood?'

'It was a valid operation.' Somerville's voice was metallic. 'They were dangerous men.'

'They were certainly dangerous men,' Stone said. 'Fighting men. But they knew that war is only a means to an end. They would have negotiated a settlement. Instead, we got young men who loved war for the sake of war. And that was what you wanted, Somerville. Because people like you thrive on uncertainty and fear and death. War is meat and drink to you. Foul meat. Rotten drink.' Stone's voice was tight, angry.

'Don't moralize at me, Stone,' Somerville said. 'You've supped enough at that table yourself.'

And then Stone had a gun in his hand. I watched Curley. He didn't move.

'The file, Jack,' Stone said. I shrugged and threw it on the ground between the two men. Neither of them moved. Instead, Curley launched himself forward, swift and vicious, a gun in his hand. Liam was quicker. He deflected Curley's gun hand and pressed the barrel of the Glock into his kidneys. I took the gun out of Curley's hand. Stone stooped swiftly and lifted the file.

'So you started all this, you little bastard,' Liam said, looking at Somerville.

'Tell him to let Curley go, Jack,' Somerville said. 'There's no percentage in it for him.'

I stared bitterly at Somerville, knowing he was right. I remembered what he had said about everyone having something they loved above all else, and wished that Somerville had something like that, something you could hold a threat over, the way he did to others. But there was something, and Liam had seen it. With sudden violence, he pushed Curley away from him and he fell to the ground. Liam levelled the Glock. Somerville saw his finger tighten on the trigger.

'No, please!' he shouted, his voice suddenly seeming high and girlish. Liam fired once, then again. Curley's kneecaps exploded in a mist of blood and shattered bone. Somerville fell to his knees beside him, moaning, suddenly oblivious to anything else. I would never have known the two men were lovers. It would have seemed too incongruous. But Liam had seen it straight away.

'I was going to say that it was for what he did to Regan,' Liam said wearily, 'but sure, he probably didn't even know who Regan was. He was just a piece of meat that he could hurt. Jesus, Jack, my world is bad, but yours is worse.'

We turned and walked back along the pier. Curley might live, if Somerville got him to a hospital in time. I didn't care one way or the other.

I told Liam to wait in the van. I went over to the Daihatsu.

Stone was about to get in. The marine was behind the wheel and when he saw my face I saw him reach carefully under the dash and I knew he was reaching for a weapon.

Stone turned to face me.

'This was never about Snyder, was it Stone?'

'Not personally, no, Jack.'

'I didn't think so. If amorality was a bar to high public office in Washington, then the place would be pretty empty, wouldn't it? So what the hell was it?'

'Simple enough, Jack. Snyder was a Democrat in a mid-term Democratic administration. Popular with the public because of his war record. Charismatic. Well-funded. The NSC was just a stepping stone for Snyder.'

'And the President couldn't go for a third term. So Snyder is a challenger for the leadership . . .'

'Was,' Stone said. 'Was a challenger.' And he tapped the folder under his arm.

'So all of this was about internal party politics?' I said. 'And that was it? That was what it was about?'

'Internal party politics?' Stone snapped, his eyes flashing. 'Is that what you call it? You don't realize what is at stake, Jack, what power is concentrated in the hands of the Chairman of the NSC, never mind the presidency. Everything is permissible in order to influence that. Everything.'

I looked at him and remembered the first time I had seen this little pier, and I thought that this gesturing, inexorable old man seemed grotesque. He must have seen it in my eyes.

'How much do you think was left to chance in this, Jack?' he said with quiet vehemence. 'I know you had a hard crossing in that little boat of yours. Did you know that you weren't alone out there? Did you know there was a submarine with you?' He was speaking between clenched teeth. 'Did you know that your life hung in the balance for hours while I went from meeting to meeting, with the consensus saying that it would be better if your boat went down and this file went with it? Do you know what favours I called in?'

But not for me, I said quietly to myself. Stone wanted the file. Ultimately he was indifferent to my fate. But it was the fact that whether I should live or die was being debated late into the night, thousands of miles away in offices along the Potomac, that seemed to unnerve and depress me to the depths of my heart. It was the thought that, while we battled for our lives against the storm, there were men, probably a few hundred metres beneath our hull, lazing on bunks, eating, working. It seemed that we had brushed up against death, and survived and forged something between ourselves in the doing of it, and had now found that none of it was real, none of it was valid. I turned away from Stone and walked tiredly back to the Commer. I climbed into the passenger seat. Liam, alone with his own thoughts, didn't look at me. He started the engine and we drove off without looking back.

19

Kate was waiting for us when we got back. It was a quiet time, and she cared for us and gave us what healing she could. Liam rang the hospital in Belfast and was told that Deirdre had recovered consciousness. A few hours later, he got through to her. He took the phone into the bedroom and spoke to her there. He came out and told me that she was doing well, but when I asked if I could speak to her, he looked embarrassed and shook his head.

'She can't speak to you yet,' he said.

I didn't press him. I was responsible for what had happened to her, and I had no claim on her.

For a few days, we slept and sat around the house. Then I had to go into Lerwick and face an inquisition about the *Castledawn*. In the end, I had to ring Stone and within hours the harbour authorities and customs had backed off with bad grace. I paid the people whose boats had been crushed and arranged for a local firm of boatbuilders to refloat her and undertake the necessary repairs to get her back to the mainland.

Liam and I didn't speak much. Kate attended to us, as if somehow we were spiritually damaged beings that needed her grave administration. Liam communicated with Stone's office about Regan's body, and how it should be conveyed back to Ireland. The mayhem at Camp Seven had been quietly cleaned up. Again, a demonstration of the power exercised by Stone. I stayed at Kate's for a week. It was a simple, almost monastic existence. Kate rose early and went to bed early. There was a rigour to her day which we copied, and which, I think, helped us.

One night, I awoke to hear some movement in the croft, a

murmur of conversation, a door shutting. The next morning, when I got up, it was clear that Kate and Liam had spent the night together, and I knew that it was time for me to go. There was a lift to Liam's step that I hadn't seen in a while, and I didn't begrudge it to him. You take your healing where you find it.

The next time I saw Kate, was on a cold, clear Sunday morning in Killeen churchyard, seven miles south of Newry. The small South Armagh church was packed and others had gathered outside. The sun was shining but there was a bitter wind that seemed to suck the breath out of your lungs. The little road leading to the church was clogged with cars, with the Hiace vans and small trucks that were used by the smugglers and small market traders of the area. Then there were the Mercedes and BMWs, many of them occupied by hard-looking men and expensively dressed women. Cars registered in Cork and Dublin, in Manchester and London. And there were many wreaths, for flamboyance was part of such occasions. And there was a helicopter, hovering in the distance over Cloghogue, watching and recording. I stood outside until I saw the hearse coming and then I went into the church. I saw Kate slip in at the back and sit down. I looked for Liam but I couldn't see him. I knew that Liam wasn't able to cross the border, that he was still wanted, but I wondered that he wasn't there. There was a stir in the church and I saw Eamon come in, limping up the aisle, leaning on his stick. More men came behind him, men in leather jackets dispersing to one side of the church and the other.

The coffin was shouldered up the aisle by four young men, nephews of Regan's, I found out later, for he had no brothers. Walking behind the coffin came Regan's wife, Marie. I hadn't expected her to look as she did. She was tall and elegant, a beautiful face made stern and melancholic by grief. She held a little dark-haired girl on either side of her and their backs were straight and dignified and your heart broke for them.

It was a simple service, soon over, and the same four men carried the coffin from the church. I waited by the door, assuming that they would be going to the graveyard beside the church. Then I felt Kate linking my arm and drawing me away towards my car. I got in and started the engine and waited. The four young men placed the coffin in the back of the hearse and we joined the cortège.

A young man in dark glasses stopped the traffic on the main road to allow the cortège to emerge and no one questioned his authority to do so. I looked back and saw the cortège snaking out behind us. It seemed there were hundreds of cars. We crossed the border at Dromad and went on for a few miles and then the cortège turned west and we climbed the little hill towards the ancient church at Faughart.

We pulled in behind the hearse. Cars were left all down the hill and the crowd pressed behind us. I looked over towards the wall of the graveyard and I saw a small, shabby figure standing there, a man in a raincoat. I wasn't the only one to see him. You could see men in the crowd looking over at Whitcroft. He ignored them. I thought he was foolhardy. There were many volatile men in the crowd behind us. Then I saw Marie walk over to him, still holding her girls by the hand. She shook Whitcroft's hand and spoke to him briefly. The message was clear. In this place of ancient sanctuary, he was to be left alone.

The same four men shouldered the coffin from the hearse. I followed them. As we passed into the graveyard, I met Deirdre. She looked pale and ill, barely able to stay on her feet. She smiled at me, but it was a distant smile, and as she faltered, Kate moved swiftly to support her.

'They're looking for you,' Deirdre said. I was pushed forward and found the rough wood of the coffin on my shoulder, as I carried it with three others towards the grave. I saw a man with a spade standing at the grave. It was Liam, and I realized it was a tradition in these parts that your friends dug your grave. He looked thinner than the last time I had seen him, honed down and serious. He looked at me with a shrewd and clear-eyed look.

We buried Regan and I left quickly afterwards. I thought I saw Deirdre looking anxiously after me. But I felt that I had brought harm to all of the people there, and the only decent thing I could do was to leave.

I returned to Kintyre. I read in the papers that Richard Snyder had retired due to health reasons. I went to Shetland and sailed the *Castledawn* back on my own, moored her in the harbour and started to work on the repairs. I worked every day until I was bone-tired, then I came back to the croft and drank Redbreast until my elderly neighbour, Jackie Irvine, felt obliged to come down and lecture me on my alcohol consumption and general refusal to engage with the world. He was right. I cut down on the Redbreast. I started walking, spending days on the heather, until I was too tired to drink at night, falling into a dreamless sleep.

Winter gave way to spring. I found myself trimming the fuchsia hedges on the way down to the harbour. I planted some ash and hazel trees. Jackie helped me, making it clear that such an important task shouldn't be left to city boys. A large cheque arrived from some foundation or other in the States, a very large cheque, for repairs to the damage caused to my boat on a scientific trip on behalf of the federal government. I thought about tearing it up, then I saw sense and lodged it in the bank. I took note of the new growth in the heather. I checked my bank account, and found that the money coming from Somerville was still flowing into it. I took that to mean I was still on call.

Then, one day in late spring, I was walking home across the heather, the dusk just light enough to see me home. I was tired and hungry and knew that there was a side of smoked wild salmon waiting for me when I got to the croft. As I came over the last brae, I saw the hire car parked outside. Closer to the house, I smelt fresh-baked bread. I pushed the door and went in. My neighbour, Jackie, was sitting at the table with a glass of whiskey in his hand. Deirdre was at the cooker, griddle wheatens cooling on wire mesh on the sink.

'I was just telling your friend,' Jackie said, hastily downing the large whiskey he'd poured himself, 'I was just telling her, smoked salmon is no use without a griddle wheaten.' He put the glass to his head and darted out of the door before I told him off about letting people into the croft. Deirdre smiled. I washed my hands and sliced the salmon. Deirdre set the table. I opened a bottle of Muscadet. She sat down opposite me. I started to say something and she put her hand to my mouth. Her face was thin and there were dark shadows under her eyes, and my heart ached that I had somehow left her like this.

'Just let me get used to being here,' she said.

We ate the salmon. We talked about Liam and Kate. She took a sly, sisterly pleasure at the thought of her brother with an older woman. But she said that Kate was good for him, and that she knew how to keep the darkness at bay. I took her hand across the table.

'You know, when I was shot . . .?' she said hesitantly. I nodded. I could still see her in that cold wheelhouse.

'I can't have children any more, Jack,' she said. 'The bullet went through my lungs and hit my ribs and went down. They told me I was lucky.'

There was terrible pain in her face. I held her hand and in the end she came towards me and leaned her head on my shoulder. We sat like that for a long time.

Eventually she looked up at me.

'I have to go to bed,' she said. 'The drugs make me sleepy.'

I could see the heaviness in her eyes. I led her to the bedroom. She kissed me on the cheek and shut the door behind her.

I lay down on the sofa and pulled a blanket over me. I

don't remember falling asleep, but I remember waking at dawn, feeling Deirdre slip in beside me. I started to say something but she stopped me.

'Just hold me,' she said.

I held her, and after a few minutes she was sleeping again. I lay awake for a while, a hand behind my head, the dawn light in the window, and the soft spring rain drumming on the roof of the croft.